DONE
FROM
LIFE

A Novel

DONE
FROM
LIFE

A Novel

Elspeth G. Bobbs

SUNSTONE
PRESS

SANTA FE

Sunstone books may be purchased for educational, business, or sales promotional use.
For information please write: Special Markets Department, Sunstone Press,
P.O. Box 2321, Santa Fe, New Mexico 87504-2321.

Book and Cover design →Vicki Ahl
Body typeface → Book Antiqua
Printed on acid free paper

Library of Congress Cataloging-in-Publication Data

Bobbs, Elspeth G. (Elspeth Grant), 1920-
 Done from life : a novel / by Elspeth G. Bobbs.
   p. cm.
 ISBN 978-0-86534-812-7 (pbk. : alk. paper)
 1. Artists--Fiction. 2. Artist colonies--New Mexico--Santa Fe--Fiction. I. Title.
 PS3602.O26D66 2011
 813'.6--dc22

                         2011014884

Published in

WWW.SUNSTONEPRESS.COM
SUNSTONE PRESS / POST OFFICE BOX 2321 / SANTA FE, NM 87504-2321 /USA
(505) 988-4418 / ORDERS ONLY (800) 243-5644 / FAX (505) 988-1025

To my dearest Howard and our darling daughters
Norrie, Margery and Sheila
in the garden of life and in the garden of memory

1

We are instinctively blind to what is not relative.
We are not cameras. We select.

— Robert Henri, "The Art Spirit"

In Villa Real, fall is the season. It is then the tourists come in single spies instead of in battalions, and those that come appreciate the old city and even know how to pronounce its name. It is quite acceptable to say Villa in the English manner, but to say Real as in 'real good' is beyond the pale, only Rayahl is correct. In summer the air is thick with ear-assaulting attempts at this Spanish name, Veelya Reel being the most popular, and worse than calling San Francisco, Frisco. But after Labor Day peace descends, again there are parking places around the Plaza, well a few, and there is time to gossip with passersby while going for the mail. This is a time-honored Villa Real habit; mail deliveries are reasonably prompt and as reliable as any other city in the United States, but few if any of us would give up our precious post office boxes. This gloriously cool crisp fall afternoon I had checked my box, but left the Villa Real Art Association box until tomorrow, when I would pick up the mail in it on my way to work. I was surprised to see in passing that my immediate boss, the curator of the Art Association, was emptying the box.

"Hi, Clem," I said cheerfully, "doing me out of a job, I see."

Mr. Dennison started slightly and dropped a letter he had in his hand. I bent over to pick it up for him, but he forestalled me and pocketed the letter quickly.

"Just checking up on something, Mary Mac, nothing important. Look, I'll leave the rest of this stuff for you." He put a pile of mail back into the box, slammed it shut and, giving me a tight smile, strode off in his neat upright way.

Now I liked Clem Dennison; he got me my job, ill paid but interesting, as general help at the Association gallery. He called me Mary Mac, instead of plain Mac, or Miss MacIntyre; this I liked too. Not mine to reason why, I thought, as I walked home enjoying the familiar sights of Villa Real on the way. As I rounded the high adobe wall of the Archbishop's garden, I saw that the pear tree jutting over it, which had delighted me in spring with its stars of white against the blue sky, was drooping, its green tired and dusty, and here and there a leaf showing a trace of dull yellow. The cottonwoods along the Alameda would soon be turning their bright gold, I thought, as I crossed the road to walk under them. I sniffed the air to catch that faint piñon smoke that is the very essence of Villa Real, and I found myself thinking with affection of Clem, as he had asked me to call him, though I stuck to Mr. Dennison while in the gallery. Returning health undoubtedly accounted for my increasing zest in life, but Clem's kindness in making a job for me helped too.

Crossing the bridge over the Rio Villa Real, which had been last year nothing but a dry ditch, but this year had run all through spring and summer to the joy of the old timers and the delight of the children who fished in it, I saw Edythe Kendall Chambers coming over on the other side. I waved and went purposefully, hoping she would not stop to yak. A middle-aged woman who I was sure had talked her husband to death and was seeking persistently for another victim, she lived very near me and was the worst bore around too. We all avoided her as much as possible, and this time most oddly she avoided me. In fact she did not seem to recognize me but hurried by with a grim look on her usually carefully bright face.

I went up Delgado, finding myself a little chilly in the shade of trees lining it, and turned off at Acequia Madre. Once this insignificant little ditch had been the main source of irrigation water for the long settled Canyon Road area, and it still ran busily in a good year, such as this was. I enjoyed its companionable chuckle as I walked close beside it and left it with reluctance at Camino Monte Sol, off which was the compound I lived in. Compound may be a strange word to use in the Spanish Southwest, since it has an oriental ring to it, but it was the only word I had ever heard used for the group of houses I surveyed now. Each house was quite separate and distinct and totally individual; all they shared was a common entrance and a common landlord, who, bless him, was not one to raise his rents at the slightest provocation. On the other hand, I reflected, he was not one to do much repair work, either. You paid low rents and were on your own at our compound.

My house was one of the smallest and least adapted to artistic pursuits, but it also had the biggest patio, surrounded by a six-foot adobe wall, and this gave me a most pleasant feeling of privacy and protection. Other houses in the compound had larger rooms, and more of them, and many had studios with coveted north lights, so necessary to a serious artist's well being. I loved my own little adobe with its sunny patio, complete with apricot tree, lilacs, wisteria and a rampant silver lace vine softening the hard edge of one wall.

As I walked through my garden, and it was mine really, because I had rescued it from weeds and the neglect of a former tenant, my eye wandered over it looking for Villa Real's daily paper, which might land anywhere from the casual toss of a newsboy's hand. It was not under the hollyhocks, now with a single last bloom at the very tips of their tall stems, not under the lilacs, still their plain green bushy summer selves, but marked for their winter death. It was not entangled in the branches of the apricot tree, showing like the Archbishop's pear an occasional yellow leaf, nor lying on the gray catmint bordering the flowerbed, nor among the vivid yellow and bronze chrysanthemums, at their peak of bloom. I grumbled to myself as I found my key under the mat and unlocked my bright blue front door.

When I get home in the evening, I like to sit down and read the paper before doing anything else, so back out I went. Failing again to find it in the garden, I opened my patio door to look outside. It was not on the ground outside, either, so I looked up, and there it was caught between a branch of the apricot tree and the wall, just too high for me to reach. I was gazing at it with annoyance when along came a neighbor, a young man whose solitary habits had aroused speculation and concern among other inmates of the compound. He sized up the situation with a glance.

"No way to deliver a paper, is it," he said with a grin. "Guess I can get it for you." He reached up and as he handed over the rolled up paper remarked casually, "Seems a shame we haven't met before, being neighbors. I'm Bill Thorpe, from New York, been here six months and love it."

"I'm Mary MacIntyre, from San Francisco, by way of Canada, been here nearly two years, and love it too."

He said in a diffident way, "I wonder if you would come in for a drink this evening, say in an hour. I'm feeling like some company now."

I agreed, rather thrilled, I must admit, because as I could see he was a personable youngish man, a bit older than I, perhaps, but not too much and certainly not the bearded beatnik bohemian type that seem to be the only young men abounding in Villa Real.

Well, I thought to myself as I sunk into my fireside chair and curled my feet under me, life is looking up all over. My eye was caught by the headline as I unrolled the paper, "Artist drowned in Tojauque," I read. I skimmed the story quickly; who was it? I knew most of the artists in Villa Real through my job, and had to know at once who it was. Oh no, I gasped aloud. Yes, it was John Graham, a delightful man, universally liked and respected old guard artist, and one of the founders and pillars of the Art Association. "Terrible," I groaned, reading on.

He had been found dead in his own swimming pool that morning by his wife, who had been aroused by the barking of their dog. He was only 50 and left, beside his wife, two daughters, both away at the time. I sighed and, putting down the paper, thought unhappily of the other two deaths of Association members that had occurred recently. Nicolai Polkoff, who lived right here in the compound, had drifted off to a peaceful enough death at 68 just last April. There had been a sudden cold spell, and a faulty gas pipe and no ventilation adds up to death. He was the first. And then after him Bela Ferency, who fell off a cliff at Puye while sketching last June. A fitting end for an artist, but with his youthful vigor and zest for life at 67 he should have more years to enjoy painting. Three of them, I thought, three of the old guard gone, and who is left to take their places and hold the Art Association together?

I shivered suddenly, and my imagination took a wild leap. Suppose these deaths were not the accidents they seemed to be, but were, say, "arranged"? So I had read far too many detective stories during my sanitarium days, so I had far too much imagination anyway, still it was odd, wasn't it? I cut out from the paper the paragraphs about John Graham's death and went to my desk to find the clippings I had put away referring to Nicolai and Bela. Sitting back again, I studied them all thoughtfully. Now that summer was over, I would have very little to do at the Art Association gallery. Clem did all the selling, Liz did the books and the secretarial work. My job was nothing much anyway and would be even less from now on. Why not do a little investigation of these three deaths, with a view to writing a mystery later on, perhaps in early spring, when Villa Real was dead itself? Of course, they were accidents, no disputing that, but the coincidence tempted my imagination.

Mentally asking each one to forgive me as I wrote his name, I ruled three columns, headed the first Nicolai Polkoff, the next column Bela Ferency, and the last John Graham. Then I ruled off a fourth column on the left side of the sheet and wrote, in descending order, Date, Time, Place, Age, Family, consulting my clippings as I did. What else, I wondered, would be relevant? I thought for a bit and added Method to the left column. Suddenly catching sight of my watch, I was reminded of that drink with Bill Thorpe. I dashed into my bedroom for a look at my face; shiny, I saw, so I repaired that, ran a brush through my hair, a touch of lipstick, and nothing more could be done, I decided.

Bill was waiting for me in his rather larger adobe up the compound from mine; at least, I amended, looking around curiously, his living room, which he used for a studio, was larger; nothing else was visible. He had obviously hurriedly straightened up a bit, but I was disappointed, both in his house, which I considered unattractive compared with mine, and his paintings. These were all over the room in various stages of progress, if that was the word, I thought ruefully. I did not feel obliged to comment on this occasion, as Bill was anxiously acting the host, pressing a drink on me and giving me the one comfortable chair.

We got to know each other very quickly, once it came out that we had both come to Villa Real to convalesce. He was 28 to my 22, I was happy to learn, and the reason he had been more or less a hermit up to now was that he had to rest for decreasing periods each day. While we chattered away, I observed that he looked tired and haggard, and I thought if he were not so tanned he would be gray. He was too thin for his framework I saw too.

To excuse my lateness, I explained that I had been shocked at the news of John Graham's death, and then on impulse, I added, "You know, that's the third of my artist friends at the Association to die within six months, and I'm wondering, maybe they were murdered."

Bill made a face combining amusement and disapproval. "Your imagination matches your freckles," he teased. "No, seriously, I knew Nick Polkoff quite well for a short time. He was the first person I met in the compound, and he used to let me watch him paint while I rested, and how he talked! And Bela, he used to come to Nick's to talk old times once a week or so; a good guy, a sweet guy, really. Nobody would want to rub them out. What for? You must be wanting to make a mystery; maybe you want to write one?"

I was casual. "You must know me too well already. I'm just

mulling this over in my mind. Maybe it'll make a detective story. Have to find something to do in the long winters here. I've read so many who-dun-its, you know how it is when you have to rest so much."

He nodded. "Sure, I do. In that case let me in on this. I'll help with alibis and such, and we can enjoy it all knowing it's just a joke. Because, sorry as I am to spoil your story, it is all imagination."

"Can't be anything else, I suppose, can it?" I asked.

"No," said Bill, "I know Henry Martin, he's not a policeman exactly, but does night duty sometimes at the main station, and he told me that despite all you hear about the corruption in the police force here, there is one thing they did do thoroughly and that was check out those accidents."

"Henry Martin?" I exclaimed in surprise. "He's an artist, a darn good one too. He paints mostly very meticulous sort of stuff, every hair is numbered, every wrinkle accounted for. Lately his work has been less hard and a lot better too."

"Oh, he's a damn good painter, all right, but as to that job of his, you've got to know what I know, then all becomes clear, in fact, predictable. Our Henry's name isn't Martin, it's Martinez."

"Really?" I asked, amused and enlightened. All political jobs in Villa Real are held by Spanish Americans, and all jobs are political. Meritocracy may be on the way but it will take a long time to conquer Villa Real. "So one of his no doubt numerous relatives is helping him out," I remarked casually. "But, Bill," I went on with more interest, "you may think I don't know nothing about painting, but perhaps you'll believe Nick, and I remember he once told me that Henry would be a very fine painter in time, he just needed experience."

"Ha, not just time or experience, but dear Nicolai Polkoff's guiding hand is what he added, I'll bet," said Bill rather sarcastically.

"Maybe," I agreed with a smile, for everybody in Villa Real knew that Nick's *amour-propre* had never been in need of propping. You could name any artist, and he would comment, 'a competent painter,' which was a term of praise, 'but . . .' and the buts were many and justified. Or he would more frequently dismiss the victim with a contemptuous 'doesn't know one end of the paint brush from the other.' Even his old friend Bela did not escape his strictures, 'a nice fellow, but never progressed an inch since his student days.'"

Bill went to fix another drink while I was thinking of Nick, and when he returned I asked him idly, "How come you didn't take lessons from Nick? He was the recognized Old Maestro 'round here."

Bill winced. "You've touched a sore spot. We got along outside painting, but I wanted to go my own way, and Nick wanted me to go his. No hurt feelings, mind you, we agreed amiably enough to disagree."

I looked again at the paintings around me, done with a very muddy palette and with a palette knife in broad heavy strokes. To Nick, who used clear fresh colors and brushes only, they would not appeal. I frowned and, realizing that Bill was expecting me to comment on them, I prevaricated.

"You take goo, and I'll take gout," I said lightly.

Bill looked puzzled for a second and then light visibly dawned, I was glad to see. "But I'd rather we had the same taste," he said, a bit hurt.

"You can't have everything," I said, getting up to leave, "after all, you're lucky I'm not one more female artist. I don't paint, never have, never wanted to, so you'll get no advice, competition or even sympathy from me."

"Miss MacIntyre . . ." Bill exclaimed dramatically.

"No," I interrupted, "call me Mac, everyone does, except Clem Dennison, and he calls me Mary Mac."

"Fine, but I prefer Mary. So Mary, you have taken a great weight off my mind. We will stick to sleuthing, and you needn't say a word about my paintings." He was smiling, but there was a distinct note of bitterness in his voice.

"Done," I said gaily, but that was not the note I wanted to leave on. So as an apology, I took his arm and smiled as warmly as I could up into his eyes. The blue eyes that met mine gave nothing away at all, but their owner smiled back at me. Encouraged, I said, "Let me know if anything occurs to you about Nick. I need help."

Bill gave himself a little shake as if to re-route his thoughts and replied rather absently, "Oh, sure, let's think about it and meet to compare ideas next weekend."

We went to the door together and, as I made as if to go, Bill stopped me. "You're sort of scrutable, aren't you? You'd better not share your wild ideas with anybody else; just keep me informed."

That suited me very well, but I did not commit myself. I just smiled and left, trying to look a bit more inscrutable. At home again, I went into my bedroom and studied my face in the tin-bordered mirror, wishing for the first time that it was a bigger and better one with perhaps two more sides and a good light so that I could see myself as others see me. Mousy hair, green eyes and freckles. With that set-up anyone would expect red hair, I thought, and made a mental note to get a rinse. Perhaps I was still too thin, but not a real string bean, luckily, so why had Bill seemed to lose interest suddenly, and when we had been hitting it off very well? I shrugged my shoulders and dived into a new Agatha Christie.

2

Persons and things are whatever
we imagine them to be.

— Robert Henri, *op. cit.*

"Hi, Mac," said Liz, when I went into the Art Association building next morning, "you look more alive than usual. Has the answer to your maiden's prayer turned up?"

"Prayer, schmayer," I growled, but with a smile; Liz certainly was observant. I had indeed taken more pains than usual with my appearance and evidently it was worth it. Liz and I got along very well, up to a point. At 37 she had quite a reputation around town; I was not told for what and did not enquire, merely noting that she was a Mrs. Elizabeth Heald and that nobody knew the invisible Mr. Heald. We joked about art and artists at work and took care not to see each other after work. Liz was the assistant to the curator and had kept that job through three changes at the top; in fact, she was appointed by the first founding board of the Art

Association and had stayed on. Very knowledgeable and efficient in her way, it was still Clem who really was the Art Association. Liz could get along with artists and keep the books and organize things, but Clem sold paintings, and that was the whole point.

"Clem in?" I asked as I plunked the batch of mail down on her desk.

"You kidding?" she replied. "He's never in this early, unless his left little toe twitches to tell him a rich bitch from Texas is on the way."

"Well, girls, my left little toe did twitch," and there right behind us was Clem. He always walked so quietly in his precise way, we should have looked before we spoke, but he was laughing, so we joined in. He shot out his small, well-kept hand and ruffed through the mail with his back to us before vanishing as quietly as he had come.

Liz stared after him. "Something on his mind?"

"Hmmm," I replied in a whisper. "He was checking the mail box yesterday afternoon and got his bookie's bill, or a billet-doux, or whatever else it is he is anxious about too."

"Not, my dear, a billet-doux, he's hardly the type." Liz looked knowing. "Bookie? No, ditto. What can it be?" Her expression changed to one of puzzled concern as she dismissed me by turning away.

Now that Labor Day had weeded out traveling parents, my work was light. In summer some of the showing fell to me. I had to take parties of school children and other obvious non-buyers around the five rooms of the Art Association Gallery and had to be on the watch to prevent anybody from touching the exhibits. After Labor Day, the Gallery actually sold more in dollar value, though fewer in numbers, than during the crowded summer season. Rarely was any painting costing over $350 sold in summer, whereas in the fall five or six $1,000 paintings would be sold, in addition to a fair number of medium priced ones. Clem was the only one to sell these profitable high priced works. Liz never really got beyond the $250 figure, and I, of course, never sold anything at all.

I put the lights on, checked to see that each painting was hung right side up and straight. In case of doubt as to which side was up, I looked for the artist's signature. I soon discovered that the more obscure the painting, the more prominent and legible was his signature. The visitor's book must be put out, pen at the ready. Once over the few pieces of sculpture lightly with a feather duster, and my morning routine was soon over.

While I was admiring a typical John Graham watercolor, Liz came in and stood beside me, looking at it.

"Damn it," she said gruffly, almost in tears, "good man, one of the best, stinking thing to happen."

I carefully kept my eyes on the painting while she blew her nose. "Terrible," I agreed. "How did it happen, do you know? "

"Yes, I saw Henry this morning, Henry Martin, and he told me that John slipped on the wet rim of his pool, struck his head and fell into the water unconscious and drowned. He took a walk around his grounds every morning with his dog and just had bad luck this one morning."

"What a shame," I said. "Of course Henry, would know because of his job. Funny you never told me he was a policeman."

Liz shrugged. "Not important, he's not a real policeman, he just mans the night desk occasionally. Decent of old Martinez, his compadre, you know, to help Henry out. Henry's got troubles."

"Troubles?"

"Who don't?" Liz said with a sigh. "Henry's a damn fine painter, I can tell, but he married the wrong woman, and, man, is she making him pay."

Some people came in then and Liz hurried off, leaving me with a lot of unanswered questions. Not that I ever questioned Liz directly. I did not need to, as she seemed to know of my intense curiosity about artists and kept me well informed. Before I had taken the Art Association job, I had been warned by an elderly acquaintance that all artists were, as she put it, dirty, immoral and irresponsible. This I had found was not true. Some artists were irresponsible, few were immoral and fewer still dirty, and fewest were all three. My analytical mind was perpetually at work trying to classify our artists and failing utterly. I could find no pattern. However, artists' wives did seem to offer a better possibility for typing, and so at this first mention of Henry's wife, I was interested.

18   _____

Clem came in, interrupting my reflections. "Mary Mac," he said, "let's take that Graham watercolor and put it on the easel in the inner room. But what shall we put up instead?"

Clem did not usually interfere with the hanging of paintings, a task that was done by a committee of members of the Art Association on the first Monday of every month; but he could and did pick out from the various other paintings left over from previous shows those to display in the inner room, where most of the sales took place. In that room, there was only an easel with the back cloth behind it, and comfortable chairs in front of it, giving the place an ambiance conducive to buying art.

"Yes, Mr. Dennison," I said, "but aren't there other Graham paintings on the storage racks?"

"No. John came in last week and removed all the six paintings he's allowed to have in here."

I was surprised. "Really? I wonder why he did that. You've always done well for him, Liz told me, and this is the beginning of the best season for his price range."

Clem looked unhappy. "Wish I knew, Mary Mac. I didn't see him."

I took down the watercolor and looked around for another painting to fill the gap. It had to be another watercolor; in art galleries there is no integration, oils go in one room and watercolors in another. In our gallery we also tried to exercise some segregation by style, a much trickier business and not for me to attempt. I saw that on one side of the gap there was an awful wishy-washy mess by Edythe Kendall Chambers, painted in the same wet method of watercolor wash as John Graham used, but there the resemblance ended.

"How in heaven's name did that ghastly daub get in?" I asked Clem, pointing.

He looked embarrassed. "Yes, I know she was turned down flat six months ago, but there was another meeting of the new members committee last week, and this time she made it."

I laughed scornfully. "Oh, I'll bet you a lunch at La Fonda, sticking only to enchiladas and beer, mind you, that our dear Paul

Humfrey was on the committee. I happen to know she's been spending pots on lessons with him."

Clem turned his hands palms up in a neat little gesture. "No takers," he said and strode off very straight-backed to his office.

This was very interesting news to me. John Graham had been, if not the one man, at least one of the very few men who had kept the Villa Real Art Association going during the first difficult years of its corporate life. There had been many other attempts at a cooperative gallery in Villa Real from time to time, but they had all come to grief, and speedily. None had lasted more than a summer. Financial problems were the obvious reason for their failures, but I surmised that behind them was the even bigger problem of the artistic temperament, made yet more quarrelsome and difficult by the altitude of Villa Real. Artists, I had observed, were uncooperative and jealous enough at sea level; at 7,000 feet up they were even more temperamental.

John Graham had several assets. Working in the field of magazine illustration, a branch of commercial art, he had made enough money to retire to Villa Real and devote himself to fine art. There is a distinction between fine and commercial art, another segregation problem, and I am not the one to draw it. John Graham was able to get the best of both worlds. After he had been recognized in Villa Real for the very fine painter he obviously was, he had inherited money and bought a large house outside the city. There he lived a very happy respectable family life and worked hard to make the Art Association a paying proposition. Other artists in Villa Real had money, but most of them had married it, not made it, and their wives were not going to waste their money in helping competition.

Yet for all John Graham had done, it was not until Clem came into town looking for a job that the Gallery had flourished. Clem had been an actor; he knew little and cared less about art; but he flung himself into his new role with enthusiasm and, spurred by the fact that his pay was dependent on his sales, proved to be a terrific salesman. The Villa Real Art Association gallery, from a struggling little amateur organization held together only by the faith and efforts of a few painters, became a prosperous concern, able to build on to its originally small adobe house an imposing sequence of showing rooms and to pay Clem Dennison an imposing salary too. All this out of the 25% charged the artists for selling their works. No wonder then to get into the Association became the ambition of every artist around.

I was wondering why John Graham had removed his paintings and hoping that it was not that he had been intending to resign from the membership in a huff, the way Nick Polkoff did regularly once a year and had to be coaxed back in again for his own good too, when Liz came in. Seeing her red-rimmed eyes, I remembered that we would probably never know the reason, and that it hardly mattered any more.

"Mac, me dear," she asked, "it's model night tomorrow; I'm just too beat to cope. The funeral will be held too. Think you could take over? Here's the folder."

"If this is a promotion, Liz," I snorted, "damned if I'll take it. Just a lot of bother for what? And that bunch of no-goodniks are as tight as my new stretch pants when it comes to paying the model's fee. I know, because I've heard them complain when they have to fork out before their paintings are hung."

Liz let her tough mask slip and asked wearily, "Please do it, I just can't."

Touched, I took up the folder and said, "Sure, Liz, anything to help," and went to the telephone to round up the model and the class. Last spring, Liz had done all this and attended the sketch class too, just to open the room and lock up after the class and crack jokes with her artist friends between. I knew from her that a lot depended upon the model. If I could find a good one, a large class would come, and everyone's contribution would be small and given without fuss, but an unattractive model meant a small class and trouble.

Once installed at the phone, I checked first the list of available models. I was lucky enough to get Dolores, a girl with an unfortunate face, ugly in fact, but a really lovely figure, full, yet still firm breasts, small waist, the generous hips that artists like. No, I had not seen her, but I had seen so many nudes of her, ranging from the green cheese effects of Nick Polkoff, to the photographic, almost pornographic studies by Henry Martin, that I knew her figure very well. Now for the class: in the folder were two lists, one headed "Members." Liz had marked a pencil cross beside the names of possible sketchers; another list, shorter, of nonmembers, who were allowed to attend, but paid double for the privilege. I was startled, first pleasurably, but then unhappily, to see Bill Thorpe's name in the nonmembers list. I allowed myself a wry smile. I was inspecting this smile in my pocket mirror, when in came Edythe Kendall Chambers. I changed my smile quickly from wry to rotgut and flipped the folder shut.

Dear Edythe was not one to notice anything, so full she was of herself, as always. Up she surged, gushing all the way.

"Oh, Mary, Liz sent me to you about the model night. I did so enjoy our little sketch group last spring. Such dear people, you know. Are we really starting again? I just adore sketching. Why, I have even sold a few nudes," she giggled. "Can you imagine what my friends back in Peoria would say?"

I could indeed, but to avoid gales of giggles I interrupted her firmly. "Tomorrow's the night, same time, same place, and a good model." I had planned to overlook her name on the nonmembers list, and I certainly was not going to bring the member's list up to date, but that little sin of omission clearly would not do now. So I went on grimly, "Yes, I hope you will come. I have got Dolores."

Edythe gushed forth again. "Why, Dolores, are you sure? What a lovely girl indeed, but a little bird told me someone we know," at this she leered at me knowingly, "was spoiling that gorgeous figure of hers."

"I'm afraid I have no idea what you are talking about, Mrs. Chambers," I replied in what I hoped was a very cold way, but as I blush easily, the attempt was not a success.

"Why, Mac, I didn't think you had any feelings."

This naturally made me furious. I picked up the folder and said, turning away, "Excuse me, I must get this phoning done."

Looking suddenly back at Edythe, I saw that her face had sagged. Instead of the rather pretty woman, there was a tired middle-aged battleaxe. I felt sorry for her, and said the first thing I could think of to cheer her up.

"So glad you're a member now, Mrs. Chambers. Welcome to the Art Association."

She did not respond to my well-meant effort, but with a haunted look on her face turned abruptly and hurried off.

3

With the model before it,
the background is transformed.
— Robert Henri, *op. cit.*

O~n~ Thursday, model night, I left work early, having prepared the meeting room for the class by setting up the model stand and arranging chairs around. I did my shopping on the way home at the little corner market on Acequia Madre and was carrying my paper bag of groceries clasped in my arms up Camino Monte Sol, when a voice called from behind me.

"Mary, Mary, here, let me carry that bag for you." It was Bill Thorpe, coming into the Camino from Canyon Road.

I could not conceal my pleasure at seeing him and handed over the bag with a large grin. "Hi, Bill. Coming to the model night? I'm to be the chaperone tonight, for a change, so you come."

He agreed to come, though without much interest. When

I invited him at my portal door for a drink and discussion, he agreed much more eagerly.

Settled down with cokes in my south-of-the-border portal chairs, we both said simultaneously, "What have <u>you</u> found out?" and we both laughed.

I surveyed my patio in the fall sunshine, every flower the more dear to me since soon the killing frost would blacken all of them overnight, and said, "It's all a lot of nonsense: Nick, Bela, John Graham, their killing frost came as it comes to all," and I shivered.

Bill was thoughtful. "Where I worked, there was a computer, a big one, and I once saw a message it returned to the programmer. It read, 'I am letting time out,' and ever since that's how I think of death, an impersonal machine letting time out; life is time, after all."

I felt rather than saw a shadow pass over his face, which I was watching intently. "You too," I stated.

Bill nodded and took from his pocket a sheet of paper on which I saw my ruled columns, with a few additions.

"Tell me what you can about these three men, will you, Mary . . . let's see if they have anything in common, besides being artists."

"Nick and Bela were old friends," I responded. "Nick came here ages ago after his wife died, perhaps to forget, and stayed on, creating quite a fancy little niche for himself as the old maestro. Bela had been here not so long. He came on a visit and stayed on too. Every year he went back East in the winter and sold, so he said, all his paintings of the summer."

"Nice work, if you can get it," said Bill admiringly.

"Bela came from a large and close-knit family," I explained. "That's an asset for any painter."

"Families ought to be investigated first. What do you know about them?" asked Bill.

"No wife in Nick's case, and Ellen, Bela's wife, would have nothing to gain from his death; she's out," I paused. "But John Graham, leaving wife, children, and a large estate, I suppose, yes, there's room for research in his case."

Bill frowned and said in an offhand way, "Well, seems to me

the only thing the three men had in common was that they were all painters. Nick and John Graham were tops, and Bela was at least well trained, if not in their class."

I nodded, "Yes, and there was a sort of polite and friendly rivalry between John and Nick; they respected each other, mind you. They took it in turns to be president of the Art Association until recently, when Paul Humfrey muscled in. But Bela, though he served on committees, was never elected to any office."

Bill shrugged, uninterested now, "I have to be off now. I'll see you tonight."

He smiled and left with a casual wave, as I sat there, contemplating with satisfaction my adobe walled patio, still lush from the unusually constant summer rains, but already foretelling winter. From the apricot tree a yellow leaf drifted unambitiously down, coming to rest on a last brave, if leggy, petunia. I sighed, and went in to wash my hair. Tonight I will shine, I said to myself. I may not have Dolores' figure, but then I have not got her face, either, praise be.

Bill, sure enough, showed up for model night, in fact he arrived early and helped me arrange the drape on the model stand. Dolores was late in arriving, but shed her clothes behind a screen with utmost dispatch. It seemed silly for me to have to admit that I was embarrassed, yet I found myself looking anywhere but at her, and certainly avoiding Bill's eye. Liz had told me to time the model, twenty minutes pose and ten minutes break, so I checked my watch as Dolores stood, hand on hip, looking over her back.

"That's O.K., hold it, Dolly," said Paul Humfrey.

I was put out. Paul was always pushing in, trying to take over. This time he had brought three women with him of various indeterminate ages, and I was not pleased to see that Edythe was one. Liz had also told me of Paul's penchant for collecting a group of adoring disciples and giving them a cheap lesson, cheap that is for him, since he had to pay the model only the small contribution required, but not cheap for the disciples.

Dolores stood like a rock. She knew her job, I thought, feeling free to inspect her now that the class was hard at work. She kept her backward gaze fixed on Paul, who, while I was watching intently, got up, adjusted the tilt of her hip and patted her fanny gently before returning to his seat.

Just one unobtrusive sort of pat, but so very familiar, it made a situation clear in a second. I glanced around at the class to see what reaction, if any, it provoked. Bill, to whom my gaze first turned, looked amused. Edythe looked angry, the other women embarrassed, and as for Dolores herself, her face never looked anything but sulky anyway.

Bill caught my eye and winked at me. A diversion saved me from having to decide whether to wink back or not. It was Henry Martin, coming in late. He ignored everybody in his usual abstracted way, sat down with his board and started right in sketching with quick sure strokes, no hesitation for him. While he was concentrating on drawing, I concentrated on him. It would be useful to know someone in the police department from whom to pick up information about procedure and such petty details that I would have to know for my mystery opus and had no other way of finding out. Henry Martinez, as I knew his real name to be, was rather strikingly handsome, about thirty or so, at a guess, still young but with lines of worry showing, dark, well built, with intent expressive brown eyes. I had seen him often enough at the Gallery and admired him too, but we had not met.

Checking my watch, I saw it was a few minutes past the allotted time and was about to say so, when Paul's loud "Lay off, Dolly," rang out with a coarse laugh. I was annoyed. Everybody got up to stretch their legs, except Dolores, who put on her robe and sat down in the chair provided beside the model stand. I went over to look at Henry Martin's sketchbook, while Bill engaged him in conversation. No doubt about it, Henry had great talent, even I could see his superiority, not an unnecessary stroke anywhere.

"Mary," it was Bill calling to me, "I want you to meet Henry Martin. Henry, this is Miss Mary MacIntyre, generally known to the Art Association as Mac."

Not only did Henry have talent, but he also had charm, the automatic kind that men successful with women often have. He held my hand longer than manners require, he looked more deeply than need be into my eyes. But he waited for me to take the lead in conversation.

I found myself babbling on of this and that and then to my horror, I said, rather loudly too, "What a shame John Graham fell into his pool, but you know, Bill and I have been amusing ourselves wondering if he was, say, helped, given a little push. Maybe someone has it in for the competent old timers of the Art Association." This with a nervous giggle.

Bill laughed it off, "Just a joke, no offense meant, Henry, boy."

"And none taken, Bill, old fellow," replied Henry, but though his mouth smiled, his eyes did not.

Paul with Edythe in his train swept up, saying, "What's this, who gave who a little push?"

With considerable tact, Bill motioned to his watch and sang out, "Time, gentlemen, pu-lease."

Obediently, Dolores took off her robe and assumed her pose, and the class took their seats. I occupied myself wondering why I had blurted out anything so foolish, and then realized that the subject of those three accidental deaths in close succession was worrying me more than I was willing to admit.

When the next break came around, Paul, the mannerless boor he quite deliberately was, stalked up to me. "Come clean, Mac, are you saying someone pushed John Graham into his pool?"

"Of course not, how stupid. I was just speculating about the coincidence of three deaths, accidents, among Art Association members. First Nick, then Bela, now John Graham."

Paul roared with laughter. "One old has-been, one never-was, and one know-it-all," he said unforgivably. "That bothering you? Relax and give credit where it is due, to providence."

We were all dumb with shock for a minute, then who knows what angry retort might have been made had not Clem and Liz walked up. Evidently they had heard most of this conversation, because Liz turned to me and said in a whisper, "Mac, you idiot, can't you shut up?"

While Clem stepped up to Paul, looking very small and tidy

beside Paul's boisterous bulk, and said in an old-maidish way, "Now, really, Paul, aren't you overdoing the part?"

Paul looked like a small boy caught in the cookie jar; I could see why he had all those female disciples. "Sorry, old man," he said in a softer voice than usual for him, "didn't mean it. Wasn't thinking. If you really want to know, I never do think."

We all, I am sure, forgave Paul then and there, until the next time he did or said something impossible, which would be soon. What a man to be able to get away with it. I was going to say get away with murder, but that clearly would be inappropriate. Like many large size men, Paul was incapable of physical violence. All that bluster and bluff was a cover-up for great guile. Oh, he got his own way, taking over the Art Association, but he got it by that shrewd thinking he claimed he never did.

Clem knew this as well as I did and was as unimpressed, but said no more to Paul because Edythe came up to him then, gushing even more than usual.

I found myself standing by Henry Martin, who turned to me from a study of his sketch and, fixing those deplorably melting brown eyes on me, said quietly, "How strange it is that I have seen you around often at the Gallery but have never really seen you until now."

I must have looked very self-conscious at this, but I was pleased. The extra care I had taken with my hair, the subtle makeup done especially for the harsh painting lights, the discreet perfume, my most becoming squaw dress, a style so kind to the thin—these were all paying off.

"Liz gets all the attention," I said lightly. "You may not have noticed me, but I have noticed you, because I truly admire your work, Mr. Martin."

"Dear Miss Mac, you know how to please an artist," he said very warmly and grasping my hand.

"It's not flattery," I insisted, "I am not capable of gush." We both looked at Edythe, still overwhelming Clem, and smiled at each other. "No, everyone knows you're good; you know too."

"Yes," he said with a bitter downward twist of his lips, "sure I know I'm good, but what's the use?" He must have sensed sympathy in my attention because he went on. "You know I have to spend the late night shift at the police desk? Look at all these other artists here," he waved his hand, "not right here, but in Villa Real, how many married money and paint in peace, but not me. I have to marry a no-good little tramp and I'm . . ." he broke off and squeezed his neck between his own powerful hands. "That's why I never get anywhere; who can take a policeman seriously?"

"Nonsense," I said briskly. "What you do for a living has nothing to do with your painting." But even as I said it, I could see his point. The greatest talent needs some freedom, in time, or in space, and certainly it must have some appreciation, financial variety, to flower.

"At least," Henry went on, "I am in a position to warn you. Lay off, Miss Mary Mac, as Paul would say. You're way out. Not my department, but I know those accidents were nothing more than that, just accidents. Too bad, they were all good painters."

Dolores was getting up onto the stand, assisted by Bill this time. I felt a distinct pang of jealousy — that figure — and turned to Henry with my warmest smile.

"Good luck," I said. "But you know, I want to make a story out of those accidents, so I'll investigate a bit more, and maybe you'll help me?"

Henry looked grave and said nothing more as he settled down to sketching again. At the next break, he was cornered by Edythe; I could see her mouth going like a teenaged gum chewer the entire break time. Henry never had a chance.

Bill came up to me, rather subdued, I thought, and said right away, "Henry's quite a charmer, isn't he? Pity he had to charm the wrong woman for him."

"You seem to know him pretty well, with your 'Henry, old boy' and his 'Bill, old fellow,'" I said sharply.

He looked at me, puzzled. "Why this interest? Henry was one of the first artists I met when I arrived, and he has been a good friend. He's had bad luck with that poor excuse of a wife of his on his neck, but he'll make the big time one day, with any luck."

Luck, I thought to myself during the next posing session. No, it's not just luck; it's often other things, too: sacrifice, judgment, work, talent to start with, of course. And how important is the choice of a wife, if wife an artist must have. You can't work at the Art Association for long without picking up all the intense gossip that goes on, I suspect, in any art colony. In Villa Real how many artists were financially successful? I would say about five out of the hundred-odd members. And the others? Either they had some other job, or they taught, or they lived very cheaply and got a lot of free drinks by providing local color at Villa Real's numerous tourist traps. Or, a better solution, their wives worked, or the best, their wives had money.

Nick Polkoff, a welcome bachelor at Villa Real's parties, peddled his own paintings with the same success he blew his own trumpet and made enough to pay his own modest but comfortable way. Bela: well, his wife had a small adequate income. John Graham: he made his money and then inherited his own too. I looked around at the artists in the sketch class. Paul Humfrey taught and did well, too, from his succession of admiring females. Henry: his situation was tough. And Bill: he must have some sort of disability pension, I thought, but that was just a guess. Judging from what I could see of his sketch board, he would never make a go of it in art. His production was firm, tight, labored, and everything a sketch ought not be. However, I gave him one point, it was recognizably a woman.

At the next and last break, Paul and Edythe converged on me together, but Edythe opened her mouth first.

"Dear little Mac, how could you say such awful things? Why, I knew dear Nick so well and I know, something tells me (I'm a real sensitive, you know) that his time had come." Her voice grew portentous. "He knew too." She leaned forward to grip my forearm. "The very day he died he said to me when I called on him, 'Edythe, time's so short, always so much to paint, so much to learn, I must work.' Why would he have said that to me if he had not been warned his life was to be shortened? He said too, 'Edythe, my dear, I'm getting old, and the older you grow, the less you know what you ought to do. Bela is coming over soon to see me and together we can decide.'"

Everybody in the room was listening to this. Edythe had an interested audience for a change. She must have sensed this because she straightened up (really, squaw dresses do nothing for the fat) and, glancing around her triumphantly, she wound up, "And why would he say that unless he knew he would die soon and he wanted to make a will?"

Why, indeed? Other reasons occurred to me, many others, but that certainly sounded plausible. As it was, he died intestate, I remembered, and a brother inherited.

At this, Henry looked in a pointed manner at his watch and said, "Maybe you have all the time in the world, but I'm just a working stiff."

So we all went guiltily back to our seats. I did the necessary mathematical computations to determine who paid what, and at the end of the last posing period collected the money and paid Dolores. Bill suggested driving me home.

"But you haven't a car," I said in surprise.

"No, I hadn't, but I have now," he said cheerfully. And sure enough, after I locked up, carefully putting all the lights out and checking the windows, there he was sitting in a very gay low-slung old convertible. I was delighted and said so.

Fortunately I had brought a *rebozo*, a fetching affair of hand-woven white wool. I wrapped this round my head and shoulders and enjoyed the ride up Canyon Road to the compound.

4

What you see is not what is over there, but what you are capable of seeing. If it is a creation of your own mind, not the model. The model is dependent on your idea of her.

— Robert Henri, *op. cit.*

Next day I walked down Camino Monte Sol later than usual. I was paid for a certain number of hours put in at the Gallery and must not exceed them, so I had to take some time off in the morning to make up for the work of the model night. As I walked, I noticed that the aspens on the Sangre de Cristos were beginning to turn their pale gold, thrown into vivid relief by the varying dark greens among and around them. Soon people from counties, even states, around would arrive in their thousands to drive up the winding dirt road from the edge of Villa Real to the ski lift almost at the top. The natives of Villa Real went elsewhere to see their aspens on weekends. If they were lucky enough to get off on a weekday, they went early in the morning. What artistic crimes have been committed in the name of aspens! So many Edythes all earnestly trying to capture that delicate fluttering gold, and at their best achieving utter banality. Only John Graham in his watercolors and Nick in his oils had managed to tread the tightrope between bad art and photography.

This train of thought lead inevitably to Bill. Now why had he seen me to my door last night, said, "See you soon," with another of those smiles and casual waves, and gone off purposefully. Should I change my hairdo, my perfume, my personality, or what? Liz caught me daydreaming in front of the mirror in her office, and to prevent any probing remarks, I asked her what she had been doing at the model night.

"Checking up on me, huh?" I said, but with a laugh to show I did not take it amiss.

She was serious. "Heaven forbid, infant, I knew you would get along like tequila down my throat." Lighting a cigarette, she seemed to change the subject by saying, "Believe me, Mac, Clem is one fine guy. He knew I'd be looking for something to soothe my savage breast last night."

She fingered the squash blossom necklace lying on that savage breast as she added, "Sometimes, you know, a man that's not for any woman is just what a woman that, damn it, seems not to be for any man, needs."

Seeing I looked puzzled, she said, "You've led a sheltered life, infant, forget it." This was undeniably true.

To distract her, as she was looking sad, I asked her what she thought of Bill.

"Mac, is that who you're dreaming about in front of the mirror?"

Annoyed at having, after all, given myself away by blushing at my question, I prevaricated, "Well, Liz, it's not just Bill, it's Henry Martin too. What a charmer, and of course, Paul still in pursuit."

Liz was all agog. "You're coming alive. Have fun, girl," she sighed and sat down to work.

The day went too slowly for me and for once I was glad to be able to leave early and walk home, this time along the Alameda to enjoy the green wildness along the Rio Villa Real. I had done the little housework necessary to keep my adobe looking attractive that morning; so changing into blue jeans and shirt, I got out my garden clippers and started tidying up the patio for winter. I worked steadily pulling dead annuals right up, shaking the soil off the roots, and snipping off the heads of dead perennials. While I was wrestling with a particularly large and tough hollyhock stem, I heard the garden gate open. Bill, I thought happily and turned with a smile, but it was Henry Martin.

"Come and help," I said, indicating the recalcitrant hollyhock. Henry was able to cut the stem at the ground with one decisive snip.

"How about a reward," I offered, "a cool drink on the portal?"

He accepted and once settled down comfortably, and after complimenting me on my garden, he asked me out to dinner, suggesting a well known dine, drink and dance place twenty miles to the south of the city. This was a wonderful opportunity to further my education, both as to police procedure and maybe, who knows, in other things too.

My second thoughts, naturally, were of what to wear. I settled on a plain but becoming black dress, in preference to the ubiquitous squaw dress, which I decided a genuine native son would not appreciate. Indeed I was rewarded for my efforts by a very intent and warm look from those brown eyes when I opened my door for him.

Henry drove fast and well along the flat open country to the old railroad town harboring our nightspot. He explained that he had been lent the car, his wife had taken his.

"Cleaned me out," he added bitterly.

Feeling strongly that I did not wish to endure a history of his matrimonial difficulties, I turned the conversation, none too subtly, to my preoccupations.

"Did you know Nick Polkoff well?" I asked.

He scowled, "Interfering old hack," he said. "Once I was his protégé, did you know? Oh yes, he was going to send me to Europe for the 'essential experience' as long as I painted his way and licked his boots. But then I sold a painting or two before he had put his seal of approval on me, and wham, there went protégé, trip to Europe and all."

I was silent, so he assumed the disapproval I in fact felt and went on, "Mind you, I don't at all question Nick's ability; he could paint, he knew more about painting than anybody else around here. That European training is something." He sounded rather wistful at this.

"Wouldn't you be touchy if you had devoted your life to painting and made sacrifices too, only to find that boys still wet behind the ears and rich widows with no training were flinging gobs of raw paint at the canvas with a house painter's brush and calling their messes art?" I asked.

"Sure," he said, "anybody would resent it. I don't blame Nick for his touchiness, but he had no reason to take it out on me."

Over drinks at the Victorian bar, where I was happy to see in the long mirror the dim lights flattered my freckly face, I pursued the subject, only to get back to Henry's gnawing grievance. It appeared that it was not really Nick's jealousy but Henry's need of money to support his wife that led to the rupture.

It was no use trying to avoid the subject, whatever I said only served to remind Henry of his wife and soon, I found myself listening to the whole story. No doubt the two drinks had loosened Henry's tongue, and perhaps lowered my guard also, for I could not help sympathizing with him. Henry, as he claimed and I could well believe, could imitate any painting style and any painter, and shortly after his marriage, which was already proving expensive, he dashed off an aspen picture in the manner of one of our lady artists whose efforts sold for $25 each to tourists who ought to have known better but who were probably delighted to find anything at all they could afford. But Henry did this on a larger canvas, put a price tag of $350 on it and put it in the Art Association show, simply because he had nothing else framed at the time. Well, it sold, and Henry from now on had to paint and sell two such meretricious productions each month to satisfy his wife. This, of course, horrified Nick, who might be misguided at times, but was always honest about painting.

My sympathy did not prevent me from enjoying the steak, nor, I could see, did Henry's troubles affect his appetite.

The jukebox was grinding out dance music by the time we had

finished our T-bones, and Henry got up to dance. I had never thought of myself as a good dancer, too little practice, but Henry was superlative. With a fine sense of rhythm, and his evident tender consideration of his partner, he was blissfully easy to follow. I relaxed and enjoyed myself; and, clearly, so did he. With breaks for dessert, for coffee, and for one final drink, the evening went very quickly and pleasantly. I was disappointed when he looked at his watch and said, "Me for the grindstone."

We had to hurry back; Henry's job left him no time to do more than nuzzle my neck quickly before I got out at my garden door, and then he drove off, leaving me to my dreams. Despite these dreams, though, I was not too starry-eyed to fail to notice Bill's lights were all on at his house back in the compound. This reminded me of our investigation, about which I had learned very little, but that little I decided to write down before I forgot, so that I could show some results to Bill.

What had I got, besides a delightful evening? Much light had been shed on Henry and a little on Nick, and I thought I could count on seeing Henry again and perhaps get some more concrete help.

With this thought in mind, I spent the next morning at home, but it was not Henry but Bill who called in midmorning. Rather diffidently, and staying firmly on the portal instead of coming in, he asked me if I would care to go for a drive with him. "Isn't this a free day for you?" he muttered hesitantly. I wondered how he knew, since only Liz and I knew my somewhat erratic schedule, but lost no time in accepting.

I hurried to grab a scarf and a short coat, as by now the days were getting colder. My eye fell upon the notes I had made of Henry's views of Nick, so I put them in my bag. They prompted me to suggest to Bill that we drive out to Puye to inspect the site of Bela's accident.

He seemed taken aback. "I thought you'd want to see some aspens," he said. "How about up to the mountains?"

I pointed out that on a weekend the one narrow dirt road would be choked with aspen lovers and there would probably be more photographers than aspens. "Also, "I said, "I know a good way round to Puye through the mountains, so we could please us both."

He agreed, though I thought not too happily, and sure enough, was soon grumbling about the road we took north out of town. It was dull and flat, but when I told him to turn off and we started climbing up into the Jemez Mountains, he fell silent. First one aspen, then two, then thousands, made a glorious fall bonfire. No startling dramatic reds, as I am told the New England fall boasts, just the pale rich yellow, in such mass and yet delicacy as to create the perfect southwestern fall picture. Bill apologized to me for his grumbling and drove very slowly along the deserted road, drinking in the scene.

I directed him when we came to an intersection and we drove up to an unexpected open flat area, surrounded with pines and deciduous trees, but no aspens now; the grass was lush and green on the ground beside a small pebbly stream, welcome sight in a dry land.

Looking up at the great cliff of Puye that reared before us with its small cliff houses at the top, Bill was astonished. I had seen the contrast before; it is dramatic, the green earth below and the dry barren cliff as a backdrop.

Clever Bill, he had brought a fried chicken, cold beer and rolls with him. We wedged our beer bottles between rocks in the stream to keep them cold in the icy water and decided to explore before eating. I had not been up to the top of the cliff. It's quite a climb, but I knew where the trail started and pointed it out to Bill. He was all for going up right away, but I had noticed with concern his flagging energy and insisted on eating first. So we stretched out companionably on a rug beside the stream and ate with our fingers.

As a way of making him rest, I showed him my notes, and when handing them over, found that I had snatched up the clippings I had saved of Nick's and Bela's deaths. While Bill read my notes, I read again the clipping about Bela's death. There was much detail.

"Bill," I said with some excitement, "We can figure out pretty well exactly what happened to Bela, and where, from this clipping. Listen . . .

The body of Mr. Bela Ferency, the
well-known Villa Real artist, was found

yesterday afternoon by his wife Ellen and Sheriff Martinez, at the foot of Puye cliff. Mr. Ferency, reported the sheriff this morning, had evidently stumbled and fell while sketching at the top of the cliff. His easel was set close to the edge of the overhang above the highest cliff dwelling, and from footprints faintly visible there and from other evidence, he is satisfied that Mr. Ferency either became dizzy and fell while taking down his easel or stepped back for some reason while doing so. His watch was smashed in the fall, according to the sheriff, so the time of death is established as occurring in the middle of the afternoon."

Bill was sad. "I didn't know Bela as well as Nick, really only saw him when he came to see Nick, once or twice a week it was. Unlike most artists, Bela didn't talk all the time about himself and his work. He always wanted to hear about what you were doing."

I remembered that too. "That's why everybody liked him," I said. "I've never heard a word against him personally. His work, yes, it was a bit old-hat, but nobody would hurt his feelings by telling him so."

Bill scrambled to his feet. "Come on," he said, "let's go up and look."

I took care to go on up the trail first, taking it very slowly and easily and glancing unobtrusively back every now and then to see how Bill was doing. Halfway, I insisted that I needed a rest and sat down to prove it.

Bill grinned. "Don't worry," he said. "I'm not about to make a fool of myself trying to impress you with my mountaineering."

I met his gaze, no melting brown eyes this time, but serious open blue ones, with smile lines at each side.

"Oh, you," I said, "it's not you I worry about. You flatter yourself," and went on up.

I think we were both equally glad to get to the top; at that altitude, I suppose nearly 8,000 feet, exertion is felt. We found the place where poor Bela must have had his easel by peering very cautiously down and finding the highest house, the best preserved of all the Puye cliff dwellings.

"The people who once lived here must have been both fine acrobats and scared stiff of somebody or something," I remarked to Bill. "Their houses were certainly as inaccessible as possible. And imagine carrying all the water, every drop of water used in the house up that trail every day."

We looked down at the green valley below and agreed it was a fine view for the cliff dwellers, and a fine view to paint too.

Bill suddenly exclaimed, "But Mary, Bela was getting on. Do you mean to tell me he walked up the way we did, carrying his painting outfit with him?"

I explained that there was a back way to the cliff dwellings too, a very old bumpy track that led off from quite another road from the one we had taken to within a short walk of the cliff.

"We didn't go that way," I went on, seeing his surprise, "because you wanted some aspens and the other road is much duller. Besides, it's on private land and you have to open gates and maybe slip a dollar to the owner. I believe that soon there'll be admission charges, guides and ticket takers here to spoil the whole thing."

We were standing directly over the highest house, and careful search brought to light three equidistant, and very distinct, holes in the ground, which we were convinced were made by Bela's combination paint box and easel. This was mounted on three extensible folding legs with sharp points on the end to keep the whole thing steady. It was Bill who found these holes and who remembered that Bela had a very old and treasured outfit he had brought back with him from France many long years ago. Bill also remembered something else. "You know, Mary, Bela was at Nick's place one day when I was there, just come in from sketching, and he had this outfit of his with him. In fact, he set it up to show Nick the painting inside. Nick said to him jokingly, 'Still the same old Bela, you never change your shadows, do you?' and then he looked at his box and added, 'Say, if you die before I do, be sure to leave me your box, won't you, and I'll leave you mine.'"

I was fascinated, "And what did Bela reply?"

"Oh," said Bill, "I don't remember exactly what, but something to the effect that he wouldn't take Nick's dinky little lady's vanity box as a gift. They were both laughing, so I guess it was an old joke."

Treading very delicately, we measured the distance from the hole in the ground nearest to the edge to a point from which we thought that a slight stumble would still result in such a horrible fall. We could see no evidence of any recent erosion in the cliff edge. On the contrary, it looked remarkably solid and tough. Any footprints or other such signs had, of course, gone permanently with the rains. We decided that it was just possible for Bela to have bent down to pack up his easel and, becoming dizzy, staggered back and fallen over the edge.

"What dreadfully bad luck," I said. "He was sensibly well in from the edge, really, and I see no reason for him to have been near enough to it just to fall over like that." I made a gesture downwards.

"Ah, I have it," Bill said. "The canvas was wet, so he'd have to prop it up carefully against something while packing up his box and before turning it face down against the lid of the box. In the painting position it would be with its back to the opened lid of the box. Now, if you look around, there's only that little stunted bush right there." He pointed at a straggly little piñon clinging to the edge of the cliff, and sure enough, it was the only "prop-able against" thing on the whole mesa.

By three he would have finished packing his box, and he'd go to pick up the painting. I said as much to Bill and there came unbidden into my head something that amused me, and I decided to see if it amused him.

"Reminds me of the worst, or really just the most unsayable lines in English poetry, 'What proppst thou ask'st, in these dull days my mind.'"

Bill was amused. "Either our Matthew had no ear or did not know what a lisp was."

Pleased that my joke was seen, I took his arm and went with him to inspect the piñon. If Bela had become dizzy putting down or picking up the painting there on the cliff's edge, the whole accident was explicable.

Bill pointed out that we would have to find out where the painting was found, and I agreed to ask Ellen.

Getting down the trail took time and care but was not so tiring as the climb. Still we were glad to collapse on the rug by the stream for a rest. Bill lay on his back with his hands clasped beneath his head and, not looking at me, said into the distance, "None of my business, you'll say, but Mary," he turned now and looked straight into my eyes, "I know you were out with Henry last night."

I was embarrassed now with those honest blue eyes searching me out, and I withdrew my gaze and nodded.

"I like Henry, women all seem to like him too, but Mary, he's not for you. Don't believe all that talk of his about his wife. He gripes and whines about her, but she has some hold on him, and he never gets free of her. They've separated so often before, but they always go back together again. When a man is through with a woman, and maybe the other way round, he's through, he just doesn't care any more, he doesn't talk about her. Henry in my book can't be through."

I pondered this and decided to play it cool, though I knew he was probably right. "I'll watch it," I said, getting up and holding out my hand to help him up.

He took it awkwardly and drove me home in silence.

5

It is true that obscurity may assist selection,
may at times force it.

— Robert Henri, *op. cit.*

Sunday was a half day at the Gallery, and my job was to cope with the obvious non-buyers, of which there were fewer than in summer, but they still outnumbered possible buyers by great odds. Clem had an uncanny instinct about whom to exert his salesmanship on. I wasn't entirely joking about his left little toe telling him when to materialize, for something did. Today his instinct told him to hang around, and as I could have predicted, we had a visit from our best customer. Mrs. Ephraim Rountree, to my way of thinking, justified the oil depreciation tax allowance all by herself. She came from Oklahoma two or three times a year and spread joy and blessings all around Villa Real with her open-handedness. Never did she fail to pay a visit to the Gallery and buy one or two, and once four, paintings from Clem. Nobody else would do for her, it had to be Clem.

I watched them together examining all the paintings earnestly. Clem could go into rapture over any painting at all at the slightest indication of interest on the part of a buyer. With no decided taste himself, he could spend ten minutes being enthusiastic over a John Graham watercolor, and then turn right round and spend another ten raving about one of Paul Humfrey's great blotchy monstrosities. He knew Mrs. Rountree's taste well from past experience, so at once he led her to the Inner Room. He snapped on the first light as he went in, a spotlight trained on the picture occupying the place of honor, the easel with a back cloth behind. Mrs. Rountree fell for this at once, and determined to have the John Graham watercolor, a masterly study of light and shadow in a Villa Real courtyard.

Clem then took down this picture and put up a small nude by Henry Martin of Dolores. I saw it was beautifully done, sexy without being offensive. His lighting focused attention on her seductive torso, her face being carefully arranged so her bad points were in shadow.

Mrs. Rountree was tempted, I could see, but she said thoughtfully, "No, Clem dear, I'd better not. Ephraim's a mite conservative, you know."

Whereupon Clem whipped that little painting off the easel and substituted a larger one. I was amused; he had planned this all along. It was Dolores again, and much the same pose and tone value, but this time she was dressed.

Clem made a quick sale on that one, I was pleased but not surprised to see, and then the two settled down to have a gossip about art and artists in Clem's office. The door was shut, so it was useless for me to try to overhear, but I did sneak up to look at the back of Henry's dressed Dolores and saw the price was $350. Good for Henry, I thought, that will pay for maybe some more dancing, as well as alimony.

Liz came in as soon as I got back to my desk at the entrance. Some non-buyers were strolling around the modern room, arguing the merits of Pop Art, which has not yet reached Villa Real, perhaps fortunately, and postimpressionism, of which we had some good examples.

"What did Mrs. R. buy?" she whispered to me. "I saw her coming in." So it was sheer curiosity that brought Liz in on her day off.

"A John Graham watercolor and that non-nude of Dolores."

Liz brightened. "Henry's?" she queried.

I nodded.

Clem bustled out importantly and went into the Inner Room where I could see him peering this way and that at the back of Henry's painting. Artists are supposed to affix a label with data and price on the upper left hand corner of any paintings for sale, but they often forget, or just scribble something illegible anywhere on the back. I had seen Henry's label, though, and it was perfectly easy to find and read. Then Clem looked at the back of John Graham's, whose label was always typed and affixed in precisely the right place, but he had the same trouble with it.

He must have felt unobserved because he quickly checked his appearance, fastidiously groomed as ever, in the mirror made by the glass of a watercolor reflecting the light, smoothed his impeccable hair down, and hurried back to his office.

Liz and I stared at each other.

"Clem's too vain to wear glasses," she said. "Men never make passes at men who wear glasses," and we both giggled, but not, I hope, unkindly.

"You go on home, if you want to, Mac. I'll close up, since I'm here."

I was glad to do so; the skies had been clouding over, and my walk home would be gray and cold.

The rain started, a gentle slow rain, by the time I reached the turnoff to the compound. I had planned to spend the rest of the afternoon cutting off the annuals that had all been killed by the first light frosts, but now I ran quickly through my patio where only the gold and bronze chrysanthemums bloomed bravely on, and hurried in to shut all my windows and light my fire. Life, I had found so far, had a way of giving one a taste for what one was obliged to do. I had enjoyed my rather solitary self-sufficient life here. I waited for that interior purr of satisfaction that usually came when I was curled up comfortably in front of my fire, allowing myself the weekly self-indulgence of a double crostic. No purr. I put down the puzzle and searched my small living room. What was missing? For the first time since moving into this delightful first house of mine, I felt lonely. Perhaps a dog or a cat? I thought. Something alive to keep me company beside the fire? This train of thought was profitless. Shaking myself mentally I went into my bedroom and took a critical look at my face and as much of the rest of me as I could see in the inadequate mirror. Yes, there was a change, Liz had been right, a light had come on inside, lending sparkle to my hair, depth to my eyes, a bloom to my cheeks. I gave myself a wink and subsided again beside the fire, happier now to await events.

It was still raining gently when I awoke next morning. I was quite pleased when Liz phoned after breakfast to tell me not to bother to come in. "Too damp for you, Mac, and nothing doing here anyway. I'm getting the accounts done for the meeting tomorrow."

That would be the regular Board meeting, I thought, which took place once a month to sign the checks to artists and generally run things. A meeting of the entire Villa Real Art Association membership took place once a year; it was then the Board was elected. The Board itself elected its own president and the Chairmen of each committee, who in turn chose non-board members for help in their duties. The president had an important job; not the least of his burdens was that of being thick-skinned, for it was to him that members went with their unending complaints. One president when the term of his office came to an end vowed that never again would he undergo such a penance, the mere thought of having to smooth down all those injured artistic egos gave him stomach ulcers just to think of it. Perhaps the most influential position after president was Chairman of the Hanging Committee. His job was to supervise the monthly gallery show. It was understood without being stipulated that he was to run the show two or three months of the year and to choose someone else to run it, someone different each month, that is, for the other months. In practice, what happened was that this chairman would choose himself to run the show for the most important months when most paintings were sold, and choose a friend who would hang his paintings in the best positions for the other months. One chairman we had once, Liz told me, hung every show each month, and so packed his jury, too, that the gallery had nothing in but almost identical huge canvasses of blots and blobs in various colors. There were complaints, and how, she said. Then another chairman, an old fellow, she said, did much the same thing but less obviously. He packed the gallery with old canvasses by himself, his wife, his friends, until we looked like a museum specializing in "the olden days," so Liz told me with amusement. More complaints. This time the Board acted. Now they submitted to the membership a change in constitution, resulting in the creation of yet another chairman. Now there was one chairman to choose and be head of the jury, and another chairman to choose and be head of the Hanging Committee. Justice, it was felt, had been done, but complaints still poured in. All members on being accepted into the Association were warned not to go to Clem with their gripes; he had threatened to leave for a better paying position if he was bothered by petty details. It was generally Liz who acted as wailing wall; she smoothed down ruffled feathers and sent the unsmoothable ones to the chairman in whose department the complaint fell.

I was curiously restless that rainy morning. I dressed with unusual care, for what I did not know, and took out my polishing rags and made a long loving job of waxing my *vargueno*. This was a specially dear piece of furniture I had picked up at a sale in a private house, a genuine old Spanish traveling desk, no earthly good for writing on, but fine for filing papers, as it had a lot of little compartments and drawers behind its folded up lid. That was where I kept my clippings and notes.

The squeak of my garden door startled me as I was rubbing the inner face of this lid to a satisfying shine. Leaving it down, I opened the door to find Edythe Kendall Chambers mincing quickly through the rain. She opened her mouth the second she saw me, and it was still open ten minutes later. By this time I sat myself down with a falsely attentive smile on my face and let the flood of I's, my's, me's, and more I's flow over me. Suddenly I caught the name "Ellen," and my attention became real.

"Poor dear Ellen, she's taking things hard, you know. I'm having her to lunch today, it's time she got out a bit. I've been through it myself, as you know, my dear, so I'm anxious to help poor Ellen."

I interrupted firmly, "How kind of you, Edythe. I haven't seen Ellen since Bela's accident, and I'd like to again, now the shock must have worn off a bit."

Edythe rose to the bait, "Why, then, dear, come along too. You'll be a help to me, since I remember you used to be quite thick with Ellen."

I was quick to accept; after all, aside from my detective aspirations, Edythe could afford to keep a good cook, and my supplies were running low. She got up after more talk finally, and, rising, her eye came to rest on my opened *vargueno*.

"What a nice piece you have there." She trotted over to make a close inspection.

Too late, I saw my pile of clippings in plain view. Nothing escaped Edythe; she pounced right on them.

"What's this?" she exclaimed. As she read, her face grew hard and for once she looked the shrewd woman that I saw she was under all that gush. She saw, too, the notes I had made, not very legible fortunately, but she had not the nerve to pick them up to read.

She turned to me and said with emphasis, "I know what you're up to, and maybe you think it's all a good joke, but just suppose," she paused and leaned forward to get her point across, "just suppose, though I'm not for a minute saying it is so, you are right. What then? We all know what you said at model night, it's allover town. If I were you, dear child, I would keep my mouth shut."

Greatly intrigued, I seized my opportunity. "It sounds to me, Mrs. Chambers, as if you do know something. What is it? "

She said with considerable dignity, "I know you think me a foolish old woman, but I have seen more of life than you have and I tell you that it is dangerous, yes dangerous, both for you and for other people too, to go about looking for trouble. Have you the least idea, you silly girl, what worry mere suspicion can cause? For every single cupboard in Villa Real there's a skeleton someone would go to endless lengths to conceal. Your joke, those three deaths, of course it's a lot of nonsense, they were accidents all right. But just by casting doubt on that you are stirring up some very, very muddy water."

I was impressed and was about to agree with her and tell her I would forget the whole thing, when her voice and manner changed abruptly and she was once more the Edythe Kendall Chambers she presented to the world, animated, flirtatious, gay and giddy.

"What a fuss to make," she said. "Now, you come along for lunch and we'll help poor Ellen forget her troubles."

She fluttered out, talking all the way, and leaving me with plenty to think about.

Ellen Ferency had married Bela late in life, in fact, not until she had retired from school teaching. Bela was father, mother, husband, son and probably pupil, too, for her. It was a companionable more than a romantic relationship. Coming into a small inheritance, Ellen had retired early on and was lucky to have Bela help her enjoy life. Bela too was lucky in having Ellen be practical for him. All he wanted to do was paint and sketch, particularly he loved sketching outdoors. Ellen enabled him to do just that. She managed things so that he could live the life he wanted. And now I observed her with sympathy, thinner, sadder and yet undaunted. She had lived alone before and could again. Though heartbroken, she would not go to pieces.

Edythe's idea of treating the newly widowed was to keep up a constant stream of reminiscence about her late husband, whom Villa Real assumed had been talked to death, but it now appeared died from overwork. I was beginning to despair of getting Ellen to myself, when a providential phone call removed Edythe from the room while we were having coffee in her large living room. I turned at once to Ellen, knowing that we would be free from interruption for some time; Edythe could never tear herself away from a phone call.

"Ellen, I'm so terribly sorry about Bela, and if it isn't reopening old wounds, I wish you'd tell me what happened. None of his friends can believe that he would have been careless, and we all think he must have become suddenly dizzy. Had you any reason to think perhaps he might have had a dizzy spell?"

Ellen turned to me thankfully. "It's funny, Edythe doesn't seem to realize that I want to talk about Bela; I want to discuss the accident. I feel I can keep him close to me by talking about him. My friends are always trying to distract me, they won't let me say the name Bela." Her voice quivered, but she raised her firm chin and went on, "I'm glad you asked me, Mac, and I'm glad to have someone to tell."

She poured it all out to me. On that June day Bela had gone off in the early morning. It was his invariable habit to sketch in the morning; he usually took his lunch with him. Then sometimes he had a little nap, if the place was cool and inviting, or he came home, but according to Ellen, he was never home later than three o'clock, and usually earlier. So that on this day when he had not returned by four, she became alarmed, and at five seriously worried enough to call the sheriff, who was sympathetic. Ellen knew where Bela had planned to go, so there was no delay in finding him. When they reached the place before the rise of the mesa and got out of the car to walk to the cliff edge, they saw at once Bela's easel set up, and then running up, they saw the canvas propped against a piñon, and then, and at this Ellen almost broke down, they looked over the edge and saw what they by now expected.

"But Mac," Ellen said intensely, "the sheriff told me, and I've not told anybody else here because I think I must have mistaken him, that Bela's watch was smashed in the fall and it stopped at three fifteen. He brought me the watch right then and I've still got it. Bela never painted in the afternoon, he didn't like the lights and shadows for sketching after morning. The car was out in the hot sun, there was no good place to nap. So he must have been feeling ill, I think. Perhaps he did have to lie down in the hot sun and got sunstroke."

Her voice dropped, "But there's another odd thing about it all. I've been sketching so many times with him and I know his routine like the back of my hand. When he finished sketching, and he never used a lot of paint, like some artists you know, he just turned the painting around and fastened it in a special slot, so that it was face down against the lid but could not touch the lid or anything else. He never had to prop a canvas up to dry out. That was something he liked about his sketching outfit. So why should he have to go right over to the edge of a cliff to prop a canvas up suddenly?"

I was soothing, "I'm afraid he wasn't himself, Ellen. You must be right, it was sunstroke."

Edythe came back then and had evidently overheard part of our conversation, because she threw me a look of concentrated dislike.

"You shouldn't talk to our little Mac," she said, "she's a troublemaker. You know what she said last model night, Ellen? Why, she said your poor Bela and dear Nick and John Graham had not died by accident, oh no, she said they had been murdered!"

I was hideously embarrassed at this and rushed in to make things worse by saying, "No, that's not so, honestly, Ellen, all I said was that those three deaths — well, I just felt it was a strange coincidence, more of a joke I was making, really."

Luckily, Ellen was an intelligent woman. She saw my embarrassment and my concern for her and kindly helped me out of a bad spot. Taking my arm, she said to Edythe, "Well, if you really want to know, I think it's more than coincidence too, and you know as well as I do that Mac wouldn't make a joke out of anybody's death, let alone Bela's."

Edythe changed her tune hastily at this and said, "Oh what a lot of nonsense we are talking, aren't we? Let's forget it all and just enjoy our little gossip."

On she went, rehashing some old stories we all knew anyway, and Ellen and I got away as soon as we decently could. Ellen insisted on giving me a ride for the short distance from Edythe's large fashionable home on the Camino to the compound and said when we were safely away, "Edythe's right, it is a lot of nonsense. I just can't bear to have Bela gone, and so I'm trying to find something or somebody to blame for it."

I impulsively kissed her cheek before getting out of the car, which pleased her, and vowed to myself not to make any more trouble.

That vow was short lived.

6

The artist should have a powerful
will. He should be powerfully
possessed by one idea.

— Robert Henri, *Op Cit.*

Restless still, I occupied myself that afternoon in rearranging my books, which is no mere ten-minute chore for me, but an afternoon's work, interspersed with compulsive dippings into some old favorites. I was completely absorbed in one of my pet anthologies, when I was startled by a knock on the door. "Come in," I called out. The door opened rather tentatively and Bill stuck his head around it. He grinned at seeing me sitting on the floor.

"A good day for staying home," he observed, wiping his damp hair back with the palm of his hand. "This rain is more like a Scotch mist, it's wet, but is it rain?"

I laughed. "The Indians call this rain the female rain, and the thundershower variety that we've had all summer is the hard pelting kind, that's the male rain. This female rain comes up from the Gulf, often at this time of year; it will be gone tomorrow probably."

I now noticed that Bill had a letter in his hand. He didn't hand it over but stuffed it in his pocket and said, "I came over to ask you to have dinner with me tonight. I will get some tamales and enchiladas in, and I have beer in the ice box. Can't take you out because my car has no top. Don't want to get you wet."

I looked around at my cozy room, and said, "It's really easier for you to bring things here. Why not come along with the food at six thirty. I'll warm it up in my oven and we'll eat by the fire."

He was clearly relieved at this and agreed, adding, "I don't want to eat surrounded by paintings, either." I made a gesture of protest, but he went on, more to himself, I think, "I *must* paint. I *know* what I'm after. I *must* get it. I *will* get it." He had become terribly intense.

I was embarrassed by his feverish emphasis and replied rather unsympathetically, "Painting well is not entirely a matter of will."

Bill fixed an intent stare on me.

"Surely if you must succeed, and you work like hell, isn't that enough?"

I said bluntly — tact is hardly my strong point, "No, hard work, training, the will to succeed, luck, they'll all help. But one other thing there must be, and that is given, not acquired, and not given to all artists, either."

Bill was still intense. "And what's that?" he asked and interrupted himself, "Talent, I suppose?"

I thought for a second. "No, it's not quite talent, it's more of a characteristic. Some people are born thinkers, some are born to love words, some people are hearers, some are doers, but artists, the best, live in their eyes."

Bill visibly slumped and with a muttered, "Be in at six thirty," walked out with a discouraged and preoccupied air.

"Damn you, Mary Mac, you and your big mouth," I said to myself. "The poor guy needs encouragement and sympathy, bread not a stone." Then I shook myself mentally and, as is my habit, learned the hard way of listening to other people's troubles, said firmly, "No skin off your nose, pal," and got up to see what I could make for dinner. I was thrilled at cooking for a man. But after chile and beer my delicious lemon chiffon pie, my bourbon charlotte russe, my devastating cheesecake would be far too rich. Anyway, on checking my ice box I saw I had little to work with. Finally, I settled on a simple but luscious green gage plum concoction. I had just put this in the icebox when there was a knock on the door again. At five forty-five, it must be Bill back again for a drink before dinner, I thought. I patted my hair in place, and went to the door to find Henry Martin standing on the portal.

"Hi, Miss Mac," he said, coming in. He saw that I had a table by the fire laid ready for dinner with two places laid and looked questioningly at me. "Company coming?"

I nodded.

"Bill's bringing over some tamales."

"Oh, well, then, some other time. I was going to invite you out dancing, but another time will do."

I thought regretfully of his divine dancing, but of course I was committed now to an evening with Bill, and I shrugged ruefully. "Sorry, Henry," I said. "I'd love to later this week."

Henry seemed in no hurry to go, so I invited him to have a small beer with me. I lit my fire again, and we sat back, glasses in hand, ostensibly relaxed. I don't know about Henry, but I was uneasy. Why couldn't I meet those warm brown eyes? I tried, but had to look away.

Nervously, I chattered disjointedly of my lunch with Edythe. Henry was attentive, but silent, so I found myself repeating Ellen's story to me. My memory is excellent, so that the conversation, or rather monologue, consisted of an almost exact repetition of Ellen's own words.

At one point, Henry fixed that warm regard on me even more intently and said suddenly, interrupting, "What, what did she say?"

I repeated Ellen's words, it was about the smashed watch. But then I stopped myself, remembering my vow, and said decisively, "That's enough about that. I've been silly, and cruel too, and I'm not going to say another word. Those deaths were just terribly sad and rotten luck and no more. I've too much imagination, I know."

Henry agreed in a rather left-handed complimentary way. "You should use that imagination to write instead of talk," he said, acutely, I realize now. He understood the creative process, which must not be frittered away in chatter, but channeled into action.

Another knock on the door saved me from the necessity of reply. This time it was Bill, who stopped in surprise on the doorstep, seeing Henry sitting by the fire.

"Come on in, Bill, old man," said Henry in a hearty, proprietorial sort of way that I rather resented. Fortunately, he added, "I'm on my way soon as I've finished this glass."

I took the Mexican casseroles Bill handed to me and went into the kitchen to put them in the oven. From there I could overhear the men talking, in a rather uneasy, mock-friendly way.

Bill said, probably to provide a distraction, I thought, "Painted anything new lately?"

Henry's tone brightened and was immediately more easy. "Sure. Like to see it?" He went to the window and peered out. "It's not raining hard enough to hurt; I'll bring it in." He did so, and I emerged from the kitchen to look.

Bill and I both gasped with pleasure together, "Wonderful, Henry," I said, and Bill chimed in, "Marvelous." Then he studied the canvas intently. It was a medium size unframed portrait of a very beautiful, sultry woman, thin face, full lips, white skin, reddish hair; she was leaning forward, so that the deep cleft between her high full breasts was shown. The whole painting was in tones of red.

I murmured to myself the lines that came unbidden to my head, "The bitter reds of love."

Bill caught this. Excited, he said, "What? Say that again."

I searched my memory. What had I been reading by my bookshelf this afternoon? Ah, I remembered. I said slowly, "Stronger than alcohol, vaster than lyres, ferment the bitter reds of love."

Bill was clearly very struck with this and asked where I got it from.

But Henry repeated it to himself and said meditatively, "I'll do another like this, all reds, I'll make them bitter too, acid bitter, and I'll put here," he made a brush stroke gesture on his painting, "a bottle, and here," he made another stroke, "I'll put in a lyre or two; heavens, what is a lyre? Well, I'll find out." He was talking to himself now, rather than to us. "Reds, and a bottle and some lyres, just suggested in the background." He turned to me, "Mac," he ordered, "find out the title of that line, or whatever."

I went obediently to the bookshelf. Now what had I been leafing through? My eye roved through my collection. Must be poetry, and if I knew it so well, then it would be in my favorite anthology, in which I wrote scraps I came across and liked enough to copy out. Sure enough, I found it quickly and showed the quotation to them.

Bill took the book and read in a very creditable accent:

> *Plus fortes que l'acool, plus vaste que nos*
> *lyres,*
> *Fermentent les rousseurs ameres de l'amour.*

Bill breathed deeply after giving full effect to the long-vowel R's and said, "Lovely, words like music."

Henry was impatient. "Come again, Bill, the only word I recognize is *l'amour*; give with the English."

Bill translated slowly with enjoyment, "Stronger than alcohol, vaster than our lyres, ferment the . . ." he hesitated. "No, ruddy reds, won't do." He looked at me.

I said, "Bitter reds is the only possible translation."

Henry was irritated. "Stop playing, you two, just give me the sense and the guy that wrote it."

Bill shrugged and handing over the book, said, "It's Rimbaud, of course. You get the sense but lose the music in English."

"Music?" said Henry. "Who wants music? Man, what a painting I can have myself." He went out quickly with his painting, not even saying goodbye or finishing his beer.

"Now that," I said to Bill, "is the true artistic temperament."

Bill flushed, annoyed, I guessed, and I changed the subject hastily.

"Sit down, Bill," I said, and I broke my vow again. "Ellen confirms your idea, you were absolutely right. Bela's canvas was propped against that bitty piñon, just as you thought."

He refused to be distracted. "Let's drop it, shall we?" he said. "Heaven knows why I've been encouraging you."

I was rather hurt at this and marched off to the kitchen.

When I came back with the casseroles, Bill was standing at my bookshelves. He came up to me eagerly, his face alight with interest, and said very happily, "Mary, what a damn nice lot of books, best I've seen around here. Most of my pets, and some I've wanted to read but haven't been able to get."

The library of Villa Real, though willing, suffers from financial anemia. So, if their tastes are off the beaten track, the few book lovers living here learn to buy what they want and share among themselves. I was mollified. "Anything you want to borrow, you take," I said warmly. "Anything except this," I pointed to the book in which I had copied the Rimbaud lines. "That's special."

"I'll take one before I go home," Bill agreed and sat down beside the fire. We had a most companionable dinner. Chile and beer and plenty to discuss all add up to a fine evening. There was none of that rather enjoyable unease I felt with Henry. I could meet Bill's blue eyes without a qualm, as we talked about books, authors, getting to the poets and writers of Villa Real, and from them inevitably to the artists.

"What do you think of Paul Humfrey?" Bill asked.

"Well," I said, considering, "as a man, or as an artist? As a man, no, not my line of country, or cup of tea; as an artist, I'd say the same. Still, he's a good teacher. Some of his pupils have gone to the top, at least here, you know."

"Huh, I heard he was going to sue one of them for copying his style and then selling better than he did," remarked Bill.

"Oh, that's just his bluff. He may be jealous, but he does O.K." I was sarcastic. "He always has his little group of female worshippers. And look how he wormed his way into the Art Association, so he can get his pupils accepted. Why, it's almost like buying a degree. You sign up with enough lessons and Paul will see that you become a member."

Bill looked uncomfortable at this, a strange look passed over his face. He suddenly forced a laugh and said, "Oh well, at least I know one of his secrets."

"And what's that?" I was interested.

Bill relaxed and said, "You saw that byplay with Dolores on model night?"

I nodded.

"That was just for effect. You all jumped to the conclusion that he'd been making out with Dolores, now didn't you?"

I nodded again, amused.

"He didn't even get to second base."

"Hmmm. How do you know?" I asked before I could stop myself.

Bill was delighted. "Jealous?" he asked.

"Don't be ridiculous," I retorted coldly. "What's it matter to me?" But betrayed by a blush, I bent down to pick a nonexistent crumb off the floor, hoping he would not see.

Bill went on, staring at the fire. "The horse's mouth, in this case, is Henry."

I sat up, surprised.

"Yes, Henry gets to any base he wants. No," he corrected himself, "that's not true; it's more that, how shall I put it, when a base is available, Henry knows?"

"More loved against than loving?" I suggested.

Bill disagreed. "Loving isn't the word, Mary. I can't explain exactly to you, you wouldn't know what I was talking about." His voice and manner were affectionate as he said this.

To cover my embarrassment, I said sharply, "I'm not the little innocent I may appear to you. You can't live in a sanitarium without picking up a lot of information about the underside of life."

Bill looked sad. "I know," he said, "but there's a difference between books and life, words and deeds, saying and doing."

What on earth induced me to blurt out, "And what makes you think I'm not one for doing?" I must have been stung by his words.

Bill got up without a word, came over to my chair, planted one hand firmly through the top of my hair, the other under my chin, and fastening his lips sideways on mine, gave me a very thorough exploratory kiss. I was rigid with shock and embarrassment. All I could think of was the taste of chile and beer and wondering if this was what it was all about. After a few seconds, which seemed like an age, Bill went back to his chair, wiped his mouth with his napkin, and remarked quite nonchalantly, "I was right," and grinned at me with perfect aplomb.

"To change the subject again," he said cheerfully, "did you know that was a portrait of Henry's wife in those bitter reds of love?"

I wiped my mouth now and, bracing myself, tried to look nonchalant. "Thought it must be," I replied, grateful for the chance to compose myself. "A very beautiful woman, too."

"All the artists wanted to paint her," said Bill, "but she would never pose for any of them, not even for Henry. He had to marry her first, and even then she was sulky about it. No nudes and five minutes sitting down at the most. Henry's painted four or five marvelous pictures from that one pose he got out of her a few years ago. And since then she's got quite fat, though she still has that fascinating face and wonderful cleavage."

"What about Nick?" I asked. "I should think he'd've been able to persuade her into posing for him. He never had the least trouble with talking everyone else into that, and getting them to pay a fat figure to buy the result, too."

Bill smiled. Nick's success with the ladies was well known. He would flatter them, get them to sit for him, and hooked, they would have to buy the portrait. No mention of money at the start of all this, but plenty at the end. "He'd have given his left finger, the one knotted up with arthritis, to paint her," Bill agreed. "But, the supreme tribute, for free. He told me so himself when I first met him. He spent most of his painting life in Paris and he used a French word—I've forgotten it—for that cleft between the breasts, and kissed his fingers enthusiastically, saying, 'Superb.'"

He gave a reminiscent chuckle. "Nick was a good friend to me. I just wish I had gone over to see him that night he died. It was early April, wasn't it? It was suddenly cold, I remember, so I didn't want to cross the compound. But damn it, I wish I had."

Nick's house was the pride of the compound. It had originally been the studio for the main house, so it had a large north light, a much envied possession in Villa Real. Though considered to be of the compound, it was so tucked away at the back as to seem separate and secluded. I wondered aloud who had it now.

Bill told me that it was empty. Empty, that is, of humans, but, he said, "Nick's stuff is still locked away there, waiting for his brother to come out and pack it up. I believe the brother is continuing to pay the rent, as storage fees, really. Meanwhile, a lot of artists and, of course, the inevitable rich widows dabbling in art were after it. I know who else wants it, and who will probably get it," added Bill. "Henry is the one my money's on."

"But can he afford it?" I asked dubiously.

"Henry, haven't you observed, seems able to afford what he wants," Bill replied truthfully.

I almost committed the crime of telling Bill about the sale of the Dolores non-nude to Mrs. Ephraim Rountree, but stopped in time, reflecting that I had been able to keep my mouth shut with Henry, who had the right to know, so I certainly must not let it out to Bill, who had no business knowing. That one thing had been impressed on me when Clem got me my job. That I must never, never tell any artists about a sale, near sale, or non-sale of his work. Nothing whatever was to be said, by anybody to anybody, or about anybody, as to sales in the Gallery. Only a check in the mail, signed by two Board members, was used to tell the artist his painting had been sold.

Bill took his leave after this remark. I went to the door with him, where he put his hands on my shoulders and kissed me gently on the cheek, giving, sort of in passing, a little nibble on the lobe of my ear, and said, "Good night, Mary, you're a nice girl," and left.

7

An artist must have imagination.
An artist who does not use his
imagination is a mechanic.

—Robert Henri, *Op Cit.*

"Nice girl, indeed," I thought wrathfully as I walked down the Camino to work the next morning. What an insult. But the clean, cool, sparkling morning was hardly conducive to injured feelings, and my familiar walk during which I watched the blue mountains as long as I could see them, put me in an expansive frame of mind. I was happy then to catch sight of Henry walking slowly and, I saw, rather aimlessly up the hill.

"Hi," I called, "you're out early."

He came over to my side of the Camino and caught my hand. "Ah, Miss Mac dear," his automatic charm on full blast, but I could see he was looking tired and strained.

I waved my hand out and around to the mountains, "The blue remembered hills," I said, which was the line that always came to me when I watched the light and shadow pattern on them in the morning.

He stared thoughtfully at them, his attention caught. "No, not really blue. I'd paint them a grayed-reddish there," he pointed, "then here a grayed ochre or yellow sienna, and plashes of violet, and some purple I see." He trailed off, still gazing intently.

Amused at his single track mind, I said goodbye, reluctantly perhaps, and with those disturbing brown eyes still fixed on me, I walked, faster now, down the hill. At the turn onto Acequia Madre, I looked back. Just as I felt, Henry was watching me. I waved and went on to the post office.

The Art Association box was empty that morning. Mine was full, which ordinarily would have pleased me. Up till now, I had enjoyed my correspondence with the many friends I had made at the sanitarium; some of them were still there and some, luckier, or perhaps unluckier, had left. We all tended, I realized then, to cling to each other until life in the less secure world outside claimed us again. I didn't bother to open any of my letters, but went on to the gallery, wondering if Clem had emptied the box, and if so, why. He had one key, Liz and I each had one too, but he had made it clear that it was my job to collect the mail and it was unlike him to bother. In fact, he had told me that he had changed the box to a new, bigger one that could be opened with a key because it annoyed him to fiddle with the combination of numbers that opened the small, older boxes.

Liz was not in by the time I arrived. This, however, was quite usual. She made no bones about being a night owl and it was well known in Villa Real that most nights she could be found in one of the bars on Canyon Road.

Clem was in his office, I saw through the open door. He put down something he had in hand on hearing me come in and called, "Liz?"

I replied hastily, "Good morning, Mr. Dennison. I guess Liz has that day-after-the-night-before headache."

Clem was tolerant "She's probably getting some coffee for it. Well, Mary Mac, find the folder with the checks and deposit slips on

Liz's desk and take it over to the bank, will you?"

Liz was a very tidy, methodical secretary, more, I suspected, from training than from character, and she had the folder ready on her desk. Glad of the excuse to go out in the exhilarating morning, I took it up and walked down Palace Avenue to the bank on the corner of the Plaza. As I let my eye drift idly over the piles of crude pottery, corn kernel necklaces, and other tourist junk displayed by the Pueblo Indian women under the portal of the Governor's Palace, I was surprised to hear a "Mary" behind me. It was Bill. I hardly recognized him until he came close; before he had always worn blue jeans and a checked shirt, clean but worn looking. Now he was in a business suit and a quiet tie. I surveyed him with approval. "Off somewhere?" I asked, and added softly, "Coming back?"

Bill gave a nervous grin. "Off to the big city. I'm going by bus, because I don't know how long I'll be away, and the old car isn't too reliable," he paused. "Oh yes, I'll be back, one way or another." He looked at his watch, patted me on the shoulder, and strode off.

At the bank, I found myself mechanically opening the folder and riffling through the numerous checks to see if they were all stamped. Most of them were to smallish sums, representing down payment, and even smaller ones representing monthly payment, but there were a few big ones, the biggest of all being Mrs. Ephraim Rountree's. I glanced at her check, enjoying the fleeting contact with great riches. It was for $1,200. After collecting the duplicate deposit slips and putting them in the folder, I hurried back to the gallery, making mental calculations on the way. John Graham's watercolor, I remembered, had been marked $750, and Henry's non-nude of Dolores, I thought, shutting my eyes briefly and trying to visualize the label, had been $350. Although arithmetic had never been my strong point, even I could add that up in my head.

"Mac, look where you're going." It was Liz, into whom I had nearly bumped as we both were converging on the entrance to the Art Association complex of adobes on Palace Avenue.

I handed over the folder to Liz when we reached her desk and asked her in what I hoped was an offhand way, "Morning, Liz. I've been to the bank for you and put in all the checks. What did our blessed Mrs. Rountree buy?"

Liz was not forthcoming; I think she was still nursing a hangover. "Look for yourself," she said, growling, and handed over another folder. What I expected to find was that Mrs. Rountree had bought as she occasionally did, an Indian painting to give to one of her grandchildren, but as I could see from the numerous entries in the folder Liz handed me, that had not been the case. It was perfectly clear, Mrs. Rountree had bought two paintings only, and the amounts were set down with no possibility for error, as I had remembered, $750 for the watercolor and $350 for the oil.

"Well," I thought, "she must have owed something from another time, or perhaps Clem had forgotten to tell Liz about another purchase." I was about to tell Liz of the mistake, but remembering her growl, decided not to approach her until the coffee had improved her disposition.

Clem did what he pleased, instinct telling him when his presence was necessary, but Liz and I had to stagger our lunch hours. When Liz was cross, I always suggested that she take her break first. This morning, she took off on the dot of twelve o'clock with a muttered, "Back soon," to me. She did return in a better temper, but I had to go off to my lunch then, so I said nothing, but sat down at my usual table in Polly's Place, the restaurant we all went to just a door or two up from the Art Association. Once there, over the cheapest and most fattening things I could find on Polly's blackboard menu, I started to think. The more I thought, the less I liked it. I was sure, of course, that someone, probably Clem, had made a mistake, but would anybody be happy if I pointed it out? Moreover, I liked my job, and wanted to keep it. Either Clem or Liz, or both together, could have me fired by the Board very easily, as I hardly earned the little money I got, not being allowed, or possibly able, to sell art anyway. Finishing the last spoonful of Polly's gloriously rich and fattening chocolate mousse and rejoicing at accomplishing that feat, I resolved to keep my mouth tightly shut for a change and wait to see what happened.

Liz was her usual buoyant self when I returned from lunch and remarking casually that she had been up late last night, asked me if I would stick around for the Board of Directors meeting to be held that night. "Paul Humfrey, the jerk, is sort of touchy about having Clem or me on hand while he does his stuff as President," Liz explained. "We wouldn't dream of trying to overhear the old biddies who think they run everything anyway, but it makes Paul feel great to have us completely out of it. So you, Mac," she smiled a bit sourly, "you can give them their coffee and free cookies, and give them, too, the illusion of importance."

I felt flattered rather than put upon and agreed eagerly. Liz spent an hour showing me exactly what to do, why and where to put what, and having made sure I knew the ropes, sent me home early. I bought the cookies she had given me money from the petty cash for, dropped them off at the gallery, and spent a little time doing my own shopping. So that by the time I arrived home, rather tired, my paper was lying in the chrysanthemums.

Sinking back into my comfortable chair, I opened the paper with a sigh of relaxation, only to be brought up with a start. *VILLA REAL WOMAN BRUTALLY ATTACKED*, I read in the headline. Then the name leaped up at me from the page, "Ellen Ferency, 57, widow of the late Bela Ferency . . ." I groaned, "No," and read hastily on, fearing to learn that she was dead. I gave next a smile of relief. It appeared from the newspaper report that the attack had failed, due to some interruption, and that though injured, and it did not specify in what way, she was resting comfortably in hospital, where her condition was reported as excellent.

A squeak of my garden door aroused me from this close scrutiny of the paper, which I flung down and went to the door to admit Edythe Kendall Chambers. She was full of the news. "Mac," she gasped, "we're none of us safe, we'll all be raped."

She was certainly upset, I thought, but did I detect a faint pleasure in the prospect before her? I made her sit down and tried to soothe her, but she was in full spate.

"No, Mac, you can't tell me not to worry. I got my doctor, he's

Ellen's too, to let me see her this afternoon. I've just come from the hospital."

I interrupted eagerly, "How is Ellen, was she badly hurt?" I hesitated, hating myself for saying it, but compelled to, "She wasn't, uh, raped, was she?"

I thought Edythe looked a little disappointed. "No, nothing like that, it was the strangest thing, Mac. She really is perfectly all right, thank heaven, she just got a bad shock. She told me all about it and I'll tell you, but you mustn't repeat it, as the police don't want anyone to know much until they can bring in the criminal. It happened rather late last night, early this morning, really. Ellen told me she thought she heard a noise in her kitchen and went down to see what it was. She's a brave and determined lady."

I agreed.

Edythe went on, "She got to the bottom of the stairs and was walking to the light switch at the front door, when she was seized by the neck from the back."

I was horrified, "How frightening, but how come she is alive, then?"

"Ah," said Edythe, "Ellen has lived in New York, and she knew what to do. She wears those old fashioned high necked night dresses with stand up collars and biggish kind of buttons at the throat, you know, and she said whoever it was had gloves on and couldn't really get a good grip on her. So very cleverly, she pretended to struggle a bit, and then puffed and collapsed in a limp heap on the floor."

I was filled with admiration. "What presence of mind. I couldn't do that, could you?"

Edythe shuddered in sympathy. "Heavens, no," she said, "but Ellen told me that, when she was teaching in New York and living alone before her marriage, she was told the various possible defenses against attack and now, here of all places, that paid off."

"But surely," I said, "didn't the attacker stop to check, and anyway, what did he want?"

Edythe frowned, "That's exactly what's bothering Ellen. This man, whoever it was, she doesn't know if it was a man, woman or child, except that it couldn't have been a small child. He seemed to wait quite still for a second, then he picked up her hand at the wrist, but let it fall directly, fortunately, as Ellen said her heart was thumping so loud she was sure he could hear it, then he ran out of the door."

"Didn't he take anything?" I asked, puzzled.

"No," answered Edythe, puzzled too, I could see. "Ellen told me she had her bag on a table by the front door. It was quite visible in the moonlight coming in from the French doors onto her patio, and she had little but nice pieces of silver on display in the dining alcove. Also, she had a wristwatch on the hand he picked up. And now she is wondering what he was doing in the kitchen, because she is sure that's where the noise was coming from."

Edythe and I looked at each other fearfully. Not rape, not robbery, what was the motive?

"Perhaps an escaped convict looking for food," I suggested. The state prison is a few miles from Villa Real, so it was a reasonable suggestion.

But Edythe shook her head. "Ellen thought of that and asked the police when they interviewed her, but that's out."

Edythe now implored me to come to stay with her, but I remained firm, though I was sorry for her. I knew she could get her regular cook in to spend a few nights sleeping in, if she paid her enough, so I felt free to refuse.

Muttering grimly, " Well, I'm going to sell my house and move to that new apartment," Edythe hurried off to get someone else to hold her hand.

Edythe had infected me with her fears. As the dark came on, I found myself nervously inspecting my windows, my doors, my locks, and blessing my high adobe wall and the squeak in my garden gate. Then I remembered I had to go out again to the board meeting. I had planned to walk into town early, treat myself to a dinner at Polly's, and snitch a ride or get a taxi back. Now it was already getting dark, and I was frightened. I ordered a taxi to come in an hour and fixed myself dinner while waiting for it.

The phone rang while I was eating. It was Liz, bless her, full of the news too, but after we had exchanged all the details we knew about Ellen, it appeared she was calling to warn me to get a taxi both ways and check my doors. "Don't let anybody in, Mac, promise me, not anybody, and get a woman taxi driver, you know the one."

I promised willingly enough and told her not to worry, but very on edge myself, I rang off.

After all the excitement, the Board meeting was an anticlimax to me, and probably to the Board members too, who shut themselves in the meeting room and seemed to get things done in record time. Liz told me to expect them to call for coffee after an hour, but it was in 45 minutes that the door opened and Paul stuck his head around and called out, "Coffee ready, Mac?"

Of course, it wasn't, but I said, "In a minute, Mr. Humfrey," and went to put the machine on. Out came the Board members after me and stood around, waiting. They all seemed fidgety and ill at ease.

"Now what's wrong?" I wondered to myself, surveying them.

Six members there were, elected by the entire membership. Paul Humfrey had been elected by the other five as the president. Nick Polkoff and John Graham had both been Board members, and on Nick's death the Board had taken in the member who had just missed getting a post on the Board at the last general meeting. That was an erstwhile pupil of Paul, who now was one of the Art Association's best sellers. A still young man, with a rather forceful and masculine personality, I suspected that conflict would now arise between Paul and his ex-pupil as it had between John Graham and Nick, and then between those two and Paul. On John Graham's death, I could see that another but current pupil of Paul's had been promoted. The other three members were holdovers from the year before and were two ladies and an old man who were known to vote exactly the way John Graham indicated. My view was that they would meekly follow whoever proved to be the leader.

I caught myself asking whoever else stood to benefit from the deaths of two Board members, Paul certainly did, but then I saw that he would have his troubles too. That ex-pupil of his was not going to be a sheep, his wife wouldn't let him, for one thing. As I was pouring out the coffee, I caught snatches of conversation around me, but it wasn't until they were all served that I was able to relax and listen closely.

Paul was booming out in his hearty way, "Damn fine tribute I wrote to John Graham, wasn't it, though I say so myself."

The two ladies and Paul's current pupil assented obediently. But the ex-pupil broke in, "One thing, Paul, why didn't you mention the Remington exhibition? That was really something to get for Villa Real, and Graham was the one who got it, arranged everything, you know."

Paul was not put out. "Well, I did think of making something out of that, but then I didn't want to revive that old disappearance bit. John suffered over that, I can tell you, and the whole business has never been explained, so I thought I'd just keep quiet."

Now I remembered that before I had come to work at the Art Association, there had been a show of Remington paintings, sculptures, prints and reproductions, right here in the gallery. That had been a big attraction and had got a lot of publicity, for the Association and for Villa Real. This particular collection had never been seen in its entirety by the public before, as the owner, a Texas oilman, wasn't very generous about letting people see it. Liz had told me a bit about this. That the collector had allowed his beloved objects to travel at all, let alone be on display, had been entirely due to John Graham's efforts. It was all the more embarrassing to him when one crate containing two paintings had disappeared for two days in transit. Luckily, the crate turned up just in time for the opening, attended by the Texan, of course, as well as everybody else with any pretensions to standing in Villa Real, in fact in the whole state, from the Governor, who was visibly bored by the fuss, through the Senator, himself an avid Remington fan and collector, and down to every last artist in Villa Real.

Paul boomed on, "Funny thing, you know, that's the last time I ever saw that bunch of old fogies together. Nick and John and Bela. Nick was pointing to something in a Remington painting, and John was examining it, and Bela seemed to be agreeing. I figured the painting must have been damaged when it went astray, it was one of those I remember, and Nick was showing John, who would have been terribly upset if that had happened. But he seemed to be shaking his head, and quite happily, so I guess he couldn't see anything wrong."

One of the old ladies broke in rather tartly, "Well, Nicolai Polkoff had far the best training of any artist round here, and if he thought there was a scratch, then my goodness, there was."

I was amused when the other lady said, "But dear, wouldn't we have heard from that loud Texas man about it, if one of his cult objects had been injured?"

Paul sneered, "That lucky bastard. (The ladies flinched.) He can't tell a print from an original. His collection is just power to him, status, maybe, not paintings to hang up, look at and enjoy. Oh no, he fell for Graham's charm once, but when he came to see the stuff got off safely, he told us there that nobody would get to look at it again. He wouldn't allow photographs, either; no, all he wanted was to be known as the collector with the most Remingtons. Why, he said so, now I think of it, before the stuff ever got here, because Graham told all of us to have a good look while we could."

This was news to me. I asked rather shyly, because I did not want to put myself forward, "I don't remember seeing anything about all this in the paper."

Paul smiled complacently. "Oh, I took care of that," he said. "The editor knew about the disappearance, all right, couldn't have been kept quiet, since the police had to know, but I pointed out to him how hard on Graham it would be if his filthy rich pal got the story. Might even cancel the exhibition, and that would've been a smack in the eye to our tourist industry. We needed the money at that time of year."

Sweet are the uses of publicity, I thought, as I started to clear up.

One of the ladies, about both of whom I felt more kindly now, came up to me and said anxiously, "My dear, we don't think you should walk home by yourself after this dreadful business with Ellen. Can we give you a ride?

I was touched by her thoughtfulness, but before I could accept, Paul broke in and said coarsely, "Who's going to bother to rape our skinny Mac?"

I blushed with rage and embarrassment and was about to accept the ride, when Paul lurched up closer and looked at me intently. "By

God, I take that back," he roared, laughing. "I mean, who's going to bother to rape Ellen when they can have Mac. You come along with me, my girl, and I'll protect you." He leered in an obvious stagy way.

I drew myself up and said coldly, "I have already ordered a taxi to call for me, thank you." I smiled gratefully at the ladies and turned away from Paul.

They all got ready to go now. I finished putting the coffee things away and went to tidy the boardroom. Liz had instructed me to remove all the papers on it and put them on her desk. This I did, but I found that a pile of checks was lying out on the table. I collected them in a neat bundle and put them in the folder marked "Checks to Artists," in which they clearly belonged. Looking nervously at the doorway to make sure I was unobserved, I took a quick look at the checks. They were in alphabetical order, and I had no difficulty in finding two made out to Henry Martin. One was for $37.50, clearly representing a monthly payment, and the other was for $262.50.

Hearing voices coming closer, I bundled all the papers together and took them to Liz's desk. Turning out the lights, locking up and seeing people were off the Association premises occupied my time until my taxi came. I was not quite too preoccupied to notice that the two ladies had waited to see me safely into the taxi before driving off, and that took the taste of Paul Humfrey's crack out of my mouth, well, to some extent.

8

The wise draftsman brings forward what he can use most effectively to present his case. His case is his special interest — his special vision. He does not repeat nature.
　　　　　　　　　— Robert Henri, *Op Cit.*

The last days of September passed slowly for me. I avoided Clem and Liz at work as much as I could, and Henry must have been avoiding me. Bill was away, as I could see by checking on his lights at night and his parked car day by day.

Even Edythe was not her ubiquitous self.

Liz noticed my preoccupation. "Hi, Mac," she said to me, coming up to gaze with me at a Humfrey painting I was straightening. "Something on your mind?"

I was evasive, "What could be?"

Liz smiled knowingly. "Only one thing, infant, at your age — men. If it's any consolation to you, I'll tell you that enquiries have been made."

I looked at her, startled. "Enquiries?"

Liz was soothing, "Relax, you don't think I'd give you away, do you?" She gestured to the painting. "Even our President," she underlined the President with mock reverence, "is interested. And Edythe has forgotten herself for a few minutes to talk about you. Oh, and Henry Martin, he really pumped me about you."

"Big deal," I said bitterly, "one chaser, one biddy, and one married man."

Liz was sympathetic. "It's all a step in the right direction. Any interest is better than none. Paul, of course, is hopeless, all talk and no do. But Henry, well, who knows, with a different wife he might make a fine husband."

I shrugged, acting bored.

But Liz was undaunted and continued. "This time he swears it's divorce. As soon as he has enough money, he's going to start proceedings and stick to it. He's said that to me before, but I really believe him now. He's changed."

"Really, Liz, less I could not care." I cast around for some distraction. "What's happening to model night?"

Liz told me that it had been temporarily suspended, as the old ladies, the backbone of the class, were nervous about being out at night after the attack on Ellen.

"Well then, could I help here next Monday?"

Liz was pleased at my interest and willingly agreed.

The first Monday of each month was hanging day. The Gallery was closed to the public, while all day artists came in with their paintings for the new show. At four o'clock, the doors were shut to all comers and the jury, selected by the jury chairman, would arrive to pick out paintings to be hung by the hanging committee, another group of three members. The jury usually consisted of the older established artists, but the hanging committee had to have at least one younger man on it, because of the sheer physical labor involved.

Liz went to her file drawers and took out a folder. "Now, let's see," she said, going through the sheets. "Here's all the dope. Juries for all the past shows, juries for the membership applications. But what they decide, you know, is filed in another folder, and the jury list for next Monday. Well, what do you know," she exclaimed, amused, "Paul has got himself appointed."

"Is that constitutional?" I asked.

"Nothing against it," replied Liz. "John Graham would never have done a thing like that, naturally, but times have changed," she sighed and picked up the folder to put it back in the drawer. As she was filing the folder, she turned and said, "The membership applications folder is the one people are interested in, but don't let anybody peek. And if I were you, I wouldn't know too much, either."

"For heaven's sake, why?" I asked.

Liz explained that membership in the Villa Real Art Association had become a valuable acquisition, paintings were sold in the other galleries that opened and shut with the predictability of the seasons, but nothing compared with the prestige and sheer volume of sales of our Gallery. Liz was proud of this. "At first, we had to take in every artist who could fork out the dues, but when Clem came and sales zoomed, the juries had a quota and were told how many to admit each session. The number just had to be kept low last year, we were getting so crowded. When an artist is rejected, he feels he must know who turned him down, and I always say I don't know, but of course I do."

"Doesn't it all appear in the reports?" I wondered.

"Oh no, that would be dynamite." She smiled and said, "But I'll let you in on a little secret to keep your mind off your troubles, infant." She picked out a sheet from the files and showed it to me. "This is the last one."

I looked carefully, interested in spite of myself. I saw first a list of names, headed by one in capitals, and that this list was the jury. Underneath was another list of those seeking to become members. Finally, just two names, and they were the ones accepted. I saw that Edythe Kendall Chambers had been accepted.

Liz was sarcastic about this. "I can tell you how Paul wangled that one," she said bitterly. "I can remember perfectly well, but I have a little system too, in case I forget in my old age." She pointed to an almost undecipherable "x" beside one name and two microscopic little dots beside two other names on the jury list. "'x' marks the boss, and the little dots are the sheep." She went on, seeing my surprise, "That applies just to some action I consider clearly unfair, in this case to admit Edythe and turn down better artists. Quite impossible to turn down this other fellow who was admitted anyway."

This gave me even more food for thought, and I was ruminating about it and my other more serious problems off and on all weekend. So worried was I by then that I could not settle down to my usual indulgence of a double crostic, but nervously kept going from chore to chore in house and garden, waiting for something to happen, but what? I was overjoyed when the phone rang on Sunday, hoping it was Henry, Bill, even Paul, anybody to provide some distraction from my increasingly somber thoughts. It was, however, Ellen. She asked me to come to see her at the hospital after visiting hours, and, surprised, I said I would be over that afternoon.

Ellen looked very well to me. She was in a private room, sitting in the armchair provided by the window, with a scarf knotted round her neck and tucked into her robe. She greeted me warmly, "How good of you to come, Mac dear," she exclaimed.

I kissed her gently on the cheek. "Oh, I wanted to come before, but I didn't know you were still in the hospital and thought you might not want to be disturbed at home."

She grimaced, "I could've gone home days ago, but really, you know, I was frightened." At this she loosened the scarf around her neck and I saw with horror and pity that her throat had an ugly fading bruise on it.

She smiled, "It wasn't bad, not dangerous, but I cannot understand why. So I've a brother of Bela's coming to pick me up here tomorrow, and I'm flying back East to stay with him for a bit." She paused. "There's something I want you to do for me, if you will."

I said quickly, "Oh anything, Ellen."

She smiled. "You're a nice girl. Would you pick out a painting of Bela's to put in the show for me? I'd like him to have one in," she said grievingly.

I hastened to agree, and we made arrangements for picking it up. Then I asked hesitantly, "Ellen, don't you think there's something very wrong here?"

She turned abruptly from her sad contemplation of the view from the window and said, looking at me intently, "Yes, Mac, I certainly do think so." She lowered her voice, glancing rather fearfully around. "I think now you were right. There's a murderer loose. My dearest Bela was murdered, I'm sure of it now. Perhaps Nick and John too, I don't know. But Bela was, and perhaps the murderer, whoever it was, thinks I know something, which I don't, though I've tried hard to remember."

Considering this, I realized it was simply confirmation of my suspicions. "Can't you say, Ellen, if it was a man or a woman who attacked you? Surely you had a glimpse of trousers, or skirt, or smelt something, like hair oil or perfume?"

She shook her head, "No, I've thought hard, and it's no good. I have no sense of smell, lost it because of a sinus operation years ago back East, and whoever it was grabbed me from the back. I deliberately fell face down, so he wouldn't see if I was shamming. I did feel something, though, the hands felt large, capable sort of hands, wearing thinnish gloves." She shuddered. "That's why I say he, it was either a strong woman or a man." She held out her left arm. "He picked up this wrist, and he must have seen my watch." She was wearing a clearly expensive diamond watch. "He could have snatched it off easily enough." Then she picked up her bag lying on the hospital table beside her. Out of it she brought an envelope. Opening the envelope and taking out something wrapped in tissue paper and handing it over, she said "Look, Mac. The sheriff gave me this on that terrible afternoon, and I'm taking it with me."

I hardly knew what to say, I felt so sorry for her. Looking carefully at the smashed watch, I said, to find an innocuous remark, "It's stopped at three seventeen, I see."

Ellen sighed and took the watch back, wrapping it up very carefully in the tissue paper and replacing it in the envelope. "Yes, the newspaper reports said three fifteen, I don't know why, and two minutes are of no significance, but they mean a lot to me."

A nurse came in then, so I took my leave, promising to deal with the painting and to write to her about it.

I walked slowly back up Palace Avenue, hardly noticing that the lilacs looked dreary, the tall trees dying visibly, the sky dark, the air cold and still. But I was cheered slightly by that most evocative of all smells to the lovers of Villa Real, the smell of burning piñon wood. Quickening my steps, I thought of home, security and a fire. But even those talismans failed to comfort me. My adobe, clean, bright and shining, welcomed me, but did nothing to make me feel secure. On the contrary, I felt too shut off and longed for someone to reassure me. When the darkness crept around my windows, I shut my curtains tight, checked all the locks, and jumped when I heard the telephone burr. This time it was Henry, and my spirits did lighten. He asked me out on Monday, but I explained that I would be busy with the Art Association, so we arranged a date for Wednesday, though Henry warned me that he could not stay out so late that night.

"That's fine. Not too much candle burning at both ends for me yet."

He didn't pay much attention to that, but asked how Ellen was.

I was in no mood to discuss Ellen, so I let it pass with an offhand, "You must know better than I do, being in the police department." But then I added, sensing that he was waiting, "She is leaving for the East tomorrow. Bela's brother is picking her up here."

Henry was interested. "Really, well, she will have to come back to give evidence when we catch the louse that did it."

"When or if?" I asked, as Villa Real's police are not known for their success in catching the young punks who are responsible for the city's bad record.

Henry was a little sharp with me. "Oh, we'll get him," he said and rang off.

Reflecting with annoyance that I muffed my opportunity to keep him talking, I fixed myself a small dinner that I did not taste and then got out my clippings, notes and pencil and paper. I was now prepared to state, instead of imply jokingly, that murder had been done. There seemed to me just too much to explain. Two deaths I might accept as coincidence, but three and one attack, surely they must be connected. It seemed to me that the attack on Ellen clinched it. She thought someone was attempting to silence her. Then she must know something, or more probably the murderer with his guilty conscience thought that she knew something. One thing might possibly be assumed about the character of the murderer, that he was better at arranging accidents than attacking directly. I decided then that I must look not for someone acting hurriedly in a brutal rage, but a clever, foresighted, cold-blooded person.

No. I interrupted my own train of thought. I must first make a list of people who could have some reason to kill three times, the one thing these three having in common being artists, members of the Art Association too. Now that, of course, brought me smack up against the one thing I had been so unwilling to face. Could Clem be getting away with the Association funds? I thought this would be quite impossible without the cooperation of Liz. And this I considered she might be willing to give, for various reasons.

Writing down "Motive" in large letters on my paper, I put down first Clement Dennison, and then leaving a space, Elizabeth Heald. I pondered, gazing for inspiration into the flames. Clem, so neat, so fastidious, so very old maidish, it would be hard for him to attack anybody. I could visualize Clem arranging a very tidy sort of accident, yes, but I could not see him seizing Ellen around the neck. Ah, but then maybe that is why he made such a bad job of Ellen. So I wrote beside Clem's name, feeling obscurely guilty as I did so that he had always been kindness itself to me, "motive, good; character, possible; opportunity?" "Investigate," I scribbled firmly underneath this.

Now for Liz. "Damn," I muttered, not to say bother, not Liz. Then I remembered that ugly bruise on Ellen's neck and wrote grimly on. Under Motive, I put "possible." And I wrote three subheadings: "1. To keep job." I knew Liz really loved being in the center of all the fascinating feuds and gallery gossip. "2. Pay-off," but I wrote "unlikely" beside this. Although she was not well paid, she didn't seem to me to be either short of money or interested in making more.

Now "3. To protect Clem." I underlined this one as being most likely. Theirs was a curious relationship and as far as I could judge, which is not very far either, they looked out for each other. Forcing myself to pursue my reasoning to its bitter end, I wrote down "Must be in this together," and turned to the consideration of opportunity.

This was much more difficult. Nick had been quietly suffocated by escaping gas one cold night in April. I would never be able to find out any more about that. Bela's death occurred in June, and that could be pinned down with exactitude and certainly offered the best bet as to alibis. Then John Graham's. I realized with sudden dismay that I knew very little about this, and from the brief report in the paper it could hardly have been murder; if it was, then it must have been the action of a desperate man, since the risks would be much higher than in the other two cases.

Beside John Graham's name, I wrote very firmly "Investigate." Beside Ellen's name, I wrote "Investigate alibis," but reflecting that it would be hard to check this, as both Clem and Liz lived alone most of the time, I put a question mark beside alibis. Then I stopped for another session of contemplation. Why those three artists, and why the two-month interval between? Nick could easily have come across some discrepancy in the Art Association accounts, and he could, in fact would, have told Bela, but then would he not have told John Graham at once, and would not Graham have equally promptly investigated? Then I corrected myself. The mistake I was making was looking at things objectively, whereas they must be looked at subjectively, through, I winced, Clem's eyes.

No sane man is going around polishing people off unless he has very good reason to think they are going to be a threat to him. Clem might be driven to desperate measures, but only, I was sure, for desperate reasons. Perhaps Nick made some remark indicating he had suspicions. Nick might certainly have told Bela something right away, but Clem would not have known that until Bela also showed that he knew. As for John Graham, he and Clem saw each other every day and Clem would know at once if John felt anything was wrong. Perhaps some accounts came up at two-month intervals. Now, I took up another sheet of paper and wrote down as heading, "Things to Investigate":

1. John Graham's death
2. Alibis, for Bela's death
3. Accounts for Art Association

At that point I almost consigned all my notes to the flames, it was so difficult for me to contemplate the possibility of Clem being a murderer. So then, I said to myself, think of who else could benefit from either one or all the deaths. Thoughtfully, I added:

4. Other possible motives:
    a. Paul Humfrey, to get control of the Board
    b. Edythe Kendall Chambers, to become a member

Two very weak reasons for wholesale slaughter, I mused sadly, but then again, I must be subjective. To Paul Humfrey, who knows, ambition might be his driving power, or it might be money, since his pupils paid him to get into the Art Association. Edythe—my mind boggled at the thought of Edythe knocking Bela over a cliff or seizing Ellen by the neck, but then again, behind that mask I knew there was a shrewd woman, perhaps a cold-blooded one.

I turned off the lights and looked out at the black night to see if it was snowing, but it was not, and finding myself imagining attackers in every shadow, I checked my locks and windows again and went to bed, only to lie awake for what seemed hours, thinking about money, art, ambition, and murder.

9

We must realize that artists are
not in competition with each other.
　　　　　　　　— Robert Henri, *Op Cit.*

Late next morning I felt rather dull and headachy, despite the invigorating sun-filled air. I walked over to Ellen's house, which was not so very far off my regular route, a short way up Canyon Road. Ellen and Bela had made a charming happy home for themselves out of an old adobe set in spacious low-walled grounds. Ellen's cleaning woman was there packing up for her and she let me in with a smile.

First I took a searching look at the kitchen, since Ellen had thought her attacker was doing something in there. I could see nothing to interest a burglar in it, just the usual appliances — gas, of course, and a furnace.

I knew that the door off the kitchen led to Bela's small studio. Perhaps he might have been looking in the studio for something, records maybe, and the noise Ellen heard really came from there. I inspected the studio with dismay. No doubt to Bela it had been arranged beautifully, but to me it was just a jumble of canvasses that were finished, unfinished, blank and in rolls. Frames of all kinds and sizes were scattered around. Two easels facing the large north light dominated the room, but I could see that the paintings on them were not finished.

I wondered where to start looking for a painting to take. It must be a fairly new one and, if possible, one that had not been exhibited before. Then my eye was caught by Bela's outdoor painting box. It was folded up, ready to go, I thought sadly, but Bela was no longer ready. As I had anticipated, Bela's last painting was inside, easily recognizable as the view from Puye cliff, since Bela painted very much what he saw.

I took it out cautiously and found it in excellent condition. Now for a frame. With so many frames of all shapes, kinds and sizes around, I was sure I could find the right one, but it took me quite a time to do so. Artists were always complaining about the difficulty of framing and now I could see why.

Since I had no idea for how to put them securely enough together, I carried the painting in one hand and the frame in the other and walked down Palace Avenue to the Art Association. Anywhere else, perhaps, it might be embarrassing to walk down a city street encumbered thus, but in Villa Real nobody gave me a second glance, nor did I feel in the least conspicuous.

After I had crossed the bridge over the Rio Villa Real, I heard a call, "Want a ride, Mac?" Pleased because I was tired, I turned to see who it was. Well, any port in a storm, I thought, as I got into Paul Humfrey's small bus, depositing the painting and frame in the main part of the bus, and clambering up to the front seat beside Paul.

"My God, Mac, you're not taking to art with a capital A too, are you?" He twisted around to look at the painting propped up against the back seats. "Now I see it's Bela's. What are you doing with that Victorian maiden's dream?"

I was about to say something nasty myself and as trying to find the right words, when fortunately I remembered his position and mine and decided discretion was indeed the better part of valor.

"Ellen asked me to put in a painting of Bela's for her," I explained. "I've just picked this up, but I don't know how to get the frame on."

Paul was unexpectedly helpful. "Poor old Bela, at least I can put a frame on his pretty-pretty stuff, even if I think it's tripe."

I felt remorseful at my dislike and my suspicion and thanked him, perhaps too warmly, because he patted my fanny in a familiar way as he helped me down from his bus. Me and Dolores, I thought savagely.

Paul did prove helpful, to my surprise and relief. He fastened the frame and painting together with the hammer and nails we kept handy in the Gallery and even typed a label to affix. "What shall we call it, Mac? From Puye Cliff?" he went on, peering at the canvas. "Funny, there's something not quite Bela." He shrugged. "Perhaps he was improving at last." He went on typing. "Price?' Well, I'll put $350, which is more than he usually got, I'll bet, but he has friends here."

He put the painting face against the wall in the main showroom and brought in his own offering of the month, a huge canvas in his older manner, grandiose building sketched in pastel colors with strong black lines placed vertically here and there to lend emphasis. This was the style he taught, and this was also the style improved on by his up and coming ex-pupil.

One of the hardest things about working in an art gallery is the task of finding something nice to say about the various paintings that one is confronted with. I cast about my repertoire for the appropriate praise of Paul's colossus. At least I liked it a lot better than his new style, which was nothing but very broad, rough, black strokes, done with a house painter's brush.

"Nice-sized canvas, Paul," I remarked. "I like that brushwork," as I pointed to a masterly black line.

Paul laughed, "Good effort, but Jesus, Mac, you needn't be polite to me."

I laughed too, liking him better and protesting, "No, really, I'm nothing if not honest."

Paul was suddenly serious, "There's such a thing as being too honest, you know. Watch it, Mac." And he lumbered off, leaving me staring after him amazed.

Liz came out of Clem's room then—I knew she must have been around somewhere—and looked at me gravely. "I heard that last line, infant, and this time he's right. Paul always looks out for Paul. When's he looking out for you too, believe him."

"Oh, I believe him," I said, "but what it's all about I wouldn't know."

Liz sat down wearily at her desk, far from her usual ebullient self. "I wish John were alive," she said, rubbing her forehead. Then she got up in sudden determination. "I'm going to leave the field to you. Remember to lock up after the hanging committee leave."

The afternoon went by enjoyably enough, because the perpetual coming and going of artists with their paintings left me no time to brood. Little old ladies brought in small carefully painted boards of aspens, burros, adobes. Bearded beatnik types carried large boldly executed creations, of what I called to myself the blob and blotch school. Conservatively dressed gentlemen brought . . . conservative canvasses. Young women dressed gaily in peasant shifts and sandals brought in oddly shaped boards of the decorative school. These young women and the bearded beatniks were an uneasy alliance. Married, unmarried, separated, divorced, the permutations and combinations were not easy to keep up with, and I was careful not to betray my ignorance of the latest developments.

Liz always knew exactly what was going on among the artists in Villa Real, and now I missed her usual commentary, as I said hello to the members as they came in and found any stored paintings they wished to remove. Each member was limited to a total of six paintings to be in the gallery at one time, either on display or stored in the racks. In practice this rule was impossible to enforce, and was not taken seriously. But Liz and I were told to remind the most persistent offenders, particularly those with the biggest canvasses, and to remove them when the occasion offered. It is hard to do this tactfully; occasion never offered itself to me in the case of any Board member. Paul himself was one of the worst offenders, and Nick when he was alive had been incorrigible. John Graham never exceeded his quota, nor did Bela, I thought sadly. Kind gentle men, both; I missed them.

At four o'clock, as Liz had instructed me, I closed the side door through which members brought and removed their paintings and put a "Closed" sign on the outside, but left it unlocked because the jury came in this way. The front door through which the public came was kept locked all day. At four thirty the jury had arrived, Paul and two cohorts. The chairman of the jury chose his other two jury members, so Paul quite predictably had chosen two loyal fans, a lady to flatter him and a young man to handle the paintings. Under orders to make myself scarce while the jury worked, I sat at Liz's desk pretending to be busy with papers, but I had left the door open just a crack so I could hear what went on. Paul worked rapidly and knowledgeably. He was ruthless with little old ladies and the more far-out of the beatnik creations, and didn't just say "in" or "out," but gave reasons for his decisions. I was rather impressed by his judgment and fairness.

He had the decency to keep in Bela's painting, and he went to the storage racks to get one of Nick's. This action he explained to his co-jurors, "Last time poor old Nick can be hung."

This was not quite true, I reflected, counting on my fingers. Any artist who dies while a member could have his paintings displayed for six months after his death, which brought me to November. Still this put Paul in a better light to me.

When I was assured that Paul had hit his stride and would not be distracted, I went to the file drawers and morosely surveyed the one marked "Accounts." This was a perfect opportunity to investigate, I reminded myself, so why hesitate? I made myself grasp the drawer handle and pull. It was rather an anticlimax when nothing happened. The whole file was locked. Stumped, I went back to Liz's desk to think.

I knew from observation that ordinarily none of the files was locked. Surely the key must be in Liz's desk, since Clem did not concern himself with such mundane matters. Or that, I thought wryly, is the impression he wants to give. Liz's desk was not locked, more, I surmised, because there was no way to lock it than because she was trusting. It did not take me long to find a bunch of keys, and from them to find the one to fit the file cabinet. However, at the end of all that, when I had looked carefully at the Accounts files, what did I find? Nothing in the least comprehensible to me. I gazed at all the sheets of figures, trying hard to make sense of it all, but it was no good. The only clear picture I got of the whole thing was that whatever was going on, Liz must know all about it. All the entries were in Liz's neat but bold writing, not in Clem's equally neat but more spidery print. Many of the sheets of figures had a signature scrawled at the bottom, and some had two. These, I saw, were always of the president of the Board, mostly John Graham's, sometimes Nick's, and recently Paul Humfrey's, and the other signature would, I deduced, be the treasurer, or another Board member. It was well known that the job of treasurer was a bit of a sinecure, as Liz did all the work.

Downcast, but in a way relieved at finding no obvious discrepancy, I locked the cabinet and replaced the keys where I had found them. Paul came in a little later, his following standing correctly in the rear, and asked me what I was doing now. "Why don't you eat with me, Mac," he boomed. "I'll send these two off, to have you to myself, but you'll be safe enough at Polly's."

I was about to refuse automatically, but stopped myself, thinking of the opportunity to pump Paul, and accepted, if a little hesitantly.

I locked up behind me and, telling Paul I must be back at seven fifteen, went up the street with him to Polly's. Remembering that Liz had told me Paul was chronically broke, since the paintings did not sell and he was dependent on his pupils, I was careful to choose the cheapest item on the menu, but at dinner none of the delicious dishes could be called really cheap. Paul, I noticed, didn't stint himself, but chose the most expensive steak.

I studied him while he was ordering. About forty, I guessed, he was a great big bear of a man, and handsome in that large scale way. He had a bush of blonde hair that was beginning to turn gray, and rather small and shrewd looking faded blue eyes. He felt my gaze on him and acted coyly, which was foolish for such a large man.

"What's the verdict, Mac?" he asked, not jokingly, but as if embarrassed.

What could I reply to that? I blurted out unthinkingly, "Verdict? Oh, as to looks, good, but conduct, not so good."

Paul was surprisingly thoughtful. "You think I'm rude, coarse, I lack the finer feelings, don't you?"

I was silent.

He went on. "That's true. I put on this act, I'm loud and coarse deliberately, because I've found from experience that's what my old biddies like." He held my eyes. "And what my old biddies like, I supply. They are my bread and butter. I have no rich wife, I don't sell many paintings, I live on what my school makes. If I want to paint, I have to get pupils to pay me, and I want to paint."

Impressed with his evident candor, I busied myself with eating the food now set before us. Paul also ate, with gusto, too, I noticed, and it was not until he finished the last crumb that he wiped his mouth and said, "And I expect Liz has told you, hasn't she, my wife — my ex-wife, that is, God damn her," he interjected bitterly, "went off with a younger man."

I gasped, "No, Paul, I'm terribly sorry, I didn't know."

Paul shook his head in a baffled way, "I wasn't enough for her, she had to have someone more . . ." he interrupted himself. "Oh well, Mac, that is past history, didn't mean to bore you." Then he was grave again. "But make no mistake, it means a lot to me to be president of the Art Association. It's not just prestige, oh no, it's money in my pocket, food to eat, and the chance to paint too."

I found myself feeling intensely sympathetic. Glancing around at the candlelit room to make sure nobody we knew was watching, I leaned forward so that my head was close to his. I wanted badly to say something kind, but nothing came. Instead I said warmly, "I'll forgive you, then, for calling me skinny Mac. You hurt my feelings, but I've misjudged you and I apologize."

Paul was amused. Surveying all of me visible above the table, he remarked, "I apologize too, I just haven't been observant lately." He put his arm around my shoulders as we were leaving to guide me through the low door.

Somehow this time I felt he was being protective and did not mind.

Alone in the gallery, I had much to consider. Paul's evident sincerity, though it endeared him to me, did nothing to reassure me as to his motives. He would stay on my suspect list and certainly needs investigation.

I was busily taking down the smaller paintings in the old show to make room for the new ones that the hanging committee would put up, when I was joined by Paul's star ex-pupil, Charles Newberg, who quickly and efficiently dealt with the larger, hard to handle pictures. A tall, thin, swarthy and still young man, he had been remarkably successful in the short time he had been exhibiting. He did not waste time in small talk, but acted with economy and precision, so that we had between us done much of the hard work of removal before the other two members arrived.

The chairman was one of the ladies who had been so solicitous of me on Board meeting night. Because she was willing to work hard for the Association, while many of her critics were not, she was in constant demand for various duties and offices, all of which she fulfilled competently. However, as far as I knew she had no strong feelings of her own about art and this was probably an asset. She would follow the most forceful leader in any group activity.

The other member was a bearded beatnik, of the type that almost invariably ducks out of any job of work to be done. But according to Liz, every now and then it was pointed out to one of these types that having been elected to membership, he owed one evening of work a year, and he was shamed into lending his needed young strength into the dull job of hanging.

I was not expected to absent myself from the work of hanging but, on the contrary, was obliged to make myself useful, at first by making room to hang the new show, and then later, I was to open the show case on the street. In between I was to stay out of the way but within calling distance. Since the old show was down, I retired into Liz's room, leaving the door ajar, but not so open that I could be seen. I reopened the file cabinet and took out the jury list folder marked

"Membership Applications." I was curious to see who had turned Edythe down the first time she applied.

That must have been in March, I figured, counting, and took out the sheet next to the last. There were the three lists. First the jury; I saw three so familiar names, John Graham's, Nick's, and Bela's. The last one was a surprise, as I knew he was not one for holding any office in the Association. The next list was of applications; Edythe's name was there as I anticipated, but so was another name, which came as an unpleasant shock, William H. Thorpe, I read with dismay. My eye ran down hastily to the list of those accepted; only two names, and neither of them the ones I sought. No wonder Bill had been bitter, I thought, disturbed. It is always hurtful to be rejected, and when you were as serious about painting as Bill seemed to be, it was a bitter pill to swallow.

Now who, I wondered did the rejecting? I looked for Liz's secret signs, and there they were, a small cross beside Nick's name, and two small dots beside John Graham's and Bela's. Oh no, I murmured to myself, horrified. Surely Nick wouldn't have turned Bill down. But then I thought less sentimentally, that it was all too probable. Nick had lived, breathed and had his being in art and would not sacrifice one artistic principle for anybody. Much as he had apparently liked Bill, he would not vote him into the Art Association if he thought Bill was not a good enough painter. I asked myself, was Bill a good painter and answer came there none.

Feeling tired now, I again locked the file cabinet and went to see what the hanging committee was doing. I was amused in spite of my cares at finding Charles very efficiently, politely and unobtrusively managing the whole thing. And managing it well, too, I reflected, as I surveyed the walls. Hanging may be the least coveted job open to members, but it is also one of the most important. Artists feel very strongly about where and next to whom they are hung. A very strong, bold painting next to a low keyed one will detract from the latter, which may make an excellent showing next to a pastel picture. Nevertheless, one must have variety, so segregation by loudness is not the answer. Charles, while being careful to defer to his lady chairman, used his excellent eye to excellent effect. Bela's painting was given a position between two undistinguished efforts where it showed up to advantage. John Graham's watercolor needed no such clever placing to put everything in the watercolor room into the shade. Nick's painting from the storage rack was one of his least happy efforts, but it too was placed to great advantage.

But my eye, as I knew all viewers' eyes would be, was caught at once by Henry Martin's, which I could see was to be put in the showcase, as it was propped up against the entrance door. It was the painting I had admired in my house. I turned it around to look at the label. I was pleased to note he had called it "Bitter Reds."

Charles saw my interest in this painting and came up to look at the label with me. "One of the best I've ever seen of Henry's. He's a damn good painter," Charles said enthusiastically. "That's an interesting title, too."

I was rather proud to explain I had given him the title from Rimbaud.

Charles was gratifyingly congratulatory and laughed, "You'll make a good wife for an artist. Titles are hell." He went on, not amused any more, "That's Henry's wife, you know, so paintable, but what a wife for anybody, let alone an artist."

Charles' wife, as I knew, was rather terrifyingly efficient, holding down a well paid job and holding Charles down too against stiff competition. I was not one to waste any efforts I was capable of on such a very married man, and turned away to see what help I could be. Charles called his colleagues over to look at Bela's painting. I joined them, wondering if he had noticed the lack of signature, but it was not that.

"Those shadows. Bela must've been using a different palette, that's just not his usual style." Charles said and gestured, "The values are wrong for Bela."

He was clearly puzzled and looked around the group for explanation or agreement. Nobody replied, so he went on studying the painting closely. "I'm sure it's the shadows, perhaps the color or the depth, or both."

Charles shrugged and turned away to survey the show. The main showroom was filled, and the small watercolor room finished too, but there were still gaps in the secondary showroom.

"Let's pick some more out," suggested Charles, and from the row of rejected paintings, Charles took out enough to round out the show. Even at one point, to make a better contrast, he put back Edythe's amateurish effort from the wall into the row of rejects, in which I knew it had not been placed by Paul. This greatly amused and interested me. Charles caught my eye while he was doing the dirty work and winked at me.

I, regrettably, winked right back. "I ain't seen nuttin'," I told Charles.

He was nonchalant. "There won't be any repercussions," he promised confidently. "I know Paul Humfrey pretty well. I worked with him for a year, you know. He's all bluster. He might bite for Paul, but he won't go to bat for our dear Edythe Kendall Chambers."

"Oh?" I asked encouragingly.

"No, he's already been paid off, you see," explained Charles, very indiscreetly. "In Edythe's case lessons weren't enough."

This time I accepted a ride home from the lady chairman, though Charles and even the bearded beatnik offered me one too, but I was tired and thought the lady would be more restful, which indeed she was. But when she dropped me at my garden door, she said earnestly, "Sometimes I wonder how the Art Association can survive without John Graham and Nick, so Mac, I hope at all costs, we can keep Clem. Will he stay, do you think?"

What could I say but a reassuring, "Oh sure."

10

Fight with yourself when you paint,
not with the model. A student is one who
struggles with himself, struggles
for order.

— Robert Henri, *Op Cit.*

Liz was very complimentary about the show next day and declared Henry's "Bitter Reds" a show stopper. It did attract a lot of attention from passersby, some of whom came to enquire about it. This was the day so many members stopped by to inspect the placement of their sacred creations, and we had a few complaints, but not as many as usual. However, Edythe was understandably vexed to find her oil rejected.

"Well," she fumed, "I happen to know Paul was the jury chairman; I'll see about this."

Trying to placate her, I pointed out that there were two other artists on the jury.

She was not appeased. "Don't take me for a fool, Mac, I know my rights."

I could almost see a tail twitching as she stalked off like a provoked pussycat. Trouble, I thought, and Liz agreed with me. "We've had troubles before, lots of them, but John Graham, backed up by Nick, could always fix them. Those two had authority, I suppose status, really. Paul hasn't got what it takes. Without a strong Board, it's hard for us to function well."

"Keep your eye on Charles Newberg," I suggested.

Liz was thoughtful. "I hope you're right," she said.

On Wednesday I left work early to give myself time for the extensive preparations necessitated by the date with Henry. I must have done a good job, judging from Henry's warm look when I opened my door to him. From my own small experience and from the warnings of girls who had had far more opportunity to learn from life than I had, I knew that there were pitfalls in asking dates in for drinks both before going out, and more especially after. So I picked up wrap and bag and went out purposefully, locking my door carefully behind me and putting the key in its customary hide-out, under a door mat at the entrance.

Henry laughed. "That's the first place any burglar would look for a key, and the second place would be under a flower pot near the door." He looked around and considered. "How about here?" he said, pointing.

I could barely reach this ledge, even standing on tiptoe, so I took a dim view of his idea. But to humor him, I obediently put the key where he indicated.

Henry drove out of town to the north, on the old two-lane winding highway that we aficionados much prefer to the new freeway, without telling me where we were going. I soon guessed that we were headed for a nightspot not far from town that had flourished for years on the strength of its unusually wide selection of good food.

"Doesn't, or rather didn't, John Graham live near here?" I asked Henry over a preliminary drink.

He was rather more expansive than on our last date and he responded to my conversation, instead of being unable to get off the subject of his wife. It appeared that he had known John very well, to the extent that he had a key to his studio. In fact, after the funeral and before she left with one of their daughters to stay with relatives in the east, Mrs. Graham had asked him to look in occasionally to see if all was well. This encouraged me to do some hinting. With all my well-known tact, reminiscent of a charging hippopotamus, I was sure, I said bluntly, "Oh, do take me with you next time you stop to check." Henry was perfectly willing and agreed to call me before his next trip out.

Henry grew even more relaxed over the excellent dinner, and I felt free to do some probing. More an incision than probing, actually. I just asked flatly, "Could John's accident possibly have been anything but an accident?"

Henry frowned and groaned, "Oh Lord, not again. For the second and last time, no, it could not."

I persisted. "That attack on Ellen, Henry, that's what made me suspicious again."

Henry seemed quite willing to discuss Ellen, surprisingly. He asked me with interest whether I had seen her, how she was, and when was she returning. Warming to his interest, I told him that I had visited her in hospital and that she had been both puzzled and frightened by the attack, as she could not think of the motive behind it.

Henry shrugged. "Just some hopped up young punk. We're investigating all the known drug addicts. Surely Ellen doesn't think it could be anything else, does she?"

I paused before replying, wondering whether to confide in Henry or not. After all, I thought, he is practically a policeman, so who could be a better confidante? "She thinks that perhaps," I was going cautiously, "it was connected with Bela's death."

Henry looked startled. "But that was an accident," he said sharply.

"Ellen has doubts too. Something is wrong there, Henry, it's no good protecting your police to me. They may have checked it out very thoroughly, but Ellen and I knew Bela, and we know there is something that doesn't fit, but we don't know what it is." I went on, remembering Charles, and before that Paul, too, at the gallery, "Why, even Bela's last painting, the one he did up on Puye cliff, even that had a false note."

Henry was immediately fascinated. "What was that?" he asked, and I told him about Paul's remark and then Charles' analysis of the shadow values. Henry grew indifferent at that. "Bela wasn't himself that day, I expect," he said. "Too much sun, or maybe he had a heart attack or a stroke." Then he got up to dance and I forgot Ellen, Bela, and everyone else.

When we paused for a drink, I felt so happy with him, never had I enjoyed dancing more, that I let my guard down even more. Forgetting to be cautious, I told him about Mrs. Rountree's purchases and the two checks and the deposit slip.

Henry was taken aback. "Now you really have something," he said, and lit a cigarette while he thought about it. "No doubt about it. My painting of that tramp Dolores, I remember that, she posed for me in my studio, for free too, " he smiled reminiscently, "and I put clothes on her later, just to see how it would look. I marked that one $350, and I got paid the right amount too, last week. After my wife, the bitch, takes her whack, I have a little left to do this with."

He swallowed his drink too fast and got up nervously to dance again. Wonderful as it was, I had to ask for a break eventually, and refused a drink in favor of coffee, but Henry ordered a drink for himself. And sipping it at first said, "What you've happened upon is maybe dynamite. It's absolute nonsense to think Clem would lay a hand on anyone, of course, that's just imagination. But when the Board discovers the gap, as they're bound to in time, who is expendable? Not Clem for sure. No, Liz will be fired. If I were you, I'd just sit back and see what happens, it's not really your business, after all."

As this was exactly the advice I had given myself, I was quick to agree, but I pointed out to Henry that jobs were not easy to find in Villa Real and I had to think of my future. If the Art Association was going to fall apart, as I feared it might, I should look around for some other job. "I have enough money to live on," I assured Henry, who was looking worried, "but the little extra is nice, and I enjoy having an interesting job."

Henry smiled affectionately at me, "You can always be my agent," he remarked cheerfully.

Dancing again, I felt very close and warm to Henry and was reluctant to leave when he looked at his watch and said, "Time's up." We drove back by another road that gave us a wonderful view of Villa Real's lights from the top of a hill. Henry pulled the car off the road and stopped.

"I love this view and I left enough time so we could look at it." With that he switched off lights and engine, and turned to me. "Let's get to know each other, shall we?"

He made out the same way he danced, expertly, tenderly, with enjoyment and consideration for his partner. I found myself responding with too much happiness to his lead and was rather relieved to find I still had some detachment, which made me remember his wife. I pulled away. Henry did not protest or press on, but simply gave me a final affectionate caress, and drove off. To myself I admitted a feeling of considerable disappointment when he dropped me off at my garden door with no more than a rather quizzical look. But I was not too bound up in my dreams of love to fail to notice that Bill's lights were on.

Pleasure rather than surprise must have been visible on my face when Bill came into the Art Association next morning. "Aren't you surprised to see me? I got in late last night."

"I saw your lights on," I explained, "when I got back with Henry." I flushed slightly, remembering.

Bill frowned and hesitated, and finally brought out, "Will you have lunch with me, Mary, how about La Fonda?"

I arranged to meet him in the bar of Villa Real's famous hotel, and he walked off. I watched him go and remarked to Liz, who had stayed in the background, "He is looking much better, isn't he?"

Liz laughed, "I hardly noticed him before, infant, but if you say so, he looks like Apollo to me. But what's this about Henry last night?"

I was embarrassed and said hastily, "Henry's such a heavenly dancer."

"Henry," Liz said, with a note of warning in her voice, "I know about Henry. Besides being a terrific painter, he is also equipped with some sort of radar. He doesn't have to hunt for opportunities, with women, that is, he knows when the plum is ripe and ready to fall and just happens to be there at the right time. Now take Dolores, to put it brutally, Henry took Dolores. It was only a matter of time, of course. We had bets on when she would fall, and bigger bets on who would profit. She was a perfectly good well-behaved girl until recently and we thought of calling the bets off, since many had tried and none was chosen. Then Henry benefited by all that preliminary groundwork other artists had done on her and scooped the market or ran away with the race, or whatever."

I remembered Paul's familiar pat and asked, "And Paul took the leavings then?"

Liz didn't approve. "That's no language to use. But you may be right."

Some promising-looking people came in and Liz hurried off to be helpful.

I did my hair with great care and checked my appearance several times before walking across to La Fonda. Bill was waiting for me in the bar and suggested staying there, a more intimate cozy room than the main dining room. We both ordered enchiladas and beer and surveyed each other while waiting for them to come.

"You're looking fine, Bill," I said first.

"And so do you, Mary," he rejoined. "What have you been doing that's been agreeing with you?"

I was evasive. "I might ask the same about you."

"Just a week of rests and tests," Bill said, and went on hurriedly, obviously changing the subject, "Any more accidents, attacks, murders or such like in Villa Real in my absence?"

I laughed, "What could happen when you are away?" I said teasingly.

He looked grim. "As long as nothing happens to you," he muttered.

I felt a bit uneasy and, to change the mood, told him about Paul and his jury and Charles and the hanging committee, making a good story out of it. Bill was gratifyingly amused. So I went on to tell him about Edythe and her reaction to this hanky panky, as I called it.

Bill was unexpectedly sympathetic to Edythe. "Damn stuck up asses," he growled, "any artist who sells more than one painting thinks he's da Vinci, Michelangelo and Picasso rolled into one."

"What an anticlimax," I said tartly. Bill was distracted at this, so I hastened to try yet another subject and told him that Ellen had gone back east.

Bill was grave. "I read about the attack in the paper, but there wasn't much detail. What happened?"

I told him all I knew about it, which was quite a lot, and found that we had both finished eating when I had tapped my excellent memory. Bill had listened with great attention, particularly to Ellen's conversation, which I was able to retail with accuracy. Seeing me looking at my watch, Bill shook himself out of what seemed to be a fit of abstraction and got up to go. He walked with me in silence to the door of the Art Association, where he stood with his eyes on Henry's "Bitter Reds."

"I'd like to come to see you again soon. There's a lot to talk about. Will you be in tomorrow?"

I told him to come around after working hours and he walked off slowly.

Liz joined me at the doorway. "You're right, he is looking much better. I'd only really spoken to him once before; he came in last spring after he had been rejected by the membership committee. He took it hard, but he was bitter, not petulant, and he didn't take it out on me, the way some of them do. Basically a good guy, I'd say."

"So would I," I agreed fervently.

Liz studied my face intently. "Which runner should I put my money on, infant?" she asked. Then she grew more serious. "Just remember one thing, no, two things. First, a married man, if he is at all decent, generally stays married, no matter what. And second, the life of an artist's wife ain't all roses. My first advice comes from experience, my second from observation, and I bet Ann Landers would say the same thing."

I laughed this off. "I'm just having fun, Liz, why be serious?"

Liz laughed too, "Why indeed?" she echoed, but her voice was sad.

I was looking forward to seeing Bill next day and had tidied up my house in preparation and even made some cookies, in case they would appeal, but that afternoon Henry came into the gallery. He looked around moodily at the show, clearly not seeing much; artists tend to be blind to all other paintings but their own. And then, seeing me, revealed the object of his visit. This was to invite me to see John Graham's place, which he planned to check right then. I obtained clearance from Liz and went off with him, only remembering my promise to Bill when we were already driving out of town. I reflected that I could not turn down an opportunity to see the scene of the crime, now could I?

The old road out to the north of town was paved just until it reached the entrance of a resort hotel and then relapsed into a far more picturesque, but dusty dirt road. Thick growth, consisting of a wild tangle of natives on the hilly side, and lush cultivated grasses and fruit trees on the valley side, made me feel like an Arab riding through an oasis. I wondered if Arabs had such valleys in their deserts. I did not bother Henry with this thought as he was driving with care around the sudden rises and sharp curves. He took a right angled turn off the road onto a narrow rough lane, crossed the little river, which I would call a stream, but any water is so precious in this land that the slightest little trickle is dignified by the name of river. From this lane Henry made another sharp turn onto a driveway, lined on each side by poplars, whose leaves had already turned and were falling. The high solid gate posts of rough rock and the tall poplars in their two rows gave an air of grandeur to the entrance, which was justified by the first sight of the house. In Villa Real the substantial older houses are hideous affairs of red brick and we of the artist colony tend to live in small adobes, so that there are not many large houses proclaiming wealth and position that fit well into the landscape. This, however, was one such, and I openly admired it.

"John spent a fortune improving this place," Henry told me, as we followed the circular drive and parked in front. "He bought it quite cheaply because it was run down, but then he worked like hell on it. So did his wife, she did the garden. I'll show you the outside later."

Henry had a key on his car key ring with which he let us in the front door.

I looked around nervously. "Nobody here?" I asked.

Henry shook his head, "No, relax and enjoy looking, this is probably as close as either of us poor peasants will ever come to gracious living."

I saw what he meant, it was lovely and expensive, every detail perfectly in harmony and showing evidence of more than money, though that was the first necessity.

Off the living room, in the left wing, were bedroom, bathroom, dressing room and small feminine sitting room. I was standing hesitantly in the doorway of the bedroom when Henry said, "Listen," and opened a window.

"Water?" I asked.

Henry shut the window. "That's the acequia, the irrigation ditch, which runs all year, right outside, and that's why Mrs. Graham didn't hear anything, any splash, for instance, when John was drowned. She said she was asleep, the window was open, and the swimming pool is a good distance down the slope anyway."

We went back through the living room to the dining room and very sunny, spacious and efficient kitchen, which I admired extravagantly, and then back through the dining room to a room with a north light, lined with books.

"Studio?" I asked.

Henry shook his head. "No, John started out with this as his studio but found it too close to the noise and activity of the kitchen and couldn't work." He walked on through the library and continued, "So he built himself this other studio."

I saw now that we were in a workshop, whereas the other studio had been a library. It was not a large room, but was very neatly arranged. No easels, I noticed, but two large tilting worktables, and a great profusion of photographic equipment, including a screen.

"This doesn't look like Bela's studio at all," I remarked.

Henry agreed, "Watercolorists don't need easels, and not much framing stuff. John did most of his work from photographs, you know, so that's why the screen and projector. And he had his framing, all glass, of course, done for him. He did his own matting." Henry pointed to a very neat rack of variously colored mat boards. Next to it was an equally neat rack of watercolors, already under glass with thin framing.

"You know something funny," I said on impulse to Henry, "John Graham removed all the pictures he had in the gallery just before he died, and Clem can't think why. Do you know the reason?"

Henry shrugged, "Perhaps he was just getting temperamental, like Nick."

I smiled. Nick's tantrums were well known. The slightest upset, such as an unacceptable placement of his painting, and in would storm Nick, calling on all and sundry to witness that he resigned. This happened two or three times a year. John Graham would be sent over to Nick's studio to calm him down. Nick would relent and all would be harmony again, until the next unavoidable insult.

"Oh no," I protested, "though I hardly knew him personally, of course, John Graham wouldn't act childishly; if he removed his paintings, it was for a very good reason." A sudden horrible thought struck me. "You don't suppose he found out something about Clem's — uh, Clem's errors?"

Henry did not seem to find the thought as horrible as I did. "You may have something there," he remarked, almost casually. "But," he went on, considering, "John wouldn't have just removed his paintings and waited, and kept quiet like you. The Art Association was very much his baby, you know. He would have done something."

"But he didn't get the opportunity to do anything," I broke in and looked at Henry in apprehension.

Henry was not impressed. "Come outside," he said. I followed him obediently out onto the kitchen patio, and from there past the car parked in the driveway, through a lilac hedge to a sunny open area. There, still filled, was the swimming pool. "Now, look, you can see for yourself, the whole thing's impossible. Can't have been anything but a damned accident. John used to take his dog around the grounds in the morning early, and this time he slipped on the tile." Henry pointed to the side of the pool, tiled in the subdued variety of Mexican tile, highly glazed, though, and I could see they could be slippery. Henry went on, "John was tile-happy for a bit. People do get that way here. But after he had put it in this one area," he pointed to one side of the pool, "he found how darn slippery it was, and rather impractical too in this climate, so he just cemented the other sides."

"Well, then, if he knew how dangerous it was, how come he walked on it?"

"Oh," Henry shrugged indifferently, "who knows why?"

"Maybe he felt safe on a fine sunny morning," I thought back carefully. Most mornings are indeed fine and bright in the late summer, early fall season in Villa Real.

"Besides," Henry continued, gesturing, "look around, this area is sheltered, but how do you suppose Clem could've driven up and parked his car unobserved and got away again. No, it's nonsense, nobody would take such a risk."

Determined to make the most of the opportunity to inspect the scene of what I was beginning to agree was an accident, I walked around the pool, observing attentively. On one side was a small adobe structure, containing, I saw as I peered in, two changing rooms. Behind this was a grove of trees, irregularly placed but concealing, as close inspection revealed, a house some 50 yards away. Lilacs hid the fence marking the boundary line separating these properties. Both lilacs and trees had already lost much of their foliage, but I could imagine the thick screen of green that would create privacy in summer. Looking up towards the house I could see first a rather wild garden, then, barely visible but audible, the acequia burbling somnolently away, and behind it the abrupt rise of the hill behind the house.

"What's back there?" I asked Henry, pointing to the hill.

"Oh, just open land, a mesa, lots of piñons, some cactus, horned toads. John owns a small stretch up to where the state park starts. Fine for horses."

On the roadside, there was just a large meadow, running down from the mixed shrub and tree grove to the fence and road. Again I could visualize the summer scene quite well, and I realized that nobody could see the pool from the road in summer. The remaining side was the driveway side, and that was made private by a cleverly staggered lilac hedge. We went through this and I surveyed the driveway, which was entirely open to view from the road, as the poplars lining the drive were tall and thin and the drive quite straight.

I said to Henry, rather truculently, I fear, "I'll agree the driveway is very visible, so, well, let's say the murderer couldn't have parked a car. But the pool itself is quite protected. The risk, then, was not in the deed but getting to the scene of the crime."

Henry was truculent too. "If you're inferring that Mrs. Graham tripped John up and threw him in the pool, you aren't certifiable," he growled.

I was at once apologetic. "My goodness, no, Henry, I'm not implying anything."

Henry was mollified. "I can see you don't really mean it. Mrs. Graham — I never called her anything else, even though I saw quite a lot of her — is what I can only call a perfect lady. Impossible to imagine her thinking of violence even. She spent all her time on her gardening and keeping John happy and comfortable. She loves this garden, with a passion you wouldn't suspect she was capable of."

I looked around appreciatively. Gardening in Villa Real is not a snap, the climate is tough, and I could see Mrs. Graham had achieved some wonderful effects, giving the semiarid valley a lush English look. "Oh well," I said, disappointed, "perhaps she caught her husband mistaking her pet delphinium for a weed." This was flippant of me, I know.

Henry chose to smile, but I could see he was not amused. "Just stop this futile speculation and see what taste and money can do," he ordered me.

I duly admired the fenced vegetable and fruit garden, irrigated by a diversion from the acequia.

"Years ago," Henry remarked, "any murder done here would be for water, and many were, too."

I looked interested, and he went on, "You rich Anglos can afford to use town water and put in your wells, so it doesn't mean anything. But we peasants, why water used to be life to us, we had no other source but these acequias, so if we came across a neighbor stealing out in the night to tap the acequia out of his turn, there'd be murder done all right, and justified too." He laughed. "Anyway, this year there's been plenty of water to go round, so we can eliminate that possibility."

"Where are the horses?" I asked. I could see stables, an obvious corral and an irrigated alfalfa meadow, but no horses.

"Mrs. Graham told me to board them at the Lodge. They had a man in several times a week from the pueblo, but he's erratic. I used to help out in the stables sometimes in return for a ride—you know, polish the bits, groom the horses and do the leather up." He sighed, "I'll miss John terribly, both for himself, and for the fringe benefits too."

It was on this somewhat egotistic note we left. Henry was subdued and silent on the drive back and did not ask me out, or himself in, as I had expected when we reached my garden door, but said goodbye warmly, at least, as I thanked him for the visit, and drove off hurriedly.

I stood there watching him drive out of the compound and reflected on that automatic warmth, which I was sure he was too absent-minded to feel on this occasion. Who should drive by too, but Bill, in his little open sports car. I waved, of course, but either he did not see me, or he did not want to, because he ignored me and swept on, hardly pausing at the compound entrance. I was hurt by this and spent the rest of the evening trying not to think. Not to think about anything, that is; it was all too puzzling, annoying or difficult.

11

*The only sensible way to regard the art life
is that it is a privilege you are willing to
pay for.*

— Robert Henri, *Op Cit.*

Life crawled flatly on for the next few days, like a home movie you've seen too many times.

Liz noticed my malaise. "You're not your usual cheerful self, Mac," she said. "Tell Aunt Liz."

So I did tell her, about the trip to the Graham house, which I raved over, and then Bill's snub and desertion.

Liz was not really sympathetic. "If that is all you worry about, you can't complain. Bill will show up again, I guarantee it."

Believing her—for Liz has a habit of being right—I immediately felt better and asked her if she had ever been out to the Graham place.

Liz looked sad and remote as she replied, "Many times, infant. I've been out on business, and to swimming parties, and sometimes John lent me a horse. He was always generous, you know. The horses needed exercising when the girls were away at college, and I think, too, he missed them, the girls, that is. He was always inviting people out, all ages. If you hadn't stayed so much in the background, he would have asked you, too, I expect."

I was defensive, "You and Clem seemed to be monopolizing him. I felt unwanted."

Liz was remorseful at this. "Yes, I suppose we did," she admitted. "He was someone special, you know. Very special," she added to herself.

I thought to myself, heaven forbid and all that, if Clem had taken the risk of going to the Graham pool that morning and arranging an accident, because of fear of imminent exposure, then Liz does not suspect it. It was clear to me Liz would not cover up for Clem if it came to murdering John Graham. Maybe anybody else, though, I surprised myself by thinking. Determined to keep my mouth shut to Liz if no one else, I busied myself with such things as I could do as far away from her as possible.

When Paul Humfrey lumbered in, looking like a mother bear whose cubs are in danger, I was tidying the meeting room, but I heard Paul's muffled roar well enough.

"Liz," he barked, "my God, Liz, what I go through."

I could hear Liz being soothing.

"It's Edythe Kendall Chambers, but again. I got her in, I admit it, you know it, now it's this painting she put in for the last show. Hell of a mess, but I did accept it, didn't I? I thought I did. Now she's mad at me about it. It seems to mean such a hell of a lot to her."

Another soothing murmur.

"But Liz, she can't paint, she never will be able to paint. But she must be in the Art Association, no matter what. Why?" Paul sounded genuinely puzzled and indignant.

I wondered furiously whether to bounce forward with an I-can-explain-everything-air, or stay discreetly out of it. Very little reflection decided me on the latter course. Eventually Paul would inquire of the hanging committee how it happened that Edythe's painting had been rejected; I would not have to tell him. As for the other question, it was as much of a puzzle to me. Edythe had money, so she did not pine to join the Art Association for financial reasons. Perhaps, I thought, it was a matter of status. If you claimed to be an artist and were not a member, a certain stigma attached itself to you, no doubt. I decided that the real question was why Edythe thought of herself as an artist. But then so many people do these days. And if someone could win an art fellowship by pasting some black squiggles on a piece of brown wrapping paper, as had happened to one of our bearded beatniks, then far be it for me to judge who is an artist and who is not. I thought on ruefully, then if you wanted to be a representational painter, your lack of training showed up very much more clearly than if you simply committed blobs, botches, squiggles and scratches.

And that, I went on thinking, was why Bill Thorpe had been rejected; he rather fell between two schools. If he had flung some paint haphazardly at a canvas, framed the result authoritatively, and acted as if he had created a masterpiece, the membership committee would have leaned over backward to keep up with the times as they did and hardly have had the nerve to turn him down. But no, he slapped his dingy colors on and worked over them, trying to produce something slightly recognizable, and that was his mistake.

Back to Bill Thorpe again, that train of thought was a mistake. I looked out cautiously to make sure Paul had gone before emerging from the meeting room. I almost bumped into Clem, who was hurrying inattentively out.

He stopped, but I could see reluctantly, and told me he had sold Bela's painting, and that he was avoiding Paul too. "Don't give me away," he said softly and pattered out neatly.

"No," I thought, "I won't give you away, not if it's just figures, but murder?" I shivered and didn't answer myself.

Plucking up my courage, plate of cookies in hand, I went over to Bill's adobe after work. I spied out the land first and knew he was home.

He answered the door, stiffly, and did not assume any air of welcome.

I marched in with a nonchalant air, handed over the cookies, and said, "Here's a peace offering. I made them for you the other day, but when Henry invited me to inspect the Graham's place, I couldn't refuse to view the scene of the crime, now could I?"

Still stiff, Bill replied, "You told me you would be in."

I shrugged, "The best laid plans of me and mice, you know. I found out quite a lot, anyway. You want to hear, don't you?"

Bill looked back at the painting he must have been working on when I interrupted him, put down his brushes, and rather ungraciously said, "Oh, all right, come in and sit down. The light's getting bad anyway."

I looked at the painting, while Bill looked at me. I simply could not think of anything to say. When all else fails, you can always say "Nice frame," but there was no frame on this muddy mess. "Vlaminck?" I asked.

Bill had a sense of humor, fortunately. He laughed, "A long way after," he said resignedly, sinking back into his armchair. "You don't have to offer anything, remember? Except cookies," he added, helping himself.

Relieved, I sank back too and wondered where to start. Then I remembered that I had not told him about the discrepancy in the accounts of the Art Association. Feeling a sense of disloyalty, but impelled to justify my suspicions, I told him now.

He was indeed impressed and agreed that the situation was serious, but he pointed out that it is a long way from a hundred dollars to three murders. He thought for a bit and then said, slowly and carefully, "You, no we, I think I'll go along with you after all."

I brightened; that was good news.

"We have really only two facts to go on. The attack on Ellen that could not possibly have been an accident, though it might have been coincidence, just a young punk. The shortage in the accounts at the gallery is a fact, but it might have no connection at all with Ellen, and might be a mistake anyway." He paused, considering, and went on, "Now the thing for you to do is to keep your eyes open at the Art Association."

I broke in here to explain that I had looked at the accounts file and it was all too complicated for me.

"In that case, don't bother with the figures, but watch Clem and Liz. Now what about alibis; shouldn't it be possible to eliminate one or the other or both?"

"But they both live alone, well, most of the time," I pointed out. "Nick's gas pipe could have been doctored any time. The attack on Ellen occurred in the early morning. If John Graham had been tripped, sandbagged and thrown into his swimming pool, that too had occurred before working hours. No, the only hope we've got is Bela's death, which to me is the most suspicious one anyway. I'll try to find out who was where on that day."

Bill seized on my statement about John Graham. "What's this? You don't really think that happened, do you?"

I defended my position, which I had not really considered before I spoke, but now seemed the truth to me. "Yes, I do," I said firmly. "Now I've seen the setup, I think he fell into some sort of trap. Whoever the murderer was washed down those slippery Mexican tiles on the one side of Graham's pool, waited for John to come by on his customary morning perambulation of the grounds, and then called urgently to him from the other side. Had John not fallen, as anticipated, it would have been easy enough to find an excuse for the summons, wouldn't it?"

Bill considered this. "What about the dog?"

"Ah, I've thought of that. 'The Dog That Didn't Bark in the Night.' Clearly, it was someone the dog knew, who had been a frequent visitor. That's no help, though, because John entertained everyone out there. Clem and Liz were practically family."

Bill was still unconvinced. "Then what about the risk of driving out there? Surely Mrs. Graham would have heard a car?"

"That is a snag," I admitted. Then light dawned. "I've got it. He—I'm just saying he for convenience—he could have parked his car somewhere along the lane outside. He would have to have a quick getaway, though, in case the dog woke Mrs. Graham. So what would he do? I know," I said triumphantly, "I bet he caught one of the

Graham's horses and used it for riding away quickly, freeing it again at the bottom of its meadow."

Bill looked dubious. "A very fancy theory, but quite impossible to prove. Besides, riding a horse bareback, even catching one sometimes is quite a feat."

Undaunted, I replied, "I know Liz rides, because John Graham used to lend her a horse; probably Clem does too, since it's the in thing here. And they both have cars, of course."

Bill threw cold water on my speculations. "No. All that effort and risk for a petty embezzlement, it just doesn't ring true to me. I think you are barking up the wrong tree. Maybe Nick's and John Graham's deaths were accidents. I think so myself. But Bela's, no. There does seem to be something fishy there, and the attack on Ellen—that's the proof. I think we should concentrate on Bela's accident."

I was a bit miffed, all my fine theories gone for nothing, but I had to agree with him. At the thought of natty dignified Clem astride a horse, bareback too, my imagination boggled.

"Besides," I went on aloud to Bill, "Clem wouldn't be fired, no matter what. He is just too valuable. He can always get another job selling paintings, he has such a gift for it. He is well paid too, I know. For a single man he gets a fine salary. He used to get commissions only, but he threatened to leave unless he was put on a salary basis."

Bill was interested. "He must have had the Board under his thumb to agree to that."

"The Board knows who has the whip hand," I replied.

"Well," Bill said, "that's that, you had better give up."

I was astonished. "Give up? Me? Never! Let's think of some other candidates."

Bill abstractedly got up, picked up a brush and added another unnecessary stroke to an already muddled canvas. Turning, he saw me looking disapproving. Unhappily, he said, "Tread softly, for you tread on my dreams."

I was unhappy too. "But Bill, is that," I pointed around at his paintings, "is that your dreams?"

Bill's mouth was a hard line. "Yes, any objections?"

Oh dear, I thought, what can I say? "Does it mean so much to you?" I asked, but with sympathy in my voice, I hoped.

Bill was even more intense and bitter. "The same answer," he said curtly.

I got up to go, thinking it was hopeless, but to my surprise, instead of seeing me to the door, Bill sat down himself and said, "No, don't go, Mary. Have a little patience, things may work out. I'll know more in a week or so, and see my way clearer then."

Casting about for something to say to put him in a better temper, I recounted Paul Humfrey's diatribe on Edythe, censoring myself hastily when it came to his description of Edythe as an artist, fearing that Bill might think of himself.

Bill greeted this subject with relief. "Well, there's another suspect for you," he pointed out cheerfully. "Say Nick's death was an accident, but it put one of Paul's stooges on the board, didn't it?"

"No," I thought carefully, "you couldn't call Charles Newberg a stooge. He is an ex-pupil of Paul's, sure, but he's done so much better than his teacher that Paul is jealous. They will come to an open clash soon."

"Still," Bill reasoned, "Paul may have thought he'd get control, but then why kill Bela? He was never on the Board."

"Bela may have suspected Paul of helping Nick out of life," I suggested.

Bill was enthusiastic now. "Yes, and then John Graham would be a menace and have to be removed for two reasons, both because he suspected Paul, and because he would thwart Paul's game of putting his pupils on the Board."

I was less enthusiastic. "That too seems to me a petty motive for such drastic deeds."

Bill disagreed. "Maybe to you it seems petty, but from what I have heard about Paul, there would be two driving impulses there: money, the root of most murder, after all, and survival, in the last analysis. What could be more important?"

I was not convinced. "No, it's just not in character. I can see Paul riding a horse bareback, and he might knock a man down in a fit of temper, though basically, like most outsize men, he is not at all violent. But I can't see him carrying through such a well plotted murder as Bela's must have been, nor would he attack Ellen, in my opinion."

Bill seemed to lose interest after this and said, "We don't seem to be getting anywhere, do we?" He picked up his paper and folded it open at the movie page. "How about dinner and a movie, if there's anything good on? I'm sure you'd rather dance, but I can't compete with Henry yet." He said this in an offhand way, but I detected a note of jealousy in his voice and was obscurely pleased.

We had a very pleasant evening, catching up on each other's pasts at dinner, and enjoying the comedy. No dancing, no handholding, and no, "Let's get to know each other, shall we?" on the drive home, but a feeling of friendship made up for the lack of excitement.

Bill stopped his car outside my garden door. I rather expected him to see me in, but he sat still and said, "You haven't told anyone else about the money business, have you?"

I was uncomfortable and had to reply honestly, "Just Henry. He's a sort of policeman, after all."

Bill frowned. "No, not really. He just allows his uncle to help him occasionally, he isn't one for regular work. No, Mary, you keep your mouth tight shut about everything we discussed. Just suppose for a minute you have got hold of something, somebody who'd already killed won't hesitate to arrange another accident. Think how easy it would be, since you live alone."

I shivered, and Bill put his arm around my shoulders, but then as if reminded of something, he quickly put his arm back. "Well, just look out," he said, dismissingly.

What a letdown, I thought to myself, as I obediently checked locks and windows and even took in my key, an obvious precaution that had not occurred to me before. Bill, I heard, did not drive up to his house until after my door slammed shut. This made me feel much more secure and I slept deep and dreamlessly.

12

*A good model is one whose lines
have meaning.*

—Robert Henri, *Op Cit.*

The gold of a million aspens on the mountains stood out clearly against the varying greens, I saw as I walked down the Camino. I hunted for a simile, preferably poetic, without much success. "Deathly yellows of consuming fire?" "Fool's gold of colder death?" Obviously, I was no poet.

I abandoned the futile effort and turned my mind to consideration of more mundane problems. By the time I had reached the post office, I had decided to find out, if possible, whether Clem and Liz were in the gallery on the afternoon of Bela's death. Considering my course of action rather than looking where I was going, I ran into Charles Newberg.

"Look where you're going, Miss MacIntyre," he said, but in a kindly way as he helped me pick up the Art Association mail I had dropped in the collision. We took the batch of assorted envelopes to a table to sort them out. Charles was openly curious, examining each envelope curiously.

I was not tactful. "What are you looking for?" I asked rudely.

At least he had the grace to look embarrassed. "I just feel something's up at the Art Association. No idea what, but I've a hunch all is not on the up and up. Clem's acting sort of queer these days. Perhaps he's dickering with a better offer from one of those rich galleries in California."

"And I have a horrid hunch you may be right," I told him, indiscreetly, I fear, and gathered up the mail firmly.

Charles stopped me by putting his hand on my arm. "No fooling, there is something wrong with Bela's painting. When's Ellen coming back? I want to see her."

This surprised me. "Oh, she hasn't written yet. I've no idea, not till next spring, I should think. But what you should worry about is that painting of Edythe's; she's on the warpath after Paul Humphrey, and it's not fair of you to let him take the blame."

Charles laughed heartlessly. "Paul can take care of himself. It's his métier," he said, with some truth, I thought.

"I'm all three monkeys when in the gallery," I told him. "I see nothing, hear nothing and I try to tell nothing, but that's the difficulty."

We both laughed at this, and I went off more at ease with myself.

Liz was not in a good mood that morning, and Clem did not appear until just before I left, so I could not find any opportunity to satisfy my curiosity as to their whereabouts on that one day in June. It was hardly possible to ask them, now was it, I reflected as I walked home, rather discouraged again. Still, Liz had asked me to be on duty for the next model night, which had been resumed now that the fuss over the attack on Ellen had died down, and that, I decided, must give me a chance to have a long look at the files.

I was even more discouraged to find Edythe in the little corner market on Acequia Madre when I went in to pick up the few odd things I needed. I would have thought that Edythe would be one to shop at the big new supermarket further down the road. Luckily she did not see me coming in, and it was not until we were both at the counter that she recognized me. Usually she fell on me with glad cries and a torrent of gush, but not that afternoon. She seemed distraught and a bit embarrassed as she put down the few and very cheap items she had selected, not her style at all, I observed as I watched. But she waited for me to pay and come out and walked along the dusty road with me.

She too asked if I had heard from Ellen, saying thoughtfully, "I want to see her. A fine woman, I wish I'd had her common sense."

This was just so unlike Edythe I was worried, and sympathetic. "Edythe, don't get upset over your painting, I'm sure Paul didn't turn it down. There must have been some mix-up," I offered in consolation.

But Edythe did not seem to be interested. "It's too late," she said, "it doesn't matter any more."

This almost frightened me. "It's never too late," I said with conviction.

Edythe had a haunted look on her still handsome, aging face. "You're young. You don't know how it is to feel life slipping out of your grasp."

Our ways parted after this, and I went on slowly, feeling uneasy at the change in Edythe. Suddenly I remembered something that might cheer her and called back, "Edythe, you'll come to model night, won't you? I'll be in charge, and I'll try to get Dolores."

She looked back listlessly, "No, Mac dear. I won't be coming any more," and walked off.

Worse and worse, I thought, what has come over her?

The phone was ringing when I reached my garden door and stopped just as I dashed in. I swore grimly to myself as I retrieved my purse and bag of groceries from the portal where I had dropped them in my rush to get to the phone. I was trying to make the garden look less untidy and picking chrysanthemums between whiles when the phone rang again. I got it this time. It was Henry, asking about model night, and upon hearing I was in charge, asked me to an early dinner beforehand. I was hoping for a ride downtown from Bill, but this was not an invitation to refuse.

"Who're you going to get for model?" Henry inquired. "Don't bother with Dolores, she won't accept. Try to get a young girl and remember it's the figure that counts. I want somebody sexy."

I was not amused. "You can't expect me to go around Villa Real inspecting all the *pachucas'* figures, can you? I have to stick to the list, and anyway, what's . . ." I stopped. I was going to say, "What's the matter with Dolores," but that clearly would have been a goof, so I hastily changed my question and said sweetly, "Surely, with your extensive knowledge you can recommend a candidate."

Henry laughed. "Jealous?" he said lightly.

I spluttered indignantly, "It's no skin off my nose, I couldn't care less, but . . ." I hesitated and Henry broke in, "But what?"

"Well," I faltered, "I have to find a model. I'm kind of responsible. If you can help, fine."

Henry would not be drawn, though, and rang off after promising to pick me up on model night.

Henry had sounded very confident of Dolores' refusal, but he turned out to be wrong. She agreed to pose; in fact, she was pleased and told me she was hunting modeling jobs, needing the money that month. I was able to get a fairly large class after much work at the phone. I went through both members and nonmembers lists, leaving out only the name of William Thorpe; I decided to make a personal call in that case. My courage failed me when it came to the point, though. I phoned instead. Bill agreed to come and he asked me out to dinner beforehand too. Very foolishly, I prevaricated and then told an outright lie about having another ride down and having to be there much earlier. I knew this was a mistake while I was saying it, but once you start to weave a tangled web, you can't really stop.

Bill got the message clearly enough and rang off with a "See you there, then."

Henry arrived rather later than he had promised on model night. I reminded him that I had to arrive a bit earlier than the class to open up and get things ready.

"Oh, we'll be in plenty of time," he said casually.

But this was not the case, as it happened. Henry took me to a chile place on Canyon Road. The food may have been delicious, but the chile sauce that everything was smothered in was more to a genuine native's taste than to a mere aficionado like me. I had to order two glasses of milk to help quench the fire in my throat, and by the time I had downed the last bit of blue tortilla, from which I had scraped as much red sauce off as I could manage, it was later than I had counted on.

"Plenty of time," said Henry. "You've got ten minutes."

That should have been ample, but when we arrived at the Art Association, we found Bill trying to get in the side door, which should have been unlocked by then. I came up first and Bill said, without seeing Henry, who was parking the car, "Oh there you are, Mary. You're a bit late. I came to help you."

Henry walked up behind me then and instead of keeping quiet as I hoped, said, "Sorry, old man, we are a bit late, but Miss Mac had a hard time eating chile the way us poor peasants like it."

Bill was taken aback and said nothing more.

Henry helped me set up the class and the model stand. Bill went around the gallery, examining the paintings carefully and staying aloof.

Dolores came in a little late and lost no time in removing her clothes and posing, a front view, hand-on-hips pose this time. Henry was visibly surprised to see her, but said nothing and stayed in the back, working hard. Paul came in with a troupe of his disciples, all female. Charles Newberg, several beatniks, a scattering of the female kind too, and the usual collection of old timers, made up the class.

It surprised me greatly when Edythe walked in rather surreptitiously and took a seat on the other side of the room from Paul and his flock.

I stayed in the room for the first posing period, watching the class rather than Dolores. Bill worked earnestly and with great intensity, but rather as warfare, attack and recoil effect. Henry worked smoothly and without any visible effort. Paul taught his class, jollying them along heartily and praising their least little squiggles. Charles Newberg, I decided, was more interested in the class than in his sketch. He looked around frequently and watched Dolores intently at intervals too, but without at once sketching what he saw. The old timers plodded on methodically.

Paul called the time, as I expected and didn't resent this time. At break, I noticed that the class seemed uneasy and not as friendly as last time. Charles went up to talk to Dolores, but I could see she was sulkier than ever and did not respond to him at all. Paul stayed in his group, the old timers in theirs. Bill went over to talk to Edythe, which I thought showed he had the right feelings, or good manners at least. Henry just went on sketching.

It was a relief when Paul's voice boomed out, "Up with you, Dolly," and I was free to leave. As unobtrusively as possible I melted out of the door and made for the office. I had just sat down at Liz's desk and was about to open the drawer in which she kept the keys to the file cabinet, when I heard steps coming toward me. I fiddled with some papers on the desk and tried to look as if I were busy.

In came Edythe, more her old self, I could see. "Mac, I must tell you, I simply must, you can it fool an old married woman like me. I've had two myself, you know."

I must have looked puzzled at this, because she explained, "Two babies, I mean. Oh yes, I have two sons. They don't want their old mother around any more, but that's neither here nor there. But I tell you, I can't be mistaken."

I still looked puzzled, and I certainly was.

She gushed on. "The signs, you can't hide them in the nude, after all. Oh yes, Mac, I know, Dolores is pregnant. I'm sure of it."

I gasped.

Edythe looked triumphant at my shock. "Well, my dear, what can you expect. She shouldn't pose in her condition, of course, but it's early yet. I don't expect anybody will notice but me." Edythe looked quite smug. "Now, who's the father, I wonder? If she knows herself she's lucky, maybe he'll marry her."

I probably looked as disgusted as I felt, because Edythe became serious.

"I'm sorry I've upset you, you're too much of a *jeune fille*, perhaps I shouldn't have told you, but it will all come out, anyway. And Mac, maybe you are the one who ought to know."

"Me?" I said, dazed.

Edythe shrugged, looking wise. "Well, we can guess who's the most likely father, can't we?"

Miserably, I shook my head. "Not me," I said, unconvincingly. "Not my business, either." I got up and looked at my watch. "Come on, Edythe. Time to get back." I was sick with dismay, remembering Henry's smile when he told me Dolores posed for him, for free too; remembering Liz's warning; remembering, too, Paul's familiar pat. It was not yet time to reassume the pose, but I wanted to stop Edythe's knowing looks.

I shook her off, kept my eyes resolutely off Henry, Bill, Dolores, Paul, and fixed upon Charles Newberg as someone safe. My hand trembled slightly as I examined his sketchbook, not seeing anything.

He was unexpectedly observant and kind. "Something's shook you up badly, I see. Compose yourself while I go on talking, nobody will see you."

He shielded me from view while keeping up a steady stream of chatter, and gradually I felt calmer. When break time was over and Dolores got up on the model stand again, tossing her robe off on the way, I could not prevent myself from watching her closely. Charles caught my intent stare and murmured, "Relax," from the side of his mouth. I flushed and tried to look at something else, but found my gaze straying back. Was Edythe right, I wondered? Perhaps there was a slight thickening in Dolores' waist, perhaps her breasts were heavier, I just wouldn't know.

I slipped out again, shutting the door firmly behind me this time. Surely Edythe wouldn't follow me this time, I breathed as I sat down at Liz's desk. I waited for the sound of steps for a few minutes. When none came, I found the key of the file cabinet and found the folder marked sales records.

After Edythe's news, I was hardly interested any more in what Clem and Liz were doing last June, but I made myself try to find out, more as a distraction than because I thought it of any importance. I was distracted when I found the record for the day in June in which I was interested. Mrs. Rountree had bought three paintings on that day. Only Clem could sell them to her, so some of his time that day was accounted for. I replaced the folder, unthinking, and sat down again at Liz's desk to put back her keys. Why was I so upset? I rubbed my forehead and looked around, seeking an answer to the question, which was one I did not want asked, let alone answered. My eye fell on the one painting in the room, which was propped up against the file cabinet with its back to me. Idly I turned it to me. It was Bela's last painting. Impulsively seizing on something to distract my unhappy thoughts, I picked it up and took it with me back to the class.

Dolores was posing when I crept in cautiously, so I put the painting face to the wall near me and waited.

As soon as Paul gave the signal for break, Edythe came over first, followed by Paul.

"What's that painting you brought in, Mac?" she twittered.

Paul lunged over and turned it around. "Oh, it's just Bela's last corn."

He was replacing it when Charles took it from him and propped it up against the model stand. "Now, look," he said, pointing, "what's wrong? See this, and this, the tone value is wrong for Bela somehow."

Everybody flocked around him, looking as he pointed. Into a buzz of talk, agreement and disagreement in equal measure, I judged, walked Clem and Liz. I had rather expected that they would: Liz hated to be left out of anything and Clem was propelled by her, no doubt. They came up curiously to the group around Bela's painting.

"Having an art seminar, Charles?" said Liz.

Clem went up very close to the painting and then backed off, starting to speak, but Liz interrupted whatever he was going to say.

"It's that painting of Bela's you sold, Clem. It was in my office. I was to take it up to Bela's old friend who bought it, remember. What's it doing here?" Liz looked at me in anger.

Defensively, I put in quickly, "Charles thinks there's something wrong with it."

"Yes," Charles said, coming to my support. "Bela had a formula, who doesn't? He was so utterly predictable, but this painting just doesn't fit. There's a false note. I think it's the shadows."

Clem shrugged and went off, bored. He never made any bones

about not being interested in the techniques of painting, but Liz was still angry. "Well," she snapped, "it's sold now, so leave it alone; put it back in my office, Mac."

I did so hastily, and when I got back, the class had resumed sketching and Clem and Liz had gone. I occupied myself with the complicated financial calculations, wondering with the back of my mind how I was going to get home. Henry was so clearly furious, I could see as I watched him slashing at his large sketchpad with sure, savage strokes. I glanced at Bill, who was not furious, but certainly unfriendly in a moody, abstracted way. I could not stand the thought of enduring Edythe's insinuations, as malicious gossip was labeled by Liz.

It was a relief, when Charles arrived at my table first. "I'll stick around and drive you home, Mac. My wife won't mind, as it's in a good cause." He grinned reassuringly, and I accepted thankfully.

Henry came up and paid without a word and went striding off. Everybody else offered me a ride, even Bill, though he did so with some reluctance, I thought, and rather sullenly. I was glad to be able to refuse them all.

Charles drove me home slowly, talking steadily all the way. "Edythe, the old witch, went and told you Dolores is pregnant, didn't she?" he started off bluntly. I nodded unhappily. "What's so upsetting to you about that? No," he interrupted himself, "don't answer that if you don't want to, it's not my business. I could see Dolores' condition. I guess I'm baby conscious; we're having one ourselves, you know, my wife's about four months along."

This was good news to me. It was common knowledge that the Newbergs wanted to start a family and were waiting until Charles could make enough by selling paintings so his wife could quit her job.

"Why, Charles, how wonderful. I'm glad to be happy about something."

Charles went on gravely, "I suppose you think Henry's the father. Well, I don't. Henry's too wily a bird to get caught that way. As for Paul, he's a possibility, but barely. His wife left him for a younger man; she wanted children, I know. If he's the father, I should think he'd be delighted and marry the girl. Bill Thorpe?" He paused so long I thought he must feel my heart thumping. "I hardly know him, just by sight. He did employ Dolores for a bit, so he's a runner, at least. But really, I think you're worrying yourself unnecessarily. It's far more likely Dolores has her eye firmly fixed on the main chance, which is marrying into a well-established family here."

"Really?" I said doubtfully.

"Oh yes," said Charles with conviction. "I don't deny that Henry was probably the pioneer, and that Paul may have tried too, later, and even succeeded. That fellow Thorpe may be the fall guy, for all I know, but if she can't get him, and he looks sensible enough to refuse to be blackmailed, her family and the padre between them will see she marries suitably." Charles smiled, and added, "And if all else fails, there is still the welfare, which carries no stigma here. But then, it isn't Dolores you worry about, I'm sure."

"Hardly," I agreed wryly. "It's all no skin off my nose, and why in hell I get so emotional about it, I don't know."

Charles took his eye off the road for a minute and looked at me. "It's high time you did get emotional. You live your own life now, not other people's. And," he added seriously, "watch out for yourself."

He saw me to my front door, looking carefully around the patio as he went, and told me to lock the door after him, checking first to see my house was empty. This frightened me; I even looked under the bed, like an old maid in Victorian jokes. But I wasn't hoping to find a man there. I even bolted my garden door, something I had never bothered to do before, and felt very alone when I heard the diminishing roar of Charles' old car go down the driveway and out into the Camino.

Later, lying awake trying to ignore my fears with a nice placid mystery in my cold hands, I heard the increasing and louder roar of Bill's little convertible coming into the driveway and past me down the compound. Strangely comforted, I slept in peace that night.

13

*Art after all is but an extension of
language to the expression of sensations
too subtle for words.*

                           —Robert Henri, *Op Cit.*

Liz did not show up at the Gallery until after lunch;
Clem was busy all morning with buyers. He sold Henry's
"Bitter Reds" to a well-known collector from the Panhandle
who always came in at the end of October, and with it a large
Charles Newberg canvas, very decorative, also emphasizing
reds, but all the warm, orangey reds, set off with black.

When Liz did come in, I could see she was in a foul
temper. "Hell, Mac," she attacked me at once, "for God's sake
why don't you mind your own business. What were you doing
in my office anyway?"

I had to be apologetic, though I was getting angry
myself. "Damn it, Liz, your office is not holy ground. I had to
get some paper, and I saw Bela's painting and remembered
Charles Newberg had said there was something a bit off about

it, so I brought it out for them all to see it, in case someone might suggest what the wrong note was."

Liz wasn't mollified. "And suppose someone had, so what?"

"Oh, no one could see what it was; Charles thinks it's the shadows, that's all."

"Nonsense," Liz said angrily. "For a bunch of artists they are a lot of phonies. It's just the lack of signature."

Unlike Clem, Liz did know a lot about the technique of painting. She had even taken lessons in oil painting at one time, but abandoned them, she had told me, when she realized she would never put in the time and effort necessary to get beyond the amateur stage.

"Well, if you say so, Liz," I said agreeably. "I'm sorry you're annoyed about it."

Liz shrugged, and I took myself off before she could find more fault with me. Walking home along the Alameda, no longer lush green now, but showing here and there its winter bareness, I was startled out of my deep thought by the sound of a car pulling up and a voice saying, "Hop in, Mary. I want to talk to you." It was Bill. Smiling with pleasure, I got in and he drove off without another word until we were out of town.

He stopped the car beside a steep cliff, and asked, "Where would you like to go?"

I waved at the cliff. "Want to go fossil hunting?" I replied. "That's a fine place. It's hard to believe all this was under water way back, but you can find plenty of evidence right there to prove it."

Bill shook his head. "Not now. It's the present and the future, particularly your future, I'm interested in, not the past." He laughed. "Well, not in such a very remote past."

He had been so grim up till then that I was relieved at his laugh. "Let's go on up to the aspens. We are on the way, and it may be our last chance; a good storm will finish them."

Bill drove in a relaxed silence up the mountain road, slowly, because loose gravel made the curves dangerous, but confidently, as if he knew the road well enough. When we came to the aspen belt, I could see that the peak of color was already over; the leaves were fluttering down in the cold winds and many were almost bare.

Bill parked the car on a track leading off the road. "Let's walk," he said and opened my door.

We walked together in silence up the tracked line with aspens, catching leaves with our cupped hands and in our hair. It was a golden dream.

I turned to Bill impulsively and said, "Funny how Houseman, the Shropshire Lad one, so very English, should suit this country so well; you know, 'the beautiful and death-struck year,' here it is 'close and dear.'" I waved my hand around.

Bill was interested. "Ah, yes, I remember, one goes through a Houseman phase. But I'd hardly call all this 'homely comforters.' Makes you think of ugly eider downs, anyway. And I hope you're not sad, are you?"

I considered. "Just the pleasurable autumn melancholy," I shrugged. "But I see what you mean, nature is hostile here, or rather indifferent; perhaps in his own shire Houseman felt nature was sympathetic. Here, never."

Bill surveyed the golden sunlit scene with frank admiration. "It's so damn beautiful, though, death-struck but not complaining, as we do."

I surveyed him, probably with as much frank admiration. Whether he reflected the gold around him, or whether it was my overcharged imagination at work, I don't know, but he blazed with light to me.

Seeing my eye on him, he took my arm and said, "You're a golden girl here too," and laughed. "How we are translated." His voice changed, "Mary, you seem to be asking for trouble. What on earth induced you to get out Bela's painting? Are you deliberately stirring things up? Why? What are you getting out of it? Think of the danger. Just suppose you have got hold of something fishy going on, then you would be the next to have an accident, wouldn't you?"

Sobered, I stopped and looked into those blue eyes. "Do you really think that our joke has turned out to be true, after all?"

Bill didn't meet my gaze, but looked back at the streams of

sunlight mingling with the gold of the aspens. "Honestly, I don't know. The joke doesn't seem to be a joke any longer, but what the truth is . . . who knows?"

He kicked a piece of decayed wood off the path and went on, "What you have done is kick a shelter out of the way, as I've done, and uncovered a nasty lot of lice underneath. Look how they scurry away for cover," he pointed.

I shuddered, "Repulsive, but that's ridiculous. Nobody we know is repulsive. You're not comparing Clem and Liz to wood lice, are you?"

Bill laughed. "That was a lousy analogy in every way. It's just that I think you have uncovered something that had to be and should have been left hidden."

"Should be? Surely you don't think murder should be kept quiet about, even embezzlement? You think anybody should get away with that?" Then I had a flash of stupidity. "You don't mean Dolores, do you? That won't be hidden much longer."

"Dolores?" Bill exclaimed in surprise. "How does she come into this?"

I said, without looking at him and as offhandedly as possible, "Don't you know she is pregnant, and not married, as far as anyone knows. Who is your candidate for papa?"

There was an awkward silence. I sneaked a small glance at Bill and could not interpret his expression, a mixture of consternation and amusement, I thought.

"Here, let's sit down," he said and pointed to a fallen log, which he inspected carefully before patting the spot for me to sit on. He sat down close beside me and leaned forward, elbows on thighs, looking straight ahead. "Don't be thinking I'm the candidate, Mary. Sure, Dolores did pose for me a couple of times in my studio, but it was strictly business. In the first place, I'm not one to pick up another's leavings, and in the second place," he grinned, "imagine having to see that face on the pillow in the morning. A lovely figure isn't enough, in my book."

I felt as if the golden afternoon had entered into my veins like champagne. I bubbled over with joy and relief. "That's just too bad," I giggled, "you would've made a lovely suspect, bumping everyone off to cover up an affair with Dolores. I'm disappointed."

Jumping up, I grasped as many aspen leaves as I could in two hands and threw them in the air, watching them fall lightly through the cool sharp sunshine.

Bill caught my hand and we started on down the trail.

"With the best will in the world, I don't see how you can link up Dolores and the three accidents. You don't surely suspect any of the old guard of . . ." he hesitated.

I rescued him, ". . . of being responsible for Dolores' interesting condition? Heavens know, the timing is out anyway. It is a pity, because it's easier to understand a murder done over seduction and illegitimacy than it is to understand one done to cover up a petty embezzlement, which is the only motive I can think of now. Except, of course, I wonder sometimes whether Paul Humfrey could have wanted to gain control of the Art Association badly enough to go to such desperate lengths."

Bill walked on silently.

So I continued, "And then there's Edythe. Her behavior has been so peculiar lately. Could she have wiped out any possible opposition so she could get into the Art Association? I'm sure she bribed Paul, and that failing, she may have thrown good money after bad, so to speak, or do I mean tried to recoup her losses. I'm confused."

Laughing, Bill said, "You are confused. You stay that way, don't try to make sense. You will be safe until you do hit upon the truth, if there is a truth to hit upon, of course. That attack on Ellen worries me. She may know of something. Suppose she writes to you about it, tell me and keep quiet." Helping me in his car, he said, "Promise?"

And I solemnly replied, "Cross my heart."

Driving back, Bill suddenly asked me if I would like to see Nicolai Polkoff's studio. "Nick gave me a key shortly before he died. It's funny, Mary, but I'd quite forgotten it until now. Come over tomorrow and we'll look in."

I thought for a minute. I had been into Nick's studio many times while he was alive, but without his gregarious, aggressive personality to give it color, what attraction was there? "I'd love to, Bill. If Clem agrees, I could pick out a painting to put in the November show; it would be the last for him."

We arranged to meet for lunch. I asked Bill in when he stopped at my garden door, but he refused. "I'm off to the big city again soon and have to clear up a bit," he explained.

I was disappointed, but it was just as well Bill had other plans, because while I was catching up on my notes—I had not forgotten my mystery in the various excitements of late; on the contrary, they were adding to my file of notes at a heady pace—there was a squeak of my garden gate and then a knock on my front door. Putting down pencil and stack of papers on my coffee table, I went to the door.

"Hi, Miss Mac, Mish-mash, Mic-Mac, how about dinner and dancing?"

I hesitated and, while I thought about it, took up my notes and put them away in my *vargueno*.

"Come on, I won't keep you out late and we won't stop to look at the lights of Villa Real." Henry smiled, "Unless, of course, you want to?" There was a question in his voice, which I thought it prudent to ignore.

"All right, Henry. You sit down and make yourself comfortable, fix a drink if you like, everything is in the kitchen, and I'll get into a dress."

I shut my bedroom door firmly and devoted half an hour to a remodeling job. Henry had already admired the plain black dress, so I wore my only other choice, a sea green semi-shift. It fitted rather more snugly than I remembered. In fact, it was quite tight in places. I looked dubiously at my reflection and decided the results were not unbecoming and that it was well made enough to stand the strain.

Henry had made himself at home. He was sipping a drink, lying back in my fireside chair with his feet up on the raised adobe hearth. "Nice place you've made of this," he said appreciatively, "comfortable, clean, good drinks. I miss having some sort of home."

"Your wife?" I asked tentatively.

He tossed off the drink and got up. "She never made a home for me anyway. We're really finished this time. I've enough money to pay a lawyer now and she won't get her claws into me again."

He suddenly seemed to see me, and whistled. "This calls for somewhere special," he said. "How about La Fonda?"

Nothing is quite so stimulating as seeing open admiration in a man's eyes. I had enjoyed a golden afternoon, and now a golden evening, with those warm brown eyes resting affectionately on me and dancing, dancing without the least feeling of uneasiness or fatigue.

As we drove home slowly through Villa Real's dark streets, Henry remarked casually, in great contrast to Bill's intensity, "Haven't heard from Ellen, have you?"

I shook my head, "Not yet."

"If you do, let me know. And keep quiet. O.K.?"

"Cross my heart," I said solemnly. I laughed, "Really, what a fuss about Ellen."

Henry shrugged. "Just in case there is something up, I don't want you to get hurt." He stopped at my garden door. "I'll see you in and then you bolt the door after me."

He took down the key from the hiding place he had found for me and opened my front door. H made a quick tour around the house with me, examining windows, window screens, and looking into the closets and under the bed. "I would offer to stay with you, just as protection, of course," he smiled mockingly, "but I have to be careful now."

The champagne bubbles inside me suddenly went flat.

"Henry," I blurted out, as we went back to the living room, "do you know Dolores is pregnant?"

He was quite casual, but annoyed too. "Sure I know, she told me. What's that got to do with you, or me, or even us?"

I did not reply; I was busy cursing myself for being such a fool.

"Oh, I know, some damned old busybody has told you I'm the father?"

I nodded miserably.

He came up to me and put his hands on my shoulders. "Look at me," he ordered.

I raised my eyes to meet his.

"You don't know much about life, do you? I know plenty. You don't think I'd put myself in the power of a tramp like Dolores, do you? Sure, I slept with her. She begged for it and got it, what do you expect? But I cannot possibly be responsible for that baby. I'm no fool."

He shook me, but gently. "Grow up," he growled and pulled me to him and started kissing me, gently at first.

But I thought of Dolores, her beautiful figure and sulky face and would not let myself respond, though I was tempted, his touch was perfect.

He let go of me, sighed and said, "Never mind, you'll get over it," and walked out.

I heard the squeak of the garden door and the noise of the car, and then silence. Locking the front door, I found myself crying in a slow, not too unhappy way. I watched the tears fall in slow motion onto my hand and said to myself, "It's your skin off your nose this time." I went to bed and to sleep.

14

It is harder to see than it is to express.

— Robert Henri, *Op Cit.*

Clem did not come into the Gallery in the morning, so I asked Liz about choosing one of Nicolai's paintings, explaining how I was able to take my pick and that it was an opportunity to give Nick a good send off.

Liz did not seem very interested. "We will probably give him a retrospective as soon as that brother of his deigns to come and deal with things. Clem wanted to put on a memorial show for him this fall, but that brother just won't even write to give permission, so he thinks next spring would be better now."

She paused to think. "No, if I were you I wouldn't even go in, let alone remove a painting. It's a tricky position, legally."

I saw her point, but it was too late to put Bill off.

Liz was in a good mood again and I was reminded by a train of thought that linked together so many things in one flash, to see if I could pin her down as to where she and Clem were on the day of Bela's accident. Very subtly, I considered, I led the conversation around to Mrs. Rountree.

"I can see Clem would want to have a show for Nick at a time when some collectors would be around, late spring and early fall, I suppose. When does Mrs. Rountree come generally?"

Liz pondered. "She was here a week or so ago, wasn't she? And then before that, let me see, she came in June, I think. Yes, I remember, it was the day poor old Bela fell off that cliff, so it was June."

"What did she buy?" I asked.

Liz did not seem very interested. "Oh, I can't remember that, she never sees me, it's Clem she likes. He knew she was in town so he was in the Gallery all day, and I was nosy. So I came in later, in the afternoon, to see how he was doing. They get along like teenagers and Beatles," she grinned.

That answered my question neatly and unequivocally. I felt a great sense of relief and could not help smiling cheerfully.

Liz was surprised. "Whatever's come over you, Mac? You come in looking like Orphan Annie, just the look, not the clothes," she hastened to soothe me, "and now suddenly you look more like your old self again." She looked at me curiously. I knew Liz was observant and intuitive but not analytical. She would not be able to reason the cause of my lift in spirits. "If you are meeting Bill for lunch and going to Nick's studio, just relax and enjoy yourselves, don't bother to come back. Clem will be in; he has an appointment with some Museum director."

Paul Humfrey came lumbering in as I was getting ready to go and, seeing us together, put his arms around us both. "My favorite women," he boomed loudly. "What are you up to? Plotting some more murders in aid of the sacred Villa Real Art Ass.?"

Liz pushed him away. "Whose Ass," she said rudely.

Paul was not subdued and squeezed me. "And my skinny little Mac, who isn't so skinny any more, snooping away?"

I pushed him away too, furious.

Paul patted my fanny. "Calm down, Mac, you haven't got red hair, you know. Heard anything from Ellen?"

The sudden question surprised me. "Not yet, but I expect to any day now."

Paul changed the subject then, as if he had given himself away and wanted to cover up. He asked me to lunch, but I had the good excuse of a prior engagement, as I told him, primly.

Liz and Paul both laughed at me. "Prior engagement," Liz mocked. "Paul, you are put in your place — how about staying there?"

I could see they were still making fun of me when I walked out. But why this interest in Ellen and her conjectural letter to me, I asked myself, undistracted.

Bill was waiting for me at Polly's place and was not as welcoming as I had hoped. After we had ordered from Polly herself, who was beaming obvious approval at my company, he plunged in, very serious. "I heard your garden gate squeak last night," he said. "I know it's none of my business, but I can't help worrying about you. I suppose you are being reasonably careful, aren't you? Don't let just anybody in."

I was embarrassed and decided to tell no more lies, anyway. "Henry took me out dancing at La Fonda last night," I said, deliberately offhand. "He looked through the house when we got back and told me to lock the door after him. I guess he's a bit worried too."

Bill was silent. I could see he wanted to say something and waited, but then, perhaps fortunately, Polly brought us our orders and stopped for a short chat. We ate in silence too, and not until we were contemplating the list of desserts posted on a blackboard, did Bill remark, "I've no right to be enquiring into your private life, forget it, but still be careful. Any news from Ellen?"

I shook my head. "Everybody is interested in Ellen suddenly, even Paul Humfrey asked if I'd had a letter from her this morning."

Bill was alert at this. "Paul? I wonder why?" he asked.

"Heaven knows," I shrugged. "It all ties in with my theory that Ellen was attacked because the murderer thought she knew something about Bela's death, something pointing to him."

Bill pursed his lips thoughtfully. "Yes, so it does, but surely Paul isn't in the running, is he?"

"Well, he is moving up. I found out today that both Clem and Liz are in the clear; they have alibis. On the day of Bela's death, Clem was in the Gallery all day, and Liz was there in the afternoon. So they are both out. Who does that leave but Paul, with Edythe as a very faint possibility?"

Bill agreed. "I can see Paul pushing poor Bela off a cliff, but barely, but I can't see Edythe doing anything out of the way at all; she is just so conventional."

"Edythe? Conventional? No, you don't know her; she isn't what she seems at all."

We drove directly to Nicolai Polkoff's studio and parked outside. Bill let us in with his key, and we were immediately struck with the very close, stuffy, musty smell of the neglected house. The studio was a fine big room with a large north light, tilted on one side to the correct angle. At one end of the room there was a fireplace, and at the opposite end a gas furnace.

"Dear old Nick, he liked to be warm," said Bill, wrinkling his nose. "That's what killed him, you know. He had every possible draft sealed off." He pointed to the scotch tape around the windows and a rubber strip attached to the bottom of the front door. "And the gas furnace on, and something went wrong."

Over the furnace end of the room there was a full-length wide balcony, more, I thought, for ornament than use, but Nick had put it to good if unaesthetic use as a storage place for his paintings, which were stacked all along it, between the curved posts acting as adornment and railing.

"Should we go up and look?" I asked, pointing. Bill helped me up the rather steep wooden stairs and together we went methodically through the canvasses that were stacked neatly and in orderly arrangement right along the balcony. Bill took out the paintings, one at a time; we both looked, commented, and I put one back while Bill took out another.

At first they were not of any special interest to either of us; early work, we decided, rather dated, of figures seated in gardens, with much green reflection. Then we came to a group of nudes, clearly painted later. We recognized Dolores. "Pity that baby can't be his," we giggled, but with a sadness.

Then Bill brought out a large canvas and exclaimed, "What's this?" He propped it up against the corner of some other paintings and stepped back with me to look at it. "My God," said Bill, "that's Henry's wife, I'd swear it. You remember that painting he showed us?"

I did and had to agree. Nick's painting was quite unlike Henry's; it was a very sensuous, seductive nude, on the green side, as all Nick's nudes were.

"Sometimes you'd think his flesh was a piece of over-ripe Roquefort," Bill remarked, "but this is perfect; the hint of decadence, but just the hint."

I was looking at the woman more than at the painting. She was lying down, on her side, one arm holding up her head, the other arm under her breasts, pushing them up and forward. Thin face, large eyes, sulky mouth were all there, and the red hair, but it was the full breasts that caught your eye, and then the swell of the hips up from the small waist.

Bill was openly impressed. "That figure is as good, or rather was as good, as Dolores', but a much more paintable face to go with it." He stopped, struck by a sudden idea. "But how come she posed for Nick? Henry told me she wouldn't even pose for him, and simply hated nudes; in fact, he really only got that one pose out of her, you know. I bet Henry doesn't know about this. It's one of the best I've ever seen of Nick's; he could sell it easily." He stopped abruptly.

"Ha," I said, "you don't imagine Henry will like that?"

Bill looked at me curiously. "Are you concerned for Henry's finer feelings?" he asked sarcastically.

I was annoyed at his tone and marched off down the stairs, taking the nude with me.

Bill clattered after me. He was rather apologetic. "Sorry, I was only joking. Let's put Henry's wife in the place of honor." He took a canvas off one of the three easels facing the north light and put up the nude. It looked wonderful, we agreed. Bill was quite reverent, gazing at it.

"Nick could paint," he said to himself. "I was wrong." Then turning to me with a laugh and his eyes straying back to the nude, "That arouses lascivious impulses, even in me." He wrenched his gaze away and took up the canvas he had removed from the easel, looking for a place to put it. He must have embarrassed himself, because he rambled on inconsequently, "Nice landscape, isn't it, but so banal. It's all been done." He placed the canvas at the bottom of another easel and sat down with me on the window seat beneath the north light to study it.

I saw that it was a landscape very like Bela's, perhaps even of the same view. "Did you see Bela's last painting?" I asked Bill.

He nodded.

"Isn't that much the same?" I pointed. There was a similarity but a great difference too. "How can two men paint, using much the same palette too, and achieve such different results?" I wondered aloud.

Bill considered the painting carefully. "I'd say it was a matter of tone values. Look at this," he gestured to a dark part of the painting, "nothing in Bela's painting was ever as dark as that. I think he generally painted in the morning, and somehow all his paintings look alike, with very little variation, and particularly not in the light and shade." Warming to his theme, he went on, "Now, this painting, if you knew the place well, you could tell whether it was morning or afternoon, couldn't you, by the heavy shadows and their length and degree of contrast and even, I think, by their color. But Bela's paintings, whenever they were done, always looked the same and you could never tell when they were done. That last painting of his must've been done, some of it, in the early afternoon, I suppose. What did his watch say? Three seventeen, wasn't it, and he would not have hung around for ages waiting for it to dry, so you could place it from that, but not from his painting." He stopped, looking puzzled. "My God, Mary, what's the matter?"

I must have gone as white as I felt. In one sickening flash I saw everything clearly, or rather I heard it. The whole mystery fell into place. It was like hitting the jackpot: the coin, the lever, the whirr, and bang, you've got it. I had it, indeed. When Bill said those words, "three seventeen," I immediately heard Ellen's voice telling me of the sheriff and the smashed watch. I saw at the same time the newspaper clipping with three fifteen written largely on it. I heard Bill's voice on Puye cliff, three seventeen again. How could he have known? How could he, unless he had seen the smashed watch? How could he have seen the smashed watch? Only the sheriff, Ellen, and later I, had seen it, and I had not told anybody. How did he know the precise time; either he had checked to see if Bela was dead, or he had smashed the watch himself at that time deliberately. I felt the blood draining from my face and had enough time to think, "I can't faint here," before I blacked out. I must have come to quickly, because Bill was still gazing at me in horror when I opened my eyes groggily.

He pushed my head down between my knees, saying, "Stay like that, Mary, I'll get some air in." He ran to open the door and by the time he got back I was feeling in control of myself again, but I stayed head down because I did not want him to see my face, which I knew must betray the horrible knowledge I had now.

It was all only too clear to me. He had been rejected by the membership committee; I remembered the cross and dots on the sheet of paper I had found. Nick had the cross, Bela and John Graham the dots. What could be more obvious? Bill blamed them for his rejection, he took his painting so dreadfully seriously, so intensely. I remembered his bitterness and the feverish stare in his blue eyes as he said, "I must succeed, I will succeed." How could he succeed here rejected by the Art Association? But how did he know who had turned him down? Nick must have told him, I thought; he was always one to be candid, brutally so. "Sorry, my dear fellow, but you're just not ready for it," would be the most he'd do to coat the pill. And then Bill would have brooded; he had nothing else to do but paint and brood, and the bitterness rose and choked him. He had to act before it strangled him.

A hand fell on my shoulder. I started up fearfully.

Bill offered me a glass of water. "Drink some of this and then I'll take you home so you can lie down. But it's just that it's so terribly stuffy in here, I'm sure." He surveyed me anxiously. "Feeling better?"

I nodded.

He helped me up and supported me with a hand under one arm as we walked across the compound to my house, which seemed a haven of refuge to me. I pointed out to Bill the key in its ledge and he opened the door for me. After sitting me down and picking my feet up to rest them on my coffee table, he opened all the windows he could find and left the door open. "You frightened me, Mary," he said, and I could hear the concern in his voice. "You just rest here and I will come back in an hour or two to see how you are."

I nodded again, unwilling to speak, and he went out. The garden door squeaked behind him. I got up and, fumbling, wrenched open my *vargueno* and hunted feverishly for my pile of notes. Though not a naturally methodical or even reasonably tidy person, I had a special place for these notes and newspaper clippings in a small drawer in the upper left hand corner of the *vargueno*. I always put the clippings on top and the papers underneath, folded together. I could see, even in my perturbation, that they had been moved. The clippings were underneath, and the papers not folded together in the same way.

I sank down in my chair wearily. This was too much to take suddenly. Now I had a burglar looking at my notes. Could he have found anything? I read through the columns of analysis, and the summaries of some conversations. I had a whole page devoted to Ellen, as I had planned to have her in my mystery and had, in fact, toyed with the idea of having her the murderess, but had not been able to think of a plausible motive yet. I had reproduced her conversation accurately, as a study in speech rhythms, and there, of course, was what I had been fearing to find, the ominous words "three seventeen." I went over the scene in my mind carefully, refreshing my memory with frequent glances at the page headed Ellen. That lunch at Edythe's, Ellen's voice ran on my ear, "Bela never painted after noon," "he never had to prop the canvas up to dry out." And there she was sitting in the hospital room, the scarf concealing the ugly bruise on her neck, and her voice again, "There's a murderer loose, my dearest Bela was murdered, I'm sure of it now. Yes, the newspaper reports said three fifteen, I don't know why, and two minutes are of no significance, but they mean a lot to me."

Two minutes, I breathed deeply, they mean a lot to me too. So much. I rubbed my head wearily. What should I do, if anything? Tell Henry? No, I flinched away from anything as drastic. Sure as I was in my own mind, I could see it was a long way from suspicion to proof. I had been suspicious of Clem and Liz, and a simple question had put to rest all my fears. Suppose, then, Bill could have a good alibi too, proving me wrong? I should give him a chance to explain himself, shouldn't I? I closed my eyes and plotted my course of action. Bill would return soon; I would pretend that nothing was wrong, it was just the lack of air in the studio, and somehow I would try to discover if Bill could account for himself that afternoon in June. It would be difficult, but surely not impossible.

A squeak of my garden door aroused me from these depressing reflections. There was a tap on my door and I called, "Come in," as gaily as I could.

"Mary," Bill said, coming up to look searchingly at me, "you look better. My God, what a fright you gave me."

I was smiling and casual, thinking to myself what a good actress I'd make, and replied, "You shouldn't have got so upset; it was simply that stuffy studio, the air must have still been bad, after all that gas in it." I went on, "I've been amusing myself with working at my mystery." I pointed at my notes. "Let's have a better think about Paul Humfrey. He certainly has the most obvious motive, now that Clem and Liz are out."

Bill settled down in the chair opposite me. I looked at him appraisingly; no one could have appeared saner. I noticed that his cheeks had filled out recently. He gave the impression of more solidity, and his tan a healthier cast. Catching my eye, he said, "Really, I thought you'd suddenly seen a ghost, perhaps Nick was returning?"

I shook my head regretfully, "I wish he had, perhaps he could tell me what I want to know."

"What do you want to know?" asked Bill, more as if humoring me than as if he wanted an answer.

I replied promptly, "Right now I want to know where Paul Humfrey was on the day of Bela's death. How can I find out? Where were you, in case that is any help?"

Bill looked surprised but unruffled. "Me? When was it?"

"The first Tuesday in June," I said, consulting my newspaper clipping.

Bill drew out a small thin-leaved notebook from his shirt pocket. "Sometimes I put down things I have to remember in this," he said, leafing through its pages. "First Tuesday in June? Yes, I have an entry, 'P.M. 2:30, at school.'" He laughed. "There's your answer. I remember now, I went to Humfrey's school, I thought I might enroll, but after I'd seen his class, no."

"Oh, joy," I said, "Paul's out too," unable to conceal my jubilation, though it was not for Paul I was rejoicing.

Surprised at the intensity of my relief, Bill asked, "You act as if I'd given you a reprieve. Why this concern for Paul Humfrey?"

I certainly was not going to tell Bill I had been suspecting him of wholesale murder, and besides, I had been so utterly sure I had the answer, unwelcome as it was, that simple caution closed my mouth. "Paul?" I said, "He's infuriating, impossible, obnoxious, but I often like him, we all do. I'd hate to think he would be so insane as to kill his way into being boss of the Art Association."

"Art Assassination?" suggested Bill.

I enjoyed his humor. "Well, that leaves our Edythe, or nobody. I'll take nobody. But in my mystery Ellen is the murderer, and she fakes that bruise on her neck, of course. Can't you suggest a plausible motive, or even a feasible one?"

Bill was amused. "You have absolutely the right person for a nice surprise at the end of a mystery. We can consider it solved. As for motive, that should be simple enough. She could have been conducting an affair with, say, Clem, and just wiped out the opposition, so to speak?"

We both giggled helplessly at the idea.

"Leave us not be just too ridiculous," I said. "It's no use flying in the face of the facts of life." More giggles. "So cease this deplorable levity. Think of Edythe, the only possibility left."

Bill amiably stopped fooling and tried to look serious.

"I don't know her as well as you do; to me she seems just a harmless old gusher."

"That's what I once thought," I agreed, "but she has been acting out of character lately, and underneath that silly mask I can see quite a shrewd woman. And a harassed one. She is not frightened, but something is worrying her."

I could see that Bill was not interested. "She probably has money trouble, who don't?"

I was persistent. "Come on, be a help. Can't you remember if she was in Paul's class when you went to see him in June at his school?"

Bill rubbed his forehead and tried to jog his memory. "Sorry," he said finally, "all I can see is a cluster of women, middle age and up, I'd say. Not a harem of harpies, more a batch of biddies. I can't see any individuals and wasn't introduced around."

This was disappointing. "What about the hours of Paul's school?" I asked. "Edythe was in faithful attendance until recently, I think. That could fix it."

Bill thought again. "That I can probably remember. Let's see, Paul gave me a schedule, I may have kept it, in case I changed my mind. Like me to go over to my place and see?"

I agreed.

Bill started off and at the door stopped and said, "How'd it be if I brought over whatever I can find in my ice box and I'll fix us something? You had better stay in this evening and take things easy."

For some reason, I was still uneasy about Bill and could think of no excuse to refuse this offer, so I had to accept, although I asked him to come back closer to dinnertime, as I wanted a rest. It was not rest I wanted, it was time to think. Unlike Liz, I am not intuitive but I am analytical, and if I had not felt a great sense of relief on learning of Bill's alibi, there must have been good reason for that absence.

What was it? I read my notes again thoroughly and carefully. All so much conjecture, but the facts that stood out were facts. The fact of the attack on Ellen, who suspected Bela was murdered, and another fact to which I had not paid sufficient attention, the general agreement that there was something wrong with Bela's last painting.

If only I had Ellen's address, I would phone her long distance and ask her if she had seen the painting, which she must have done, and if so, had she noticed anything wrong. Unless the sheriff had packed the painting box up. Who would have Ellen's address here, I asked myself and decided to go over to her house some time soon to see if her maid knew.

Taking out a fresh sheet of paper, I wrote a list of things to find out and headed it "Ellen's address?" Underneath, I wrote, "Who bought Bela's painting?" And then, "Where is it now?" And finally, "Check with Charles Newberg." This sheet I put on top of my other notes and clipped them together, ready to put back in the *vargueno*.

While opening the hinged front, though, I was reminded of the different order I had found the material in and, disturbed, shut the lid and paused for consideration. I must find a better hiding place. I may be imagining things after all, but just in case I am not, then it would be foolish to put what may be dynamite back in such an easily discoverable place. Where else could I hide them? The obvious and best place would be in the fire, I thought ruefully, and shivered; it was cold suddenly and I knew I would be lighting my fire very soon. But I did not want to burn the notes, so I put them down on the bookcase while I busied myself with the fire and some tidying. Inspiration came with warmth, as the sun arouses the hibernating animal, I thought, and I carefully put the newspaper clippings back where they were in the *vargueno*, but I separated my notes and stuck the various pages interleaved among other sheets and clippings in my favorite anthology. Fine camouflage work, I decided. I surveyed the result approvingly and replaced the book, not noticeably untidier or much fatter, with its fellows. I congratulated myself upon my ingenuity.

Suppose Bill remarked on the absence of notes, though? Concluding I would deal with that contretemps if and when it arose, I went into my bedroom, planning to spend the remaining time before Bill was due to return on my appearance, which I inspected carefully for signs of suspicion. I did not detect any. My cheeks did not look white under their spattering of freckles, my green eyes gazed back calmly enough at me, and my hands were steady while I arranged my hair as becomingly as I could. But inside I felt uneasy, apprehensive, of what I could not tell. The garden door's protest startled me from these reflections upon my reflection and I hurried out to open the door.

Clem Dennison came slowly but precisely up the garden to my portal.

"Well, this is a nice surprise, Clem," I said, putting warmth and welcome into my voice. "Come in and have a drink by the fire."

He smiled rather vaguely, but walked in.

As I was shutting the door behind him, I heard the sound of a collision. Turning, I saw Clem rubbing his ankle, which I could see he had hit against the projecting legs of my coffee table.

"Damn it," Clem said petulantly. "Sorry, Mac, I wasn't looking where I was going."

He sat down and handed me a letter, which I put on the top of my *vargueno* without looking.

"This was in the Art Association mail box, and I thought I'd stop by with it while I was walking home."

It was so unlike Clem, so neat, tidy, and precise, to trip over anything that my first thought was that he must have been drinking, but that was unlike him too. When I had first come to Villa Real, Clem Dennison was one of the first friends I had made, a very delicate and limited friendship, certainly, more of uncle and niece relationship, or to put it exactly, if brutally, a maiden aunt and niece. Clem looked out for me, he made a job for me, and in the early days of it, he used to give me a ride home after work whenever we left together. For some reason he had abandoned that helpful habit some months ago; I had thought because I had become so obviously quite healthy enough to walk. Sometimes, but not lately, he had invited me to his very correct little parties, where carefully chosen wines would be served to carefully chosen people, but decorum invariably prevailed. I had enjoyed the food and drink and the well-bred air of these gatherings, but somehow felt not quite at home with his other guests, perhaps because I was always the youngest present. Usually there was a youngish man invited to balance the table, but that man would be the type who could have no possible interest in me, or I in him.

I offered Clem a glass of sherry rather tentatively. His voice was perfectly normal, clipped, well modulated and exact. I decided I had misjudged him and went into the kitchen to find my best glasses and my one good sherry. When I came back, Clem was sitting straight but at ease, feet on the hearth and elbows on the arms of the chair, tapping his fingers against each other nervously.

"You've been so busy, Mary Mac, I haven't seen much of you lately. How's everything?"

I responded to his interest. "Everything's just fine, Clem, not a complaint in the world."

He smiled at his fingers. "Nice to meet someone who hasn't a care."

"What about you?" I asked, but keeping any note of real curiosity out of my voice.

Clem shrugged wearily, "Don't quote me, but the Art Association ain't what she used to be."

"Oh?" I encouraged.

"I'm still selling, the financial outlook is pretty good, but somehow the direction has gone. I miss John Graham. I don't know how we will get along without him, Mary Mac, if we get along at all."

I sat silent, hoping to elicit more confidences, and Clem went on, "You know me, Mary Mac, I don't pretend to be a leader, I just seem to have this talent for selling. John had the ideas to promote the gallery. He organized the traveling shows and the lectures. He got publicity for us all over the Southwest. Why, that Remington exhibition, it brought in three times what it cost in sales. People came to see the show and stayed to buy local stuff. Of course, it took John's charm to get the exhibition at all, and then work and patience to set it up. John suffered agonies over it. Did I tell you about that one crate getting mislaid? John worked day and night to find it. I thought his hair would turn white, he worried so, but it turned up just in time, thank heaven, and it all went smoothly after all. Now who is going to do that much work for the Art Association again? Voluntary effort, too?"

I could only reply, "No one, Clem. No one right now, but I have hopes of Charles Newberg."

Clem brightened. "You really think so? Well, I could get along better with him than with Paul." He swallowed his sherry in neat, appreciative tastes. "Good choice," he said, lifting his glass to me. "You've got a nice place for yourself. Are you happy?"

Quickly I assured him I was.

"If I were you, Mary Mac," he said, eyes on the fire, "I wouldn't be in any hurry to throw all this away on some struggling artist who'll move in to share all you can provide and expect you to work to keep it coming too, while he produces yet more masterpieces for me to foist on an unwilling world."

Clem sounded unusually bitter, perhaps, I thought, because his role was beginning to bore him. I have observed that actors have a low boring point. Fortunately, a knock on the door saved me from having to reply to his advice, well meant, I was sure, but not calculated to please me. This time it was Bill, arriving with his arms full of assorted food and drink.

"You remember Bill Thorpe, don't you, Clem?" I said, as I relieved Bill of his burden. "We are sharing a makeshift sort of dinner from our respective ice boxes; if you would care to join us, we would love to have you."

Clem smiled vaguely again, finished his sherry, and got up to go. "Thank you for the invitation, but I have dinner awaiting me," he said dryly.

And no picnic by a fire, I thought, but a proper, well-served meal. Single men with good incomes could always buy service. But was that life? Not the life I wanted, I decided firmly, then and there, and I saw Clem out, one hand on his arm, affectionately, but with pity.

"Where does Mr. Dennison live?" asked Bill. "There's no car outside, so he must be walking. Should I offer him a ride?"

"Nice of you to think of it, but he has a car, I know, so if he is not using it, he has his reasons. I don't think you need bother. He lives up the Camino, by the Museum, not very far, lovely place too. House, car, service, he has everything, and no need to snitch an extra hundred or so here and there. I just can't understand it."

Bill said, with some hesitation, "He's a friend of yours, isn't he?"

I nodded.

"Don't think I'm being critical, but the kind of person he is, and the kind of life he leads, he may be open to blackmail."

I frowned. "Blackmail? Clem? Whatever for?"

Bill shrugged and changed the subject. "Well, I've brought over plenty. I'm off to the city tomorrow, be back as soon as I can, but I don't know when, so I cleaned out my ice box."

We surveyed the conglomeration of edibles and potables Bill had brought over.

"Bill," I said, with decision, "leave this to me. Go and sit down and I'll bring you a drink."

Obediently, Bill went, and I brought him some sherry. On the way back to the kitchen, my eye was caught by the letter Clem had given me. I took a quick look to see who it was from. Ellen's flowing schoolteacher cursive was immediately recognizable to me. With my back to Bill, I flipped open the letter, but then decided against reading it and left it face up where it was on the *vargueno*.

It did not take me long to concoct a passable dinner from the various oddments. When I emerged from the kitchen with the first course, Bill was standing by my bookshelf replacing a book.

"Found something else you'd like to borrow?"

"Not now. Things are too uncertain for me."

We ate companionably by the fire and Bill talked freely of everything but his immediate past and his future and evaded all my efforts to find out what he had been doing for the year before he arrived in Villa Real and what he intended to do in the future. I was tempted, I must confess, to favor him with a lecture on the financial hazards of an artist's life, but something in his expression when I entered upon the subject of art and money deterred me.

Over after-dinner coffee, which I made at the table in a fascinating little espresso machine, Bill said suddenly, "Oh, before I forget, here's that schedule for Paul's school you wanted." He handed over a sheet of paper. The summer sessions were clear enough. I could see Paul worked hard; the only half days were Tuesday and Thursday, he held a class from two till five on those days. Other weekdays he had classes all day, and on weekends he took out sketching groups.

"Well, at least he works at his school, if not for the Art Association," I observed.

Bill disagreed. "I've watched Paul teaching, and I've talked with his pupils and ex-pupils and he's not really a teacher; he just jollies his old biddies along. It was his wife, his ex-wife, rather, who built up the school. Paul is just coasting along on the reputation she made for it. And now it's beginning to get around that it is not as good as it was; he has fewer and worse pupils all the time."

I felt sorry for Paul and said so.

Bill disagreed with this too. "No, Mary, don't waste your sympathy. Paul still gets his flock of silly sheep who'll pay him to get them into the Art Association. Besides, he is no fool. He will get in another teacher somehow, a good one. He will either marry again, or get someone like Charles Newberg with energy and ambition to keep the school going."

I laughed, "He could marry Dolores and with her as a free model, he'd have it made."

Bill was amused too. "But you forget these Spanish girls go off very quickly once they start having babies. Still, provided Paul could keep Dolores in line, that would be her one and only baby, I bet."

I thought it tactful not to pursue that aspect of Paul's, and any conjectural wife's, future. "If, by any chance that baby is his, it would give Paul an even better reason for wanting to control the Art Association, now wouldn't it?" I suggested.

Bill was not very interested. "Sure, but he has an alibi for the only time we can pin down, so you'd better concentrate on finding a motive for Edythe. She's your only hope."

He got up and offered to help with the dishes, but I told him that I felt perfectly normal and would rather do them myself. An unusual and curious constraint fell upon us. Bill wandered around the room picking things up and putting them down. I started off to the kitchen with the coffee things and, looking back, saw him fiddling with my *santo* on the *vargueno*.

"Ah, Bill," I said, going up to join him, "you see, here is the little infant Jesus, between His mother and father. If you want something really badly you must take out the Child, and hide Him and tell his parents that you will not return him until they grant your desire. See, He is removable."

To my surprise, Bill remained serious and constrained. "Mary, I do want something very badly. Can I try?"

"Sure, but you must take Him out yourself and breathe your own prayer without telling anybody what it is, and I suppose you had better hide the Child yourself too. I'll go away and leave you to it."

I went off to the kitchen and started stacking and soaking the dishes.

Bill joined me in a few minutes. "All done," he said, but soberly.

I dried my hands and followed him to the *vargueno*, where my *santo* stood without the small figure of the infant Jesus in the middle. "You must bring Him back when your wish is granted," I said.

"It will be," Bill grinned nervously. "Have you ever tried it?" he asked.

"No," I said ruefully, "there hasn't been anything I wanted badly enough to put it to the test. I'm happy as I am."

Bill stared enquiringly at me. "Really happy, Mary? You've got everything you want?"

"Almost," I said, with a sidelong glance at him. Bill leaned forward and put one hand on my shoulder. I really thought he was going to kiss me, so I lifted my face up encouragingly, but he just squeezed my shoulder and said, "Well, in that case . . . I'll get off. Take care of yourself, Mary." And he vanished.

Muttering imprecations under my breath, I washed up slowly and thoroughly, finding the routine a sedative I needed. When I had finished, I went to my *santo* on the *vargueno* and said, "Now mind you give him what he wants, and then do something for me." Tired and discouraged, I slunk off miserably to bath and bed.

15

*After all, the error rests in the mistaken
idea that the subject of a painting is the
object painted.*

— Robert Henri, *Op Cit.*

It turned cold in the night, very cold. I woke up in
the night and raised the temperature of my electric blanket,
hating to remove my hand from underneath its insufficient
warmth.

As I lay there, letting the obedient heat lull me back to
sleep, I thought regretfully of the final blow to my garden
and wondered if it was going to snow. It was still cold when I
woke late the next morning. It was Sunday, I remembered, as
I looked at my watch. No hurry. So I allowed myself time to
gather my energies for the hurried dash to turn my two gas
furnaces on, and then back to a warm bed to wait until the
rooms warmed up. I drew back the curtains for a brief look at
the patio. It had not snowed, but the killing frost had finished
off every last chrysanthemum; there was nothing left alive. A

bleak scene indeed, I thought, and planned to have a bonfire if the snow held off.

When the house had warmed up, I got up and made myself a large Sunday breakfast to eat beside the window that caught the morning sun, bright as ever, if not warm. I took Ellen's letter from the *vargueno* to read while I enjoyed my last cup of coffee.

My dear Mac, How are you? I miss Villa Real already, but here I am well looked after and I am not reminded all the time of my dearest Bela, yet I can talk about him to his many relatives living here, and that is what I need. It does me good to see how much they thought of him. I really believe they miss him almost as much as I do. I can only regret we did not meet earlier in life, so that we could have had a longer time together.

These are useless regrets, I know, but I wish I could feel certain that it was God's will that Bela died. I have thought and thought about it, and it still seems to me that it could not have been an accident. If God had wanted Bela and called him, then I could not complain, could I? But I do not feel that; I feel, on the contrary, that it could not have been an inevitable accident that happened because Bela had a heart attack or a fainting spell. No, I still feel that there was something unexplained, and inexplicable, about the way he died.

Why do I feel this way? Apart from the fact that Bela never worked on a sketch after noon, and that he never propped a painting up to dry, the only other indication of falsity I can find is his brushes in the painting box. The sheriff brought the outfit back to me that evening, but I didn't look at it until much later. When I did, I found that his brushes were quite clean. During our honeymoon I used to clean his brushes, he liked to have them done with soap and water, so I made that my job for him. Then it got to be a habit with him to wrap his brushes in a paint rag after sketching without cleaning them, so I could do a good job at home. Darling Bela, he had that habit for years. He would not have forgotten it suddenly.

Do not breathe a word of this to anybody, Mac dear, but keep your eyes and ears open and tell me anything you can discover when I come back. You must not be attacked the way I was, so please be careful, and burn this letter after reading it.

My coffee was cold by the time I had finished reading and rereading this explosive material. Now, if Bela had been taken sick suddenly, sunstroke, perhaps, or a minor stroke, then it might be possible for him to have neglected to clean his brushes, although he had always done so before, but surely if he had never cleaned his brushes for years, an indisposition would hardly make him clean them, would it? It was just the wrong way round.

Ellen's letter struck me as being evidence, evidence too valuable to be burnt as she asked. I folded the two sheets of paper together carefully and replaced them in the envelope, looking for a place to keep it. What I should do was a question not to be considered yet, but to burn the letter and forget it was not a course open to me. Sheer curiosity, if nothing else, would drive me to some action. But first, I decided, I must think. I put the letter in my wallet, and the wallet back in my purse.

Nothing is quite so conducive to thought as the monotonous routine of housework. After getting into blue jeans and checked shirt, I tackled some accumulated ironing and let my mind dwell on Ellen's letter and the possibilities it evoked and presented. As a premise, I told myself, forget this business of sudden flashes and jackpots, intuition is out, let the light of pure reason reign. Guess work, yes, if it is based on reason, just as when filling in a double crostic, to a non-addict it may look like intuition, but it is actually an educated guess when you fill in a whole word from one letter and the shape of the blanks. Well, then, I told myself, start making educated guesses; you have more than a few letters here and there, make sense of them.

Ironing away abstractedly, I started with the fact of Bela's brushes being clean. If he did not clean them, someone else did. Why did someone else clean his brushes? Because he was using them. Why would someone else use Bela's brushes? Because he was painting. Painting what? That stumped me through a whole blouse. The only possible answer was that he was painting Bela's picture. That did not make sense; try again. Bela had someone else, another artist sketching with him, someone with a very tidy mind who could not bear to see dirty brushes, so he cleaned them and went away ignoring poor Bela's body at the bottom of the cliff; that is ridiculous. Well, back to the original line, why was someone painting Bela's picture?

I remembered Charles' exposition in front of Bela's canvas, something wrong with the shadows, he thought it was. Why paint on Bela's shadows? There must be a reason, a good reason to tamper with another artist's work. I looked up from the ironing board and saw that the sun traveling on had left the window where I had sat with my coffee; there was no pool of sunlight there any longer. Sunlight, shadows, time, it all came together in my mind. Shadows indicate time, so this someone painted on Bela's canvas to change the time. Bela's works always looked much the same because they were all painted at the same time, before noon. This one would be changed, then, for what reason? Ah, I had it, to look as if it were painted after noon. After noon, afternoon, the time when all my short and hopeless list of suspects had alibis anyway.

I checked myself, remembering the watch. The smashed watch, three seventeen, that was what fixed the time of Bela's death. That could be faked easily enough by somebody sufficiently cold blooded to scramble down the trail, see if poor Bela were thoroughly dead, take off the watch from his body, set it to three seventeen, smash it, and replace it.

I turned cold thinking about it, a gruesome chain of actions, but I was sure now I was on the right track. It would be in the morning, that June morning — Bill, I still had to put him first; Paul; Edythe; or perhaps Liz; not Clem, he was in the gallery all day, I remembered — that someone had come upon Bela while he was sketching up there on the top of the cliff, enticed him to the very edge and pushed him over. Then what would he have done? Added some touches to the painting to make it appear as if it had been done later in the day, just a few brush strokes, propped the painting up against the piñon, cleaned the brushes.

I stopped; why clean the brushes? Probably, I surmised, from habit. When he had surveyed the scene to make sure all was arranged as he wanted, the someone would have hurried down the trail and gone through that gruesome business with the watch and rushed off to establish the afternoon alibi. Now there was another point, I interrupted myself, how about the coming and going?

Paul, I knew, had a bus; Liz had a very small car; Edythe, I frowned, not remembering whether I had seen her driving; and Bill, here I felt more cheerful, Bill did not have any car in June. Still, there are ways to get around that, men seem to be able to borrow cars, and then you can rent a car for a month, say, or perhaps there are busses along the main road from which the lane to Puye cliff turns off. No, I cannot eliminate Bill, much as I would like to, just because of the transportation difficulty. Anyone with the brains and determination of this murderer would not let a mere trifle like the lack of his own car stand in his way, now would he?

Another thought struck me, the climb up the trail: would not that eliminate all but the young and fit? The murderer would have to park his car at the bottom of the cliff somewhere, walk up, spend say ten minutes doing the horrible crime, fixing the painting and cleaning the brushes, and then walk down to tamper with the watch before driving off. But then, he could take it easy walking up the trail, which is the hard part. Bill had managed the climb easily enough a few weeks ago, despite my misgivings. I had no idea what he was recovering from. It might be something that had no effect on his climbing abilities anyway. Edythe was a different proposition, but such exertion was probably not beyond her as far as I knew. As for Paul and Liz, they could do the climb without turning a hair. My suspect list remained the same, with the exception of Clem, whom I had never seriously considered at any time. In fact, I had not before seriously considered anyone, except Bill, for one horrible flash of time.

Now the situation had changed. Ellen's letter had turned a joking speculation into a fearful probability.

Pulling on a heavy sweater, I went outside and started a bonfire. There had been no rain since that long female rain weeks back, and no snow, so everything was dry enough to burn readily. First I put on just twigs and leaves, and then I cut up the tough fibrous hollyhock stems and had to keep snipping busily at the dead chrysanthemums to keep the small fire fed. I was beginning to get warm from the fire and the exercise and was thinking of shedding my sweater, when my garden door opened with its attention-catching noise and Edythe poked her head around it.

"I saw your smoke, Mac, and thought I'd just stop by to say hello."

"I'll just finish collecting the stuff to burn, and then you come in and have some coffee with me," I invited her hospitably, but with far from hospitable motives.

She came in and tried to help me feed the fire.

"Edythe, you're no gardener," I had to say. "Leaves are fine for starting a fire, but it's a waste to burn them all. Just leave them scattered around; I'm going to heap them over the rose bushes after I've pruned them, and then next spring I'll dig them in."

Edythe stopped her well-meant efforts gladly and went to sit down on the portal, where I joined her and we watched the fire burn out.

"I declare," puffed Edythe, "the least little exertion and I get tired here; perhaps it's my weight." She peered down at her plump form smugly.

"Everybody feels the altitude," I replied. "Bill Thorpe and I climbed that trail up Puye cliff not long ago, and I found it quite enough for me. Ever been there?"

Edythe thought for a minute. "Puye cliff? Oh yes, I remember I went there with Paul Humfrey, a sketch group, you know, and some of us climbed down the trail. I thought I would never make it back again, but I did."

"We must go again some time," I suggested in an offhand way, "but you know, I have no car. You have, haven't you?"

To this innocent remark, Edythe looked a bit embarrassed. "Well, my dear, I did have one, but really it's not necessary here, is it? So I sold it a few months ago and honestly, Mac, I haven't missed it."

"I suppose you go out on Paul Humfrey's sketching trips a lot. He has that bus of his to transport his pupils?" I said, trying hard to keep the offhand tone.

But Edythe was curiously indignant at this. "You don't think I'd continue with Paul after he turned down my painting, do you? No, when I'm through, I'm through. I'm not one to throw good money after bad. I may seem to you foolish, but when I have made a mistake, Mac, I admit it."

This sounded honest to me, even sensible, but that was not to say that Edythe might have come to her senses after losing them. Could she have lost them to the extent of pushing Bela off a cliff in a fit of rage? I looked at her plump body sitting there and decided it was ridiculous.

"I've had a letter from Ellen at last, Edythe," I told her impulsively. Edythe was immediately her old self and chattered on about Ellen for five minutes, hardly stopping for breath. Finally she wound up with, "and what did poor dear Ellen say about coming back?" She looked very bright and inquisitive, like a dog hearing a refrigerator door open.

I decided to hand her a bone to chew on. "It's funny, Ellen isn't satisfied that Bela's death has been properly accounted for. She says that she thinks the sheriff's office should have made a more thorough investigation and she is going to have something to tell the sheriff when she comes back."

Edythe was gratifyingly impressed. "Mac, you don't say. Perhaps you were right, after all. I warned you not to go meddling and prying, but this isn't your fault now. Still, you leave this to Ellen and keep your nose out of it." She was unusually sharp and forceful.

I looked suitably penitent and said, with some truth, "Oh, I'm terribly sorry now I ever said anything, but Ellen's ideas are all hers, not mine, and I don't know what she has in mind to tell the sheriff; she just sort of drops hints, you know."

"Hints? What hints?" Edythe asked rather shrilly.

"Oh, nothing I could make head or tail of," I said casually. "Come in and have some coffee." I wondered if Edythe would have the nerve to ask me to show her Ellen's letter. I could almost feel her curiosity, but she said no more about it. Usually when I was with Edythe I just let her torrent of twitter flow over me, but this time she seemed subdued and abstracted. I had to cast about for topics of conversation to interest her. I even mentioned Dolores, but that brought no answering flood of gossip, speculation and insinuations, as I had anticipated.

As soon as she had finished her cup of coffee, she got up to go, looking around at my house as if observing it for the first time. "What a dear little place you have here, Mac. I should have taken a place like this, really." She sighed and went out, even omitting her customary prolonged leave-takings.

My little bonfire was now nothing but a heap of gray ash. I poked at it moodily, considering Edythe's uncharacteristic behavior, when my garden door warned me of intrusion. This time it was Henry.

"Shush," he said, stealthily, "I was waiting until Old Faithful left."

I laughed. "Edythe? She hardly gushed at all the whole time she was here. Something's on her mind."

Henry was scornful. "What could be on it, if it exists?"

"It exists, all right," I said dryly, but I did not want to get into an argument with Henry, so I went on quickly, "Well, what's on yours? I won't add the second question."

Henry smiled coldly. "I was looking for Bill Thorpe. He's not in his place, and his car's gone. Thought you might know when he'll be back."

"He's gone to the big city for a few days, indefinite. He just told me he'd be back as soon as he could."

Henry said, "Hell," with a grimace of disappointment. "I need some cobalt blue. I'm in the middle of something good. Why don't you come along and see."

Henry had never told me where he lived, and I welcomed the chance to find out. "Love to, Henry," I said. "And then why not look at Paul Humfrey's; he's sure to have the paint."

Henry looked less disgruntled. "That's a good idea."

"Come on." I snatched up my purse and ran out after him.

Henry was living in the guest studio of a very imposing house on Old Pecos Trail, owned by an amateur artist, an oldish divorcee who had lent Henry the studio.

"A nice place to land on your feet in," I remarked tartly as I got out of his car, also lent to him, I knew.

The studio itself could have been an artist's dream, but right then it was a mess. Not just an artist's mess, either; some of that is inevitable and forgivable, but a living mess too. It even smelled slightly. Paying as little attention as I could manage to the unmade bed in a corner, the dirty dishes in another, and the unwashed clothes all over, I picked my way carefully to the painting on the one easel.

I forgot the sordid surroundings. "Oh, Henry, wonderful," I whispered and gazed entranced at the painting. It was a landscape, and even I could see very much the view chosen by Bela for his last painting, and Nick Polkoff for the landscape Bill and I had seen in his studio, but so unlike theirs, unlike indeed the actual scene. Henry had transformed without abstraction, by the skillful use of color, mostly shades of blue. He had made a dream landscape, remote, yet nostalgic.

"Give me a title for this one," Henry commanded.

But I could think of nothing. "I need time for that," I said, looking around now, curiously.

Beside the easel, Henry had a table on which his palette rested with a great array of brushes scattered, all loaded with various paints. Henry picked one of these up, put one stroke on the canvas, and dropped the brush down on the table.

"Don't you ever clean your brushes?" I asked, thinking of Ellen's letter.

Henry shrugged indifferently. "Oh, sometimes I have a good clean up and do them all, but not often. I like to be able to pick up a brush as I go by and add a stroke here and there. I don't work to any time table."

"What about these?" I pointed to a row of four canvasses, all of aspens, identical in color and tone values, but varying slightly in the composition. All were at exactly the same stage, being, it seemed, about half finished.

Henry looked a bit put out. "Those are my bread and butter, being careful not to flood the market, of course. Come on, let's go over to Paul's. I want to finish my blue landscape while I can see it."

Submissively, I walked out and got into the car, feeling unable to comment on Henry's assembly line.

He noticed my shock. Putting his arm around me and drawing me close to him, he said, "You don't like my aspens, do you? Nick didn't either."

I met his eyes. "It ain't art," I said stubbornly.

Henry laughed. "Maybe not, but it's what sells, and if I can keep my wife off my neck that way, so that I can paint what I want to sometimes, they serve a good purpose." He kissed me gently, disturbingly. "Cheer up, Mic Mac, ideals are all very well for some people, but a poor peasant like me can't afford them."

He drove off suddenly and fast, and we reached the door of

Paul's studio in record time and without further conversation. Paul had a large place off Canyon Road, a rambling series of buildings, old adobes converted to large and small studios, Paul's school, and behind them Paul's own house. Paul was home. He came to the door with a paintbrush in one hand and paint rag in another.

"Well," he roared heartily on seeing us, "Look who's here, Don Juan Martinez and our little Mac." He looked closely at Henry, "And isn't that lipstick on your mouth, Henry boy? You watch it, Mac, he's a fast worker, successful too." He laughed with gusto, Henry looked smug, and I smiled without any amusement at all.

"Come on in, have a beer. I'll clean my brushes and join you." He dipped the brush he was carrying into a jar on a table beside his easel.

But Henry stopped him. "No, Paul, we can't stay, sorry, but I'm in the middle of something. I've run out of cobalt blue. Got any to lend me?"

Paul went on dipping brushes and wiping them on his paint rag. "Cobalt? Never use the stuff myself; don't keep it for the school, either. How about ultra marine?" He picked up a tube from his table.

Henry frowned and shook his head. "Sorry, Paul, cobalt or nothing."

Paul was put out. "Well, take your pick of any of my blues. Not painting Mac, are you?" He looked appraisingly at me. "She won't make a nude, but I'd like to see her anyway, can I come?"

Henry laughed. "Never stop trying, do you, Paul?" He emphasized the "trying" in a sneering sort of way. "Come on, Mac, let's go. Sorry, Paul."

We walked out quickly and shut the door.

"That wasn't very kind of you, Henry," I said severely, when we got into the car.

Henry was impenitent. "He's such a big blowhard, all wind. Make's out he's God's own gift to women, but he couldn't even keep his own wife."

"You have your illusions, I'm sure," I replied sharply. "Let him keep his, at least he's harmless." I was thinking of Dolores.

Henry looked around at me intently. I don't know what he was looking for, but he said quite gently, "I'd hate to be harmless, what would be the point of life?"

I smiled, "What life, what joy, without golden Aphrodite?"

Henry's expression was complacently reminiscent. "That's it, Mish Mash," and he took my hand and twisting it around, kissed the inside of my wrist.

"Henry," I said quickly to distract him, "I've got an idea. Can you get into Nick's old studio? I bet he has your blue, and nobody's using it. He wouldn't mind if you took one tube, I mean if he knew."

Henry was diverted. "Good idea, but how can we get in?"

"That's a snag," I said, considering. "Everything's sort of sealed up, scotch tape around the windows. I suppose you haven't a key?"

"Key?" Henry struck his forehead lightly with a closed fist. "Key? You know, I believe I have. Way back, Nick gave me a key so I could get out paintings for him, when he was away. Don't remember ever giving it back, either."

"Well, then, where is it?" I asked impatiently.

Henry closed his eyes in thought. "I've moved around so much, it is probably lost, or my wife has it." He smiled sourly. "If she has it, I'm not going to get it back. I'll look around my stuff."

At his studio door he told me to wait in the car, he wouldn't be long, and he was not. He returned in five minutes, carrying a key triumphantly. "The advantage of traveling light," he said.

"Nick must've scattered his keys around rather generously," I remarked. "Bill Thorpe has one too, and they didn't know each other so very long, either."

"Really?" Henry sounded interested. "I wouldn't't've thought so." Driving down to the Camino, he said idly, "What did you go back to tell Paul?"

"Just to say I'd had a letter from Ellen Ferency. He wanted to know." I stopped myself, apologetically. "Sorry, I forgot to tell you first in the excitement of the paint hunt."

Henry was angry. He frowned and drove faster. "Don't you remember, I asked you to tell me, and no one else."

"But," I said, on the defensive, "it's nothing important, really. She still thinks Bela's death was not properly explained, but she can't explain it herself."

Henry braked sharply at the door of Nicolai Polkoff's studio.

"Really, Mish Mash, you have loused things up. Why don't you keep your mouth shut? Now tell me exactly what Ellen wrote. If it's anything important, I can tell the sheriff, but probably she's imagining things anyway."

I handed over Ellen's letter from my purse without speaking.

Henry read it slowly and thoroughly, frowning. "Seems a lot of hooey to me," he said, handing it back. "I think he had sunstroke and wasn't acting normally." He turned to look at me. "What did you tell Paul? Have you told anyone else?"

Resenting his dictatorial manner, I replied coldly, "I told Paul I'd had a letter, that's all, and Edythe knows too."

"Edythe?" Henry was surprised.

"Well, Edythe is a great friend of Ellen's," I pointed out, "but I didn't show her the letter, she's such a gossip."

Henry was still annoyed, in a tired, defeated way now. He sighed and said, "You are a damn fool, you know. I don't know what to do."

We sat there in Henry's borrowed car, Henry silent and moody, I thinking furiously of how to placate him.

"Henry," I started rather timidly, "you see, I have an idea. I want things settled one way or another. I thought I would tell the few people I suspect that I've had this letter and that Ellen knows something, I won't say what, of course. If any of them has a guilty conscience, surely they will try to get the letter to see what Ellen suspects, won't he?" There was no reply, so I added, "or she."

I wanted to tell him that I could not bear the horrible suspicion I had of Bill, and wanted to end that anyway, but this I felt would not be tactful.

Henry turned around to face me. "So you want to get yourself killed, too?" he asked.

"Well, why can't you or someone from the sheriff's office be on guard outside my house tomorrow?" I suggested. "Seems to me it's a legitimate use of the taxpayers' money," I added, nettled by Henry's attitude.

Henry unexpectedly melted at that. His manner changed and he smiled at me, his brown eyes affectionate. "Now you've got something. You be the sacrificial lamb, to attract our tiger, and I will be there to save you? Is that the idea? You're nuts. But I see the damage has been done. You have told Paul and Edythe already. Who else is there?"

I hesitated and finally decided on half the truth. "Well, Clem's in the clear; he was busy all day in the gallery. So it really leaves Liz. She was at work too, but only in the afternoon."

"You're not being very intelligent, Mish Mash, that clears Liz too. I was in the sheriff's office from two till eight the day of Bela's death myself, so I know all about it. The sheriff told me."

"No, Henry, I'm being intelligent, all right. I've figured it all out. Whoever did it—pushed Bela over the cliff, that is—was intelligent too. He or she did it in the morning and fixed the watch and the painting to look as if it was done in the afternoon, and then had an alibi for the fixed time. Paul and Edythe at his art school, Liz in the Gallery, and . . ." I stopped myself in time.

Henry was disgusted. "Can't you forget all this? It's nothing but your overheated imagination, anyway. Still," he sounded indifferent now, "if you must meddle, then I must see you don't suffer. I'll get someone from the office to watch your house, if I can't do it myself, tonight and tomorrow night."

Whatever had I got myself into with my ill-considered plans? I wanted to back out then, but Henry was getting out of the car and it was too late to backtrack. We went into Nick's studio together, Henry going ahead and making a beeline for the table on which Nick's painting things were still laid. Standing with his back to the easels, he looked around, opened a drawer, and found a tube, which he took out. "Ah, I've got it. Nick can't use it any more, poor old fellow, so I might as well take it." He pocketed the tube and turned to go, looking around as he did so.

Too late, I remembered the painting Bill and I had taken down from the balcony and put up on one easel.

Now Henry's eye lighted on it. He stopped still suddenly and stared at it. Apprehensively, I watched him. His face flushed a dark angry red and then grew slowly white as he stood there, staring. "My God," he said, his voice shaking, "that's my wife, the bitch." He strode stiffly up to the easel as if he could not trust his coordination. "Look at that," he said, in a whisper, more to himself, I thought, than to me, "look at the mole there." His hand trembled as he put one finger lightly on the canvas, and then brushed his whole palm over the painted figure. Stepping slowly backwards in the same stiff held-in way, like a pointing gun dog, he cursed in a monotonous gritty undertone, using words I did not recognize. He came up against the window seat and sat down heavily, slumping forward, his eyes never leaving the painting on the easel.

"The bitch, the beautiful come-hither-touch-me-not-bitch. Nick got it, he got it all, those damn great tits stuck out at you, what do they say but come in? But he's got the eyes too, those damn eyes, they say leave me alone, you bore me. Look at those cold contemptuous eyes. Oh, Nick was clever, how he got her. She wouldn't pose for me like that. I tried to make her, I tried so hard, maybe I'd get her there like that, and I'd put my hand on her," he made a cupping motion with one hand, "to harden her nipples, and she'd get up when she felt me and shut herself up in the bathroom with a headache, she said. How do you suppose Nick managed?" He laughed sardonically. "She must've felt safe with Nick. I'm not jealous of Nick, not of an old dead man like Nick. That's a fine painting. But I'd do as well. I'd do better. She never would let me, and now she's fat. She's got those tits still, and those despising eyes, but she'll never be like this again. Why wouldn't she let me paint her?"

He closed his eyes and put a hand over them, blotting out the picture. "Sometimes, when she thought she was alone, she would watch herself in the mirror, taking off her clothes for herself; she'd stand there twisting this way and that and enjoying herself. I'd come in quietly and want to join in the fun, and then it was always 'leave me alone' and the eyes, those eyes said 'go away.' The only time she'd shut those eyes and let me in, let me feel her, was when I brought back a nice big check for her, a reward for being a good donkey; even then she used to snatch the carrot out of my reach sometimes."

He gazed at the painting again and went on, still whispering to himself, oblivious of my presence, a hideously embarrassed presence too. "What did she get from Nick, I wonder? No, it's all past history. I don't care any more, it's over. But I should've done that, not Nick."

He gave a tired, discouraged sigh and walked out, not seeing me. I followed him quickly, banging the door behind me. He started on hearing that and suddenly saw me again.

"God, I'm sorry," he said slowly; I could hear still the suppressed rage in his voice. "Just keep your mouth shut about everything. I mean everything, will you? Promise?" He looked compellingly at me. I nodded, not trusting myself to speak. He drove off, leaving me staring after him in dismay.

16

The exterior of the model is not the model.

—Robert Henri, *Op Cit.*

The rest of that interminable Sunday afternoon I spent planting bulbs in my patio garden and thinking with pity and anxiety of Henry. As I stabbed at hard dry earth with my trowel, I remembered Bill's comment on Henry and his wife and agreed there was no indifference there. Henry cared, but whether just as an artist, or as a man, or both, I could reach no conclusion. What was clear to me was that Henry needed looking after, someone to tidy his life up, giving him more freedom to paint.

As I put a large pinch of bulb food down in the hole I had made and set the bulb carefully on a mound in it and filled it all up again, I reflected that I was doing all this to have a week or two of beauty next spring. Surely Henry deserved some care too, to produce beauty for others to enjoy.

Snorting at myself for my sentimental nonsense, I turned

my thoughts to my own problems. I had no doubt that Henry would forget all about his promise to have me protected. I had already alerted Paul and Edythe, and it was possible that either might want to know what Ellen's letter divulged. Should I stay at home and await a visit? Outside in the afternoon sun I could contemplate such passivity, but I knew that as soon as darkness fell, I would be frightened. Edythe I could cope with here. Though I had never suspected him of violence before, if Paul chose to exert his strength, he would be formidable.

I smoothed the disturbed earth and shook a branch of the apricot tree to dislodge a few more leaves, which drifted down slowly and with finality upon the hidden bulbs. The sun was going down and the patio became cold in the shade. I shivered and went indoors to order a taxi, deciding to stay the night at the hotel.

Before I left, I ate a scratch meal, because I did not wish to encounter anyone I knew in the hotel dining room. The bar would be closed, a circumstance that would eliminate most of the people I wished to avoid, but I was not taking any chances. I took Ellen's letter from its envelope and tucked it away in my wallet. The envelope went on top of my *vargueno* face up, flap folded in. Then I sprinkled talcum powder around it, which was a messy operation requiring several tries before it was a light enough dusting not to be obvious. Well pleased with my trap, I locked up carefully and thoroughly, but I left the key under the mat.

That night I slept well, feeling perfectly secure, but woke up early with a feeling of apprehension. It was a gray cold morning and I walked fast to keep warm, as well as to get home quickly to see if my trap had been sprung. Looking back as I neared the top of the hill up the Camino, I saw the Sangre de Cristo Mountains were invisible under a dark gray cloud and thought to myself that it would snow before nightfall. I remembered that it was the last day of October, Halloween, and I must be prepared for the flocks of roaming children demanding ransom.

My trap had not been sprung, everything was exactly as I had left it, talcum powder and all. I felt more than a little ridiculous. Why was I disappointed? Bill I wanted eliminated, but did I really suspect Paul or Edythe? Liz would be my only hope now, and hope was hardly the word. Yet of all my suspects, Liz seemed to me to be the one capable of action, violent action, if there was sufficient reason for it. Paul had the most compelling motive on the face of it, but perhaps Liz was also under some compulsion about which I knew nothing.

Still thinking about Liz, I walked back to work. While was crossing the bridge over the Rio Villa Real, I saw Clem walking towards me down the Alameda. I waved, but he did not notice, so I waited for him and as he came up said, "Good morning, Clem, what a morning to be walking. Car broken down?"

Clem seemed to be startled, but he walked along with me pleasantly enough. "Oh, no, I like to walk too sometimes, you know; healthy exercise and all that," he added, unconvincingly.

"Liz has been a bit moody lately, hasn't she?" I remarked in what I hoped was a disinterested though sympathetic manner.

Clem agreed. "She's worried, I think. Well, so am I. But it's more than that. You know, don't you, that she was in love with John Graham?"

"Love?" I exclaimed in surprise.

Clem smiled and said affectionately, "You're so young. I suppose you thought John Graham an old man, and Liz, what do you know about Liz?"

"Not as much as I thought, evidently," I said.

Clem nodded. "Liz and John Graham were thrown together because of their Art Association work, of course. Liz had always been, shall we say, a free spirit. She worshipped John, probably because he was a gentleman, a type of man she had not ever known before."

I was very interested. "And John?" I asked encouragingly.

"John behaved just the way you'd've expected him to. He treated Liz like a favorite daughter, as part of the family, really, and accepted her devotion as if it were from a daughter or a student. He could so easily have drifted into an affair with her, which is what she wanted, but he wouldn't let her stop playing that part of a member of the family. She told me. People tell me things." He smiled ruefully, and went on, "I hated to see Liz hurt, I depend on her. But she would have been even more hurt if he had come down to her level, so to speak, wouldn't she?"

"You mean it gave her something to live up to?" I asked.

Clem looked sad as he replied, "Yes, and now what has she got? She looks *after* me, not *up to* me."

"Well," I said comfortingly, "she will look after the Art Association as John's memorial. That's what it is, really."

Clem was not comforted. "It may not survive, Mary Mac, who knows?"

We parted at the Post Office, where Clem asked me to bring him the mail first. An unusual request, but I did so after first glancing through the batch out of curiosity. I noticed a letter addressed to Clem from Mrs. Ephraim Rountree, but nothing to provoke any suspicions in my mind.

Liz was in her office when I arrived at the Gallery. "Hi, Mac," she called as I walked past her, "where are you going?"

"Just a minute," I replied hastily and went on to Clem's room with the mail.

When I came back, Liz was indignant. "Why are you bypassing me?" she asked.

It was contrary to our accepted procedure, so I explained that Clem had told me to give him the mail first.

Liz seemed to understand at once and said no more.

But I was curious and pursued the subject. "What's up, Liz?"

Liz sighed. "Clem's got troubles, bad ones. You're so young, you don't know what the word trouble means."

I was indignant. "Don't I just," I spluttered. "You know what happened yesterday? Henry blew a fuse in Nicolai's studio," and I proceeded to tell her the whole story, but omitting any reference to Ellen's letter.

Liz was both entranced and amused. "You can't say I didn't warn you, Mac, now can you? I know Henry well, very well," she smiled reminiscently, much the same smile I had seen on Henry's face when he was talking about Dolores. "I told you he might make a good husband if he could get rid of that wife of his, but I didn't say he would or could do that. As long as he can't conquer her, he can't get rid of her. Conquest is too easy for him, he wants resistance." Her smile became bitter. "Advice to the lovelorn, by Aunt Liz — resist."

I laughed nervously. "Oh, I'm resisting like mad, Liz. But unfortunately there is nothing to resist, damn it."

Liz was sympathetic. "Horrible situation," she agreed, "but cheer up, things are bound to improve. You look in the mirror; you've changed in the last two months."

I went over and looked at myself. It was true, I saw, as I smiled at the green eyes in the mirror. Turning away, rather embarrassed under Liz's gaze, I tripped over a painting propped up against the file cabinet. When I straightened it, I saw that it was Bela's painting, his last one. "Still here?" I asked Liz, pointing to it.

"I'm supposed to deliver it, but the buyer hasn't phoned when, so it can stay there for the time being."

I picked it up and set it against the wall opposite the window. "Look, Liz, Charles Newberg is right, you know, those shadows are not Bela's usual nothing muches."

Liz was not interested. "Oh, come off it, Mac," she said irritably. "Do stop harping on things wrong. Haven't we got enough troubles as it is?"

But I was persistent. "I got a letter from Ellen yesterday, Liz, and she knows something. She didn't tell me exactly what it was, but she hints. She says she has remembered something about the painting box that proved Bela was pushed off the cliff.

Liz was furious at this. "For God's sake, why does she have to make trouble? It's a lot of baloney, anyway. I don't believe a word of it." Liz got up and put the painting back where it had been. "And you just shut up about Ellen and her letter. Don't say a word about it to anyone. I won't have you making trouble too." She walked off angrily to Clem's room at this.

By the time Liz emerged, I had opened the Gallery, and had done all my usual small jobs of straightening, tidying, dusting, and was in the watercolor room looking gloomily around. Without John Graham's paintings there was not much to tempt a buyer.

Liz joined me there looking very much more cheerful. "Sorry I was angry with you, Mac, forget it, will you? Forget everything, Ellen and all, I mean. If we all just keep quiet, things will settle down and we may survive and keep our jobs." She followed my gaze around the room. "Pretty poor show, isn't it? Watercolors just don't sell well, and when they do, it's for so little. Painters can't be bothered with them. John was in a class by himself."

"Wonder why he removed all his paintings," I remarked absently.

Liz frowned. "That's just one of the things Clem and I have been worrying about. When his wife comes back, we'll ask her, and try and get them back."

We went out together and Liz looked out of her window. "Why don't you get off home" Nothing much to do, and it looks like snow to me."

"I've got to get in a lot of Halloween stuff. I had so many of the greedy grasping kind of child in last year, I ran out. This year I'm going to have plenty of small candies and give them out myself."

Liz was surprised. "Thanks for reminding me, I'd forgotten. Well, I hope the weather will keep the mischief down a bit. Last year I had shaving cream all over my car and a squashy pumpkin on my doorstep. But that was better than the broken window of the year before last."

On my way home, I went out of my usual route to pick up a large bag of cheap candy at the market and another bag of small wrapped chocolates, and I asked for my change all in pennies. These preparations made, I went home in the increasingly dark but warmer air to light a fire and await events.

I could not leave my house on Halloween night. Apart from enjoying the parade of masked and excited children, the delinquent element might take revenge by window breaking or other mischief, so I hoped Henry would remember that he had promised to give me some protection.

I was becoming resigned to the thought that it must be Bill who killed Bela. Hard as this was to accept, it was harder still to fit Liz, Edythe, or Paul into the murderer's shoes. Motive was lacking in Liz's case, and better but still insufficient in Paul's. Edythe just wasn't the type. In Bill's case, the motive indeed seemed pitiful, but then he did not seem quite sane on the subject of painting, and perhaps it was some sort of disabling head injury from which he was recovering. This explanation did not satisfy me, but I could think of no other.

Deciding that in my book I was certainly going to have Ellen the murderer, I settled down to write to her reassuringly, but found it impossible, since I was so far from reassured myself. All afternoon I wandered restlessly from room to room, from book to book, from window to window, watching the sky get darker. When the phone rang, I jumped nervously and found my heart thumping when I picked the receiver up.

It was Bill, calling from the city. "Are you all right, Mary?" he asked.

"Sure, Bill, why not?" I replied, trying to sound confident.

"Heard from Ellen yet?"

"Yes, I got her letter. She knows what's wrong now, she is quite explicit."

"Really? What is it?" Bill sounded anxious.

"Oh, I can't tell you now. I'll show you the letter when you get back."

"Haven't told anybody else, have you?"

I took a breath and lied with great conviction, "Heavens no, it would be dangerous, wouldn't it?"

"Well, sit tight until I get back. I'll hurry, but probably I'll be late. I can't leave until after dinner."

"Don't forget it's Halloween. You ought to be here."

Bill was surprised, like Liz. "I never thought of that. Well, it's too late now, I can't get away, but you be careful, won't you?"

I said I would and he hung up abruptly.

This brief exchange upset me badly. Why was he so anxious about Ellen's letter? Why did he want me to sit tight? Why was I not to tell anybody else? I looked out of the window on the dark garden and was soothed at the sight of the first snowflakes fluttering tentatively down and melting almost immediately they came to rest. The first snow, a magical time for an exiled Northerner. Enchanted, I watched the snowflakes fall and the sky grow dark.

Then I remembered that the small children would be coming early because of the snow and went out to open my garden door to invite them in. It was not very cold outside, but I was glad to get in again because the air was so ominously still it increased my apprehension. I put on my outside light and set out two bowls of candy and several piles of pennies on a table beside the front door. It was not long before I heard little steps and muffled giggles coming up the garden path. More and louder giggles and then a small knock on the front door. I opened with a flourish and looked down to see a small group of very small children, shepherded by an older one, all with masks on of varying degrees of horribleness.

"Trick or treat!" they said in a ragged chorus of squeaks.

"My," I said with mock dismay, "you are a frightening lot, aren't you? I'll have to give you the treat, won't I?" I carefully put four candies in each held-out paper bag. They giggled and nudged each other and ran away. Peering out, I could see a car parked outside my garden door and realized that some responsible parent was driving a group of children around the more reliable parts of town.

Several more such groups followed. As it became quite dark and the snow fell faster and thicker, groups of older children arrived, rather less appealing and certainly more demanding. Some now said "Treek or Treat!" in the soft Spanish way. I gave them extra candies. Some made to grab a handful, but I forestalled such action by hastily removing the bowls from under the greedy hand.

"Have to leave some for the others," I said soothingly. This occupied me and my thoughts until I suddenly felt hungry and realized it was past my usual dinner time. I looked out and heard and saw no imminent arrivals, so I started to fix myself a dinner from the oddments in the ice box.

While I was considering the assortment, I heard some rather more solid sounding footsteps coming up the garden path, no giggles either. The knock on the door was not the tentative, hesitant Halloween variety, either. Rather frightened, I opened the door and was taken aback to see Clem and Liz on the doorstep. They smiled and both said, "Trick or Treat!" with their hands out.

I laughed with them and said, "Come in and have an adult treat." They looked quite happy and normal standing there. I felt ashamed of my suspicions and bustled about with extra good will to make up for it.

When we were all settled down with various drinks and snacks by the fire, I said appreciatively, "This is a nice treat for me. What's the trick?"

Liz laughed and said, "You may well ask." She went on seriously, "Clem and I thought you deserved an explanation of some things that may have been worrying you, and now Clem sees his way clear, he wanted to come right out to see you and tell you."

This was puzzling. "Whatever are you talking about?" I said, frowning. Surely they had not brought me news that Bela's murderer had been caught?

Speaking precisely and clearly, Clem said, "My eyes have been bothering me lately, haven't you noticed? I can't drive any more and it's been hell wondering whether I was going blind and what to do. I told Liz in the end. I had to because I thought it was beginning to be obvious, and she has been wonderful." Clem looked at Liz and smiled at her. "She made me find out what was the matter, and although it is bad, it could be worse. She covered up for me at the Gallery. I made one bad mistake, though. Lucky you didn't see it, Mary Mac, or you might have thought I was embezzling the Association money."

I smiled in a "what an impossibility" way and felt even more ashamed of myself.

"I charged Mrs. Rountree, of all people, too much for a painting. Liz found the mistake and that's how it all came out, really, and luckily for me."

Clem paused and Liz broke in, "Poor Clem, he's been through hell, but after an operation and a rest he'll just have to wear glasses, contacts, he won't be blind, which is what he feared."

Clem resumed his explanation. "Well, I thought I was going to be blind, and I remembered that one of the inducements that the big gallery in California had offered me was a pension and health insurance scheme, so I wrote to see if the position was still open."

"Oh, that's why you were so anxious to get the mail."

Clem nodded. "So you did notice that, did you? Yes, that was one reason."

There was a gentle knock on the door at this, so I got up to dispense more candy. This time it was two older children with badges pinned onto their costumes. Seeing this, I gave them both pennies in their collecting boxes and candy in the paper bags they carried behind their backs.

"Sorry," I said, sitting down again, "was there another reason? Good heavens," I said, interrupting myself, "you are not leaving us, are you?"

Clem brightened. "No, but one thing at a time. I had to write to Mrs. Rountree to explain my mistake and refund the money. She is such a nice, generous old girl, I was sure she would understand, and she did."

Liz interpolated quickly, "And how! Know what she's done? She arranged to have Clem stay with her after the operation, which she has already set up and promised to pay for, too."

"But," I said rudely, without thinking, "surely, Clem, you can afford . . ." I stopped, embarrassed.

Clem looked sheepish. "I've always lived up to my income, I mean since I've had one, you know, the house, car, servants, and so on, and then I support my mother. But if I can get another good job or keep this one, which is what I hope will happen, I shall certainly pay Mrs. Rountree back, but nothing can repay her for taking me in, of course."

"Oh, I'm sure the Art Association will want you to come back when you can see again."

Clem sighed. "If I can see again, you mean."

Liz broke in irritably, "Now, Clem, stop being sorry for yourself. The doctor practically guaranteed success, you know he did, so you don't have to worry."

Clem went on placatingly, "I know, Liz, but how can I help

worrying. If John Graham were alive, I would feel better, but the present Board, who knows, they may fire me. Anyway, I can always get a job in that California gallery, but I'd rather stay here because the climate is better for me."

"I'm quite sure the Art Association will welcome you back with open arms, glasses and all," I said warmly, remembering the comment of the old lady Board member who had given me a ride home a few weeks ago. "They know that you are the reason for the success of the Gallery."

They got up to go and Liz explained, "We have to be getting back, Mac. I don't like to leave my house for long. My neighbor promised to keep an eye open, but on a night like this, what can she see or do?"

I watched them walk down the garden path, now with a film of snow on it, Liz with her hand on Clem's arm, guiding him lightly.

"Shall I shut the door?" Liz called.

"Not yet, too early," I said and waved goodbye to her, thinking with remorse of my unworthy suspicions.

There goes Liz, I said to myself, as I mentally struck her off the list of suspects, greatly relieved in a way, but I did not like the way things were narrowing down.

I was dealing with a very greedy older boy in a dirty sheet who tried to take a whole bowl of candy to put in his already bulging pillow case, when up the garden path lumbered Paul Humfrey. One look from him and the boy vanished, with only his quote, too, and no tricks.

"Thanks for the presence, Paul," I said, as he came up to me on the portal, "but surely you are not coming for this?" I waved my hand at the candies and pennies.

Paul laughed amiably. "No, but I wouldn't say no to another sort of treat, perhaps a drink by the fire?"

How could I possibly refuse? I was frightened, but I stepped aside and invited him in. Keeping a careful eye upon him, I made drinks for us and settled him opposite me in front of the fire.

Paul plunged right in. "What did you hear from Ellen?"

I sipped my drink, thinking furiously. "Why are you so anxious to know?" I replied bluntly.

Paul was clearly at a loss for an answer. He fiddled with his glass, took some cheese and crackers, and finally stared into the fire.

I waited in silence.

"Guess I might as well tell you," Paul said slowly. "Somehow you got hold of part of it, anyway. The damage may have been done, I don't know. But shortly before Bela fell off that cliff he came to see me, or rather we bumped into each other in the Gallery. We were both looking at one of Nicolai Polkoff's paintings, and Bela asked me to La Fonda for a cup of coffee. He told me a queer tale, which I sort of forgot until you brought all this stuff up about his painting being wrong and Ellen's letter and so on, acting as if you knew something."

He paused, and I stayed quiet, to encourage him to get down to it.

"I didn't pay much attention at the time, so I may not have it right, but I think what Bela was getting at was that he and Nick both thought that there was something fishy going on at the Art Association."

"Fishy?" I said.

"Yes, that was the word he used. At the time, frankly, it sounded like a red herring to me," he laughed boomingly. "It was a lot of baloney about the Remington exhibition, you know, when a crate with two paintings in it got lost."

"But what did he say about them?" I asked impatiently. But I was on my guard, thinking Paul might be distracting my attention from some nefarious design of his, even though the conjunction of big bear Paul and a nefarious design struck me as incongruous.

"That's just it, Mac, I really can't remember exactly. I wasn't very interested, after all. But I remember he said he and Nick had told John Graham about it, whatever it was they knew, and John hadn't agreed, so they kept quiet, but that he, Bela, that is, was sure Nick was right."

This was tantalizing. "Come on, Paul, think," I commanded brusquely, "it might be important."

Paul scratched his bushy hair and said, "Sorry, Mac, all I can remember is that it was about the crate with the Remington paintings in, and Bela said that it wasn't just mislaid, it must have been stolen. But why and how he and Nick thought so, I don't think he said.

Bela was pretty vague and apologetic about all this. He said that he didn't want to make trouble, and was only telling me because I was president of the Art Association and if any question came up about the Remingtons, then I ought to know."

Paul stretched his long legs out and put his feet up. "Now you see why I want to know about Ellen's letter. You are being a bit mysterious about it. Why?"

Was Paul dragging a tempting red herring in front of me to distract my attention from him? I looked at him critically, and decided I would have to risk that. "Ellen is sure Bela was murdered," I said abruptly.

Paul was visibly startled and then dubious. "But why?"

"Why was he murdered, or why does Ellen think he was murdered?" I asked pedantically.

"Both," Paul said with a frown.

"I can't answer the first question, can you? But the second is simple. Bela's brushes were cleaned when she found them in the painting box, but he never did clean them when sketching, he left them for her to do."

Paul looked rather relieved. "Oh, that's not a reason, just a guess. Maybe he just wasn't acting normally that day, sunstroke or something."

"But then how do you account for the difference in his painting, the one you saw in the gallery?" I asked firmly.

Paul shrugged. "Same reason, he wasn't himself."

A knock on the door summoned me, and I left to deal with a large group of children, but I kept my eye on Paul, looking back frequently to see what he was up to, thinking wildly of pills in my drink or poison on my cheese. The "thank yous" from the children died away as I turned back to Paul, who had stayed quite still, as far as I could see.

He looked up at me, worried. "This may be dynamite," he said, and I agreed.

The phone burr-burred suddenly, making me jump. I picked it up quickly, keeping my eye on Paul. "Hi, Mic Mac," said a voice. "I'm on the job, and I've got something to tell you too. Get rid of your company as soon as you can and come on over to Nick's studio, will you? And don't say anything, just come."

"O.K.," I said, and hung up.

Paul looked enquiring.

"Nothing important. Just Bill Thorpe saying he would be later than he thought." The lie came on the spur of the moment, and I had time to wonder after I had said it how I had become such a ready and accomplished liar.

Paul accepted this but made no move to go. I was contemplating asking him to leave, such was my impatience to learn what Henry had to tell me, when another knock came. To my great surprise, this time it was Dolores, who stood uncertainly on the portal.

"Hello, Dolores," I said, "won't you come in?"

Paul came lumbering up at my words. We stood there looking at each other, in an embarrassed silence. Dolores awkwardly gave each of us an envelope and waited. Paul tore his open clumsily and took it under the portal light to read the card inside. I followed him.

He suddenly roared delightedly. "Dolly, you made it," and clapping me on the back, said, "Bye, Mac, thanks for the drink. Forget all that stuff I said," and went off with his arm round Dolores.

Well, I murmured, now what? I read the card. It was a very formal engraved invitation to the wedding of Dolores and some Spanish-named boy — in church, reception later, the usual form. I smiled happily, another loose end tied off, so to speak.

The snow was falling heavily now, so I put on my fur-lined coat and a scarf around my head, turned off all my lights, even the outside one, as I did not want any late-coming Halloween visitors to be disappointed by my absence. The remaining candy I put in one bowl and set it on the outer edge of the portal, just in case. As I did so I noticed that the snow was not melting any more but resting thickly on the garden and already obscuring the footprints on the path, so I went back to put on my winter boots. By the time I had found them, shaken the mothballs out and put them on, another five minutes had passed.

I was impatiently rushing to the front door when the phone

burred again. "Hello, Mary," said a voice. "I'm leaving for Villa Real now. Are you all right?"

Bill again, I thought in despair. Why is he so anxious? "Yes, of course, Bill," I said impatiently.

"Well, don't forget, sit tight until I get back. Won't be long."

"Sure," I said and hung up. Everything now pointed to Bill, this anxiety about me, most of all. Still I owed him some sort of explanation for my whereabouts, didn't I? I got out pencil and paper and wrote in large letters, "At Nick's studio, back around 11 o'clock." I looked at my watch. That would give him time to get up here, and me an hour and a half to see Henry and warn him to watch the house while Bill was around too.

I put the note under the bowl of candy and hurried off.

17

*It is not enough to have thought great
things before doing the work. The brush
stroke at the moment of contact carries
inevitably.*

—Robert Henri, *Op Cit.*

Snowflakes fell gently on my face as I walked across the
compound to Nick's studio. Childishly, I put out my tongue to
catch some and then looked around quickly to see if anyone
was watching. There was no eye upon me that I could detect
in the glow from all the outside lights. Nick's studio, though,
was in total darkness, not even a chink of light showed in the
windows. I knocked on the door nervously and then tried the
handle, but it was locked. To my relief, it really was Henry
who opened the door to me. I half expected an ambush by
some utterly strange and devilish personage. "Henry," I cried,
my heart thumping.

"What's the matter, Mish Mash," he said, drawing me in,
his arm around me.

"I'm frightened," I said candidly.

Henry untied my headscarf and took it off, shaking the snowflakes from it. "Why?" he asked indifferently, yet with a watchful sort of tenderness. "Nothing to be frightened of, really, is there?"

"Oh, yes, there is," I interrupted him. "That was Paul I had visiting me, and even he is suspicious now."

Henry took my coat and put it on the window seat. "Paul?" he said, astonished. "For God's sake, what's eating him?" He lead me to a chair in front of the gas furnace, which was on full blast.

"How come the gas is still on?" I said, prevaricating.

Henry was impatient. "It was never turned off. But what did Paul say? You didn't tell him you were coming here to meet me, did you?" He looked at me intently.

"Of course not," I assured him.

He came over and kissed me rather absently. "Good girl," he said. "Want to take your boots off? He bent down and pulled them off for me.

Wriggling my toes in front of the warmth from the furnace, I said, "Well, this is very nice and cozy, in fact, it's downright stuffy." I sniffed; the air was very close.

"Have a drink," Henry urged. "I've got it all ready for you."

Beside us on a table were two full glasses and some potato chips. Henry handed me a glass and smiled. "Let's have a toast. Here's to art. You can drink to art for art's sake and I'll drink to art for money's sake. Then we'll both be happy."

I held my glass to his and sipped. I had already had two drinks, one with Clem and Liz and one with Paul, and having a weak head, I did not really want another, besides it tasted terrible. I made a face. "Whatever did you put in this?" I asked.

Henry was annoyed. "It's just a weak Tom Collins, best I could do with no ice. Come on, drink it up."

"Are you trying to make me drunk?" I teased.

Henry smiled wryly. "Are you accusing me of plying you with liquor so I can seduce the innocent maiden? Come off it, I like my women all there and cooperative." He changed his smile. "And I get them that way too."

"Is that a statement or a boast?"

"Both," replied Henry, stretching with a complacent air. "Now come on, stop dithering, what did Paul say?"

I took a handful of potato chips, hoping that some food would make me feel less peculiar. "You know, we really have got something. Bela saw Paul shortly before he was pushed off the cliff and told Paul that he and Nick knew that there was some dirty work over the Remington paintings, the ones that were mislaid before the exhibition. They weren't mislaid. They were stolen."

Henry was suitably shocked. I thought he was angry more than surprised. He took a long swallow of his drink and then said carefully, "Stolen? Nonsense, because they came back. Nothing missing, nothing stolen, simple."

He got up and came over to me, taking my glass on the way. He bent down and kissed my neck, and then put the glass in my hand and said, "What shall we drink to, your heart's desire?" He looked at me smiling. "I know you have one, your Infant Jesus is missing from your *santo*, what are you hiding Him for?"

I was first surprised and lifted my glass absentmindedly, but then I put it down, thinking hard. "Henry, how do you know about my *santo*? Bill took the Infant Jesus away, when was it, Saturday, and you haven't been in my house since then. Not by my invitation, that is, have you?"

I could see Henry was very angry, but he pretended that he was not and spoke softly, "You asked me to protect you, didn't you, darling, so I did."

That "darling" rang very false to me. I took some more potato chips and nibbled away angrily. "When did you go into my house, and why?" I asked, in what I intended to be a very cold manner, but it came out sounding sleepy. "Couldn't you turn the gas down and open a window? I'm feeling dizzy."

Henry smiled very sweetly at me. "Let's polish these off and then we'll go over to your house."

182 _____

This I did not want to do, so I roused myself with an effort and said, "What did you have to tell me?"

Henry shrugged, "Nothing, really, I just wanted to see you and keep you safe somewhere comfortable. I didn't want to hang around in the snow."

Suddenly there swept over me the conviction that Henry's behavior all evening had been peculiar and his speech false. I shook my head to clear it and looked at him. He was watching me with those brown eyes fixed intently on me. There was no real affection in them. I decided his expression was more like that of a cat watching a mouse. Why? No jackpot this time, no coins, levers and whirs, but a sudden blinding conviction that the name of my murderer was Henry Martin. Just as at a point in double crostics the name of the author emerges from a vague scattering of isolated letters, to make the only name that will fit, so did I put the name Henry Martin in my puzzle and it, too, was the only one. This happened in a second, and instead of becoming faint, as I had when the jackpot spelled Bill, I felt a rush of energy. My brain worked furiously, I felt cold with anger and determination, as I reviewed the very few courses open to me. I took some more potato chips to cover my expression.

Henry said with vexation, "God, Mish Mash, stop eating, what's the matter with you, drink that up and we'll go."

Well, there was a clue. He badly wants me to finish the drink, and it tastes peculiar. He must have doped it, probably with sleeping pills. I obediently took a very small sip. Inspiration came while I played with the smallest possible swallow.

"Did I tell you, Henry," I said sleepily, "there's another canvas of Nick's that Bill and I found, we think it's of your wife too." I pointed to a spot in the balcony directly opposite me. "You could probably find it from here and pull it out, you are so tall."

Henry took the bait and got up to look. He had to turn his back to me to pull each canvas out. I quickly poured some of my drink into my boot, which was on the floor beside me. When he turned around after each look, I pretended to be drinking. Lucky my boots are waterproof, I said to myself, after pouring my third libation in them. I was not so frightened as I had been, my heart was not beating unduly fast or hard. In fact I felt quite cool and detached, as if I were watching a scene played by others in a movie.

Henry gave up in disgust after I got my drink down to a third of the glass left.

"Was somewhere round there," I waved a hand up groggily. "Le'ss go." I got up and collapsed back in the chair, shutting my eyes and opening them with an effort. I slurred my words with care, "Henry, have you doped me? Don't feel right. Must've doped me. Why?" I shut my eyes and dropped my head, then looked at him and allowed an expression of drunken cunning to appear on my face. "Henry, why did you dope me? Henry, did you push Bela off the cliff?" Then I collapsed completely, letting my hand holding the glass fall back on the table, knocking over the rest of the drink. I allowed my head to fall naturally, eyes shut and relaxed. That should fetch him, I thought, proud of my acting. Now what?

Henry spoke. He answered me in the same gritty undertone he had talked about his wife in this studio, the same note of suppressed anger was there, bitter and harsh.

"You fool, you damned little fool, why couldn't you keep out of this? I don't want to hurt you, but I have to shut your mouth, I have to. What else can I do? Damned idiot."

His voice changed and became more normal. "We could have had such fun together too, I was enjoying you. I always hoped you would stop prying and meddling, but now it's too late."

A note of pleading crept in as his voice came closer, "Oh, Mic-Mac, I hate this, I hate myself, I hate my bitch wife, it's her fault, you know, not mine." He called louder, "Mic-Mac," and pulled at my hand.

I judged it politic to allow my eyes to open but with a great effort, and I pretended I could not focus them. "What?" I muttered.

Henry was very close to me, trying to catch my feeble attention. "Listen, Mic-Mac, I've got to do this, but I didn't kill anybody, truly not, I never laid a hand on anybody except Ellen and that was a mistake anyway. Nick was nothing to do with me, nothing, I swear it."

I looked at him very dopily and said, "Bela?"

Henry went on pleadingly, "That wasn't my fault. He knew something about me and I followed him to find out what it was. I went up the cliff and talked to him, guess I frightened him, but he fell off the cliff. I didn't push him, believe me, you must believe me."

I opened my eyes with another great effort and said, "Why?"

Henry was angry at this. "Why, you always want to know why. Well, you'll be dead to the world soon, I can see, and then your world will be dead to you, so if you want to know, I'll tell you. I must tell someone, I can't bear it by myself."

He took my hand, I would have thought in a loving manner if his voice had only matched, but it became harsh again, low and forced. "Listen to me, I took those Remingtons. I didn't steal them, I just borrowed them, that's all, nothing wrong with borrowing, is there? I was going to copy them and put the copies in the exhibition and keep the originals, but there wasn't time, so I kept the copies, good ones, too. But I saw Nick and Bela and John Graham together looking at a painting. They couldn't have seen anything wrong, because there wasn't anything, but they looked, and then they looked at me. I think Nick guessed I'd kept them, but be never said a word. He died, poor Nick, and I felt safe again."

He let go of my hand, which I let fall, inert. His voice now sounded heavy and tired. "It was good to feel safe, but then Bela behaved strangely to me. I think Nick told him something. He dropped hints to me, very round about, but I got the message. When we were on that cliff, I asked him what he knew. He was afraid of me and backed off the cliff." His voice came nearer me. "What could I do?" The pleading note came back. "How could I explain what I was doing up there? So I fixed his painting, and I wiped his brushes off because I figured that's what he would do, and I went down the trail and fixed his watch. That was horrible, but I had to do it, didn't I?"

There was a silence, worse than speech. I had to strain to keep my eyes shut and my hands still. I heard footsteps going off, and then the gas furnace suddenly shut off. This was a relief to me, as the room was getting so hot, but after an interval I smelt that ominous smell of escaping gas, and then I knew what my fate was to be.

Henry came back and started talking again, more to himself, in a low feverish mutter that I could barely hear. "And then all for nothing. John avoided me, never asked me out any more. He must have known something too, but he didn't say anything. Not to me. I could have left it, wish I had, but I had to know." He came nearer again and took my hand. "Didn't I, darling?" I stayed relaxed, remembering to keep my breathing deep, slow and even. Then he stroked my face. I pretended to struggle to open my eyes but failed.

He started talking again in the gritty whisper. "Damn John, with his patronizing airs, letting me ride his horses, so I had to groom them for him. I'm as good as him, I paint as well as he did, why should he patronize me? So I went out one morning early to find out what he knew. I left my car on the road and walked up the meadow. One of the horses followed me, because I always rode that one, and I gave it sugar. I saw John by the pool and I called him. He hurried over to me, anxiously, and fell." The pleading note returned. "What could I do? I couldn't explain why I was there, could I? So I rolled him into the pool. The dog started barking then, so I grabbed the horse and rode down the meadow and got away."

He sounded pleased with himself now. "Everything worked out well for me, didn't it? Nobody saw anything, nobody suspected anything. It was all meant to be. Then you had to start snooping, and started Ellen thinking too." He sounded sad. "It's too much. I'll find you here dead tomorrow morning and I'll leave town, heartbroken." I caught the mockery. "Then I'll disappear, leave my beautiful bitch, and won't have to fake Remingtons, after all. Life is odd, all for nothing, but I thought I could keep the bitch if I made more money, and now I know she isn't worth it. You might be, but she isn't."

I heard footsteps going off, the sound of a door opening and closing firmly and, worse, the sound of a key being turned in the lock. I lay there, not daring to move, with the gas smell making me sick, and the fear I had been too occupied to feel crept over me like a drowning wave.

I lost consciousness, but it could not have been for long, and it was lucky I did, because when I very gradually came to, I heard footsteps coming up to me. I resumed my very slow, even breathing with an effort. There was a confused noise near me and the gas smell suddenly became intensified. Then with a kind of dreamlike horror I felt flesh on my cheek and lips on my lips, just brushing mine, and my cheek was wet.

"Goodnight, darling Mic-Mac," said Henry's voice, with no mockery at all, just sadness.

It was all I could do to stay still, shuddering inside.

There was a clink of glasses and footsteps receding. The door opened and closed again, the key turned, and I allowed myself to shudder. I waited, counted out 60 seconds, and opened my eyes. The intensified gas smell was coming from a piece of rubber tubing attached to the gas furnace pipe, the other end on the arm of the chair in which I was huddled. I put that end down cautiously on the floor and thought quickly but not very clearly, since I was feeling the effects of the gas and the small amount of dope I had taken. Dazed, I inspected the furnace as well as I could in the light of one table lamp left on by the window seat. I could see the knob that turned it on and off, crept up quietly and turned the knob. Nothing happened. I bit my lips hard to rouse myself. The room was filling up with gas.

I could hardly breathe. What next? I staggered to the door and, trying to be quiet, turned the handle and pulled. It stayed locked. Should I break a window?

Surely Henry must be waiting in hiding out there. If I pulled a curtain back, he would see and come in. I could not risk that. He must think I was unconscious. Leaning against an easel for support, I looked at my watch and found I could not focus on it, so I reeled up to the light and bent down under it with my face almost on the watch. I thought it said 10:30, but wasn't sure.

I thought of Bill; he would not get up here until eleven o'clock at the earliest. Could I stand the gas until then or would I be collapsed and dead by the time he arrived? Shaking my head in a vain effort to clear it, I decided I could not last much longer. I must turn the gas off.

Drunkenly, I got over to the furnace, like a ship wallowing in a storm. Unable to think clearly what to do, I tried to see where the gas pipe went, and my eye fell on a silver cigarette lighter in a niche beside the furnace. "Gas, fire," I muttered, "light gas, big fire, somebody'll come." Then I had a second blurry thought. "Don't want to get burnt, get water." I stood swaying, looking around for water, lighter in hand. "Water, water, anywhere," I said stupidly and was aroused from my torpor by a crash and tinkle. There was a rush of cold air behind me, which immediately made me feel less stupid. I breathed deeply, face to the air coming from behind the curtain, below which a few scattered pieces of broken glass caught the dim light. Ah, rescue, and waited, clutching the heavy curtain with one hand and the cigarette lighter in the other. But there was no sudden noise, no loud knockings or hammerings on the door such as I hoped for. Instead, the key turned in the lock. Henry, I thought, with a sudden surge of fear and got behind the curtain, clutching the cigarette lighter despairingly while I gasped in the cool draft of air. The door opened stealthily. I peered around the curtain with fearful clumsiness. It was Henry, looking for me feverishly. I threw the cigarette lighter at the furnace, aiming for the end of the rubber tubing on the floor. It had mercifully caught on the first flick.

I don't know what I hit, but there was a soft roar as a sheet of flame billowed up and out. I flung my arm over my eyes and fell back against the curtain, feeling the hot rush of fire close to me, but it receded at once. I opened my eyes and saw Henry standing by the open door, paralyzed. Opposite him there was a wall of flame filling a quarter of the room. Henry came to life and ran up to the flame, looking around wildly. I cowered back against the curtain. Henry ran back past me, muttering as he ran. I caught three words in passing, "Not this way" He went out of the door and I started to pull myself together to go out after him, but my eye was caught by a sudden difference in the size and sound of the fire. I realized that the gas had been turned off.

I waited, watching the balcony above the furnace burn and saw that the pile of rags in the corner had caught and was blazing furiously. Henry came running back and, still not seeing me, though I was standing out in the room, seized Nick's painting of his wife off the easel and another beside it and threw them outside the front door. I let him run back again before going out myself.

Once outside in the cold my head cleared. As I stood there in the doorway, confused but beginning to feel more normal, a compound neighbor came running up. "I've called the fire engine," he shouted. "Anyone in there?"

I waved feebly at the studio and said, with an effort at clarity, "He's getting paintings out."

There was a squeal of brakes and Bill's car was right in front of me. Bill saw me and his face cleared momentarily. He asked, "All right? Stay there," and ran through the door.

More people came through the snow and I felt foolish leaning there against the wall. Also, I was suddenly aware that my feet were very cold. Looking down fuzzily at them, I saw I had no shoes on, so I weaved my way back into the studio, dodging my compound neighbor, the man who arrived on the scene first. I found my coat on the window seat, but my boots were nowhere to be seen in the confusion of flame and milling figures. I shook my head again to clear it and made out the form of Henry pulling canvasses down from the burning balcony, with Bill carrying them outside. He caught sight of me through the smoke on his way back and checked himself to come over. "Get out, Mary," and he grabbed me to pull me to the door.

"Boots," I slurred, pointing, and Bill frowned impatiently and tried to get me to go. But I looked away at the balcony, searching blurrily for my boots. That was why I saw the huge beam that supported the balcony had burnt away at one end, directly over the furnace. Henry was standing under the beam at the other end. My mind was still working slowly, and when Paul came charging in through the front door, shouting, "Mac? Mac?" I became confused and at first I couldn't speak. I just lifted my arm with an effort and pointed. Then speech came to me in a scream, "Henry," and Bill and Paul both looked where I was pointing at the beam and saw at once the danger and yelled, "Henry, get back." Henry looked around at them. I think he must have heard the shouts outside of people trying to get water, and he saw Bill and Paul standing there near the door. Like a trapped animal he swung his head from side to side. "Here," I screamed desperately, seeing the beam start to fall, and Bill dropped my arm and made as if to run to the balcony, but I seized him, and as he wrenched free, the beam fell in a shower of sparks and smoke. "No," I groaned, and shut my eyes and let myself go.

The next thing I remembered was a pain being pushed into my head. I opened my eyes in indignation and saw a strange man bending over me, feeling the back of my head. He smiled reassuringly at me and said distinctly, "You'll be all right," and then I felt a prick in my arm and soon the pain stopped.

When I woke up again, with a dull ache in my head and a dry throat, I opened my eyes cautiously and looked around at a perfectly strange room, in which the curtains were all drawn, but through them came enough light to see that someone was sitting in a chair by me. Who was it? I gave a sort of croak, which was all that I could manage, and the figure came over to me. It was Edythe. She took my hand and said, "Well, Mac dear, you're in my house." I must have looked puzzled, because she added, "I'm Edythe. We took you to my house because we thought you would not want to wake up in hospital. You just lie still and rest. I had the doctor come last night and you are perfectly all right, you know."

I croaked, "Water," and she gave me a glass and helped me sit up to drink, and then it all came back to me. "Bill?" I asked fearfully.

Edythe had been looking anxious, but now she brightened.

"Oh, Bill's fine, he got you here, he and Paul, and now he's waiting to see you."

I started to shake my head, but that hurt, so I said, "Don't want to see anybody."

Edythe looked sympathetic as she wiped my forehead with a damp cloth, but she said, "You'll have to soon. The sheriff and the fire chief want to see you, of course, but Bill first."

I looked at my watch and then at myself, as much of me as was visible above the bedclothes. I was wearing a strange over-sized nightdress.

Edythe saw my surprise at both the time and my attire. "Yes, it's Tuesday afternoon," she said, going to the window and drawing back the curtain, "and you're wearing one of my best nightdresses. Can you manage to get up? You could freshen up here," she pointed to an open door that led to a bathroom, "and I'll get you some coffee."

Obediently, I got up with care and found I could manage the trip to the bathroom and back. It was only my head that hurt, as I found when I tried to brush my hair in front of Edythe's mirror. I looked pale but there was no visible damage.

Edythe brought me a cup of coffee and a bed jacket, and I settled myself back cautiously in the pillows she arranged for me. The coffee revived me and I started thinking hard, but without much success, as to what I would have to tell the authorities, when Edythe brought Bill in. He sat down in a chair beside the bed and looked at me. His hands were both bandaged, and his eyebrows and hair had been singed.

"Were you hurt, Bill?" I asked, unhappily.

He shook his head, not smiling. "Just my hands, not badly."

There was a silence. I could see that Bill was hunting around the room for words. Finally he brought out, "How are you feeling?"

I grimaced, "Could be worse."

Bill blurted out awkwardly, "Can you take some bad news? I hate to tell you, you must've loved him, but you'll have to know. Henry," he paused, and I waited. He took my hand, gravely. "Henry's dead." He watched me, holding one of my hands in both of his bandaged ones. "I'm sorry, Mary, we tried to save him, but just too late. He didn't suffer."

I must have known what was coming, subconsciously anyway, because I felt no surprise, rather relief. "Maybe it's for the best," I said, but my lips trembled and tears began falling down my cheeks. I was reminded of Henry's wet cheek on mine and pulled myself together. "I killed him, Bill. But he was going to kill me." I took some more coffee and wiped my eyes.

Bill had not looked at all surprised when I said this, just sad.

Feeling stronger, I sat back in the pillows and told him the whole story and started crying again when I reached the point when I felt his wet cheek on mine. But I struggled on to the end, Bill watching me closely.

He nodded at times as if I was confirming what he had already guessed. "Did you love him very much, Mary?" Bill said, but hesitantly, as if he feared the answer.

This was, I knew, a case for honesty, so I said, thinking and choosing my words with care. "Love? I don't think I know what love is, do you? He attracted me, I was sorry for him, but I realized he was tied to his wife somehow, so I didn't allow myself to become affectionate as he wanted." I continued, my voice becoming stronger, "No, I thought of you first, not Henry, and that's an indication of something, now isn't it?" I was being as honest as I could, without thinking of the effect on Bill.

He squeezed my hand and smiled with pleasure. "That's my answer," he said and then gave a little groan. "I forgot my hands," he explained, looking at them. "That hurt. Now," he said briskly, "What are you going to tell the sheriff and the fire chief? I think Edythe and the doctor between them can stall them off until tomorrow morning, so we have time to concoct a story."

I frowned, hurting my head. "I suppose the truth won't do?" I enquired, with a note of doubt.

Bill shrugged, "Well, think, poor Henry's dead. Couldn't we spare his family, and his name? Let his paintings live on, untarnished by a bad name, perhaps?"

"That's good of you, Bill, but how on earth can I explain the fire, and why was I there, with no coat and no shoes on, either, and probably looking drunk too."

Bill gave a reminiscent grin. "You sure did."

"Damn it," I retorted, annoyed. "Surely you don't want me to tell the sheriff that Henry and I were having a drinking and, by inference, a necking party in Nick's studio and set the place alight in our drunken revels?"

Bill was penitent. "No, not quite. Don't be angry, Mary. After all, I had already guessed some of what you told me. So had Paul, which is why he came so promptly. He knew Henry was up to no good and was worried about you. Even Edythe suspects the story is not that simple. And the doctor told her that you were not drunk, but had taken a drug of some kind."

"Well, that's worse, in a way," I pointed out. "I don't want to be known as a dope addict, either."

Bill smiled, "None of your friends would ever believe that of you."

I thought for a bit. "Well, the first thing is to account for our presence in Nick's studio at all. Sorry, Bill, I just can't think of anything," I said, feeling the back of my aching head where I encountered a particularly sore spot. "How did I get this?"

Bill looked rather sheepish. "Paul and I both let you go and ran to Henry, and you fell and hit your head on the corner of the window seat. The firemen arrived while we were trying to get Henry out from under. They took over and Paul carried you to his car and drove you to Edythe's." He gestured downwards. "Besides the sheriff and the fire inspector, you have newspaper reporters awaiting you."

I groaned, "Oh, no, Bill, this is awful. I wish I'd left well enough alone. It's all my fault. Henry was right, first he blamed me and then his wife, but in the end I'm the one who killed him."

Bill got up, looking anxious. "I was afraid you'd take it this way." He walked over to the uncurtained window and looked out. "It stopped snowing not long ago, and everything looks so clean and lovely." He turned back and looked at me affectionately. "Don't let this spoil your life. Just remember that Henry told you he was responsible for two deaths. He would have gone on trying to cover up, wouldn't he? Ellen would not have been safe; he might have arranged another accident for her, and maybe for Paul too. Once he started to conceal his tracks and had already killed once, why and where would he stop?"

Bill sat down again by me. "No, Mary, don't blame yourself. You may have saved other lives."

I replied to this more cheerfully, "Then what we want to do is to cover up the Remington business and Henry's part in Bela's and John Graham's death, but we need not whitewash him completely, I suppose. Could he be trying to make out with me in Nick's studio and giving me a doctored drink, but no question of gassing me, of course?"

Bill agreed with this. "You'll find that the sheriff, who is some sort of relation of Henry's, and the fire chief, who is very buddy-buddy with him, of course, won't be too anxious to go into details."

"Particularly if I tell them that Henry gave me to understand he was on duty, guarding the studio from Halloween pranks?" That reminded me of a question still unanswered. "Who broke the window, then?" I wondered aloud.

Bill turned his bandaged hands palm upwards. "Who knows? You were saved by Halloween probably."

I laughed with caution, "All those treats I gave out paying off in a trick, no doubt."

Bill was serious. "Thank God," he said fervently. "You know something," he put his hand clumsily into his pocket and drew out an object wrapped in a handkerchief, which he put on the bedside table. "Here's your Infant Jesus back. It worked."

"Oh?" I enquired, but Bill did not pursue the subject.

"Now then," he said abruptly, "suppose you tell the truth up to a point, that Henry invited you over to Nick's studio, saying he had been guarding the compound and he was cold, and you went to keep him company and did not like the taste of the drink he had ready for you and found yourself becoming faint, so you asked Henry to turn off the gas, which he did." Bill was warming to his theme and sounded as if he believed himself. "But you smelled gas and feeling very strange, you didn't know what to do about it. You told Henry that there must be an escape of gas, and he laughed at you, but you insisted, so he struck a match right beside the furnace to prove that you were imagining things, and there was an explosion." Bill stopped, out of breath.

"Bill," I said thankfully, "that's wonderful. It sounds quite plausible, really. That's what I'll tell them, skating over the details, because what with the doped drink and the gas, I was hopelessly confused, as of course, I was. Do you think they will accept the story?"

"If they really wanted to know what happened, probably not, but they, the sheriff, anyway, will want to protect Henry to some extent. He would rather have Henry die as a hero rescuing Nick's paintings than as a murderer and forger."

"But what about as a heel, then?" I pointed out. "Plying me with a doped drink and blowing up the place in a drunken fit of stupidity?"

Bill smiled. "The sheriff will manage to gloss over that aspect, I'll bet, and I think we can leave him to deal with the reporters. You keep your end up, look pale and helpless and touching, the way you are now, and you won't have any trouble." He came over, kissed me very gently and carefully, and said, "It's over, put it behind you, the best is yet to come." He grinned at me and went out.

18

Nothing should be negative, or trying to
get away, brush strokes irresolute, words
you did not mean.

              — Robert Henri, *Op Cit.*

Later that afternoon Edythe's doctor came back, strange no longer. "Well, young lady," he said kindly, "another good night's sleep and you'll be as good as new, maybe better." He pointed to the telltale scar on my chest. "Seen your own doctor lately?"

I told him that I had not got one in Villa Real.

He frowned, and said, "I don't think it's unethical, then, to tell you that I think you are perfectly fit now. Feel free to marry and have children and live a normal life, but stay in this sort of climate. I speak from experience; nearly died twenty years ago myself, now look at me."

I looked and felt heartened by his assurance. He gave me some sleeping pills and told me I could return to my own house the next day.

Edythe was unnaturally subdued as she looked after me in a very competent way. Though I could see she was longing to talk, she repressed herself with a very evident exercise of will power.

After breakfast I felt so much better that I invited her flood of talk. "Edythe, you've been just wonderful to me, and I know that you must be curious as to what actually happened . . ."

Edythe interrupted me eagerly, "Mac, don't tell me anything. Of course, I'm crazy to know, but then I'm such a gossip and whatever I promised, I know I wouldn't be able to keep my mouth shut. Anyway, my dear, I'm sure it wasn't your fault." I was silent, so she went on happily. "And, my dear, when you came to and asked about Mr. Thorpe first, I felt much better. I went and told him. He was just wild with anxiety about you and that calmed him a bit."

This was thin ice to me and I skated rapidly away. "You'd make a wonderful nurse, Edythe."

She made a face, as much of a face as her plump, good-natured features could manage. "Better nurse than artist, is what you mean, I expect."

I couldn't deny that.

She sat down beside my bed and started a torrent of talk, to which I paid attention, at first from gratitude and then from interest. The late Mr. Chambers, it appeared, had neither been talked to death, as Villa Real thought, nor died from overwork, as Edythe had let drop, but had been a hopeless alcoholic. After he had drunk himself to death, Edythe had come into some insurance. This she put into her ostentatious house and art lessons. Her dream was, she told me, to be a patroness of the arts in Villa Real. She had read some books about that kind of life that fired her imagination. But she reckoned without the expense of getting into the Art Association. Paul had taken what he thought the traffic could bear, and she did not blame him for misinterpreting the situation. She had to sell her car first, and her house was up for sale.

She smiled at me, bravely, I thought. "You've helped me come to my senses, Mac, and I've kissed that dream goodbye and applied for a job in the hospital."

"Oh, Edythe," I said, nearly crying. The death of a dream is still a death. "I'm so terribly sorry."

"Don't be," she said with determination. "As you say, I'll make a good nurse, and I didn't make a good artist, now, did I? You seem to be one for facing facts, and that encouraged me to face mine."

"Yes," I said slowly, "you can and must lie to other people sometimes, but you must be honest with yourself." I was thinking of Bill and his dreams, and I sighed.

The interview with the sheriff went off smoothly enough, more because he was anxious to believe me than because I was a fluent liar, though I played my part well enough, I thought.

The strain of acting, as I preferred to think of my lying, left me tired and depressed, a feeling that the brief visit Liz paid me did nothing to dispel. She was kind enough, but her conversation kept returning to Henry and his painting, his already substantial achievements, and his great promise, now cut off. It would be easy for me to justify myself by telling Liz the truth, and I was sorely tempted to do so when she remarked that it was a pity Henry had to sacrifice himself to Nicolai's paintings, when Henry would have been twice the artist Nick was.

"Liz," I asked, choosing my words with care, "do you believe that art, any art, is more important than the individual life?"

Liz looked surprised. "Of course, who doesn't? After all, it doesn't matter to us in the least what a rotten life, say . . ." she searched for an example.

"Rimbaud, Verlaine, Poe, perhaps Whitman," I suggested.

"Yes, that's right," Liz agreed. "Even Shakespeare wasn't a good man, good morally, I mean. What do we care? It's the result that counts, isn't it?"

"In the long run, yes," I agreed, "but in the short, I mean, at the time, who's to judge?"

Liz looked puzzled; fortunately her intuition wasn't set at the receiving position because she passed that over, and I was able to keep my mouth shut. Liz noticed my silence and got up to go.

"Cheer up, infant," she said, "I won't be calling you that much longer, you're growing up fast. Whatever happened, I know you did your best, it wasn't your fault. It's just a damned shame."

What if I told her Henry killed John Graham, I thought bitterly, she wouldn't be so mawkish about Henry's lost masterpieces, then, would she?

When Bill came to take me home, he called a taxi because he could not drive with his heavily bandaged hands. It was an easy walk from Edythe's house to the compound, but we did not want to be waylaid by reporters.

I carried out my Infant Jesus still wrapped up in Bill's handkerchief. Edythe lent me some overshoes for the short trip.

I kissed Edythe warmly on parting, and when I thanked her, she turned away my stammered but real gratitude with a kind, if untrue, "You've helped me too, Mac dear."

My garden looked very precious to me, bedraggled as it was, snow on the ground underneath the trees and shrubs and in the shade of the wall, and mud in the sun. The garden path was slushy under our feet. Bill picked up the damp stained note I had left him; it was still under the bowl from which the candy had been taken.

"How come you arrived so soon," I asked curiously. "I figured you couldn't get back before eleven o'clock. And anyway, why were you so anxious?"

Bill opened my door for me and pulled back the curtains from my living room windows. He didn't answer my questions, but pointed to the array of empty glasses on my coffee table. "Henry didn't come here, did he?"

"No," I replied, as I tidied up the mess. "First it was Clem and Liz, and then Paul. I was scared of Paul, you know, he was always a suspect."

Bill laughed. "You're easily scareable. It was lucky you didn't suspect me."

I laughed too, but very hollowly. "You didn't answer my questions," I said hastily.

Bill sat down. "Ask me no more for fear I should reply," he said with a grin. He went on seriously, "You don't imagine I was going to let Henry get my girl, do you? And as for your first question, I phoned you from Bernalillo and then drove like hell. It was snowing on La Bajada but I made the best time ever, I guess. I knew Henry, fairly well, and thought he was up to something more than his usual easy conquests."

"My girl," I said to myself, as I walked off to the kitchen to hide the glow of happiness that enveloped me.

When I returned, Bill was looking around intently. "Where did you put your notes for your very own mystery?" he asked casually. I took out the book in which I had hidden the odd sheets and put it down on the table beside which he sat.

"Henry must have been in here snooping around, but I don't think he found anything. I really didn't suspect him, anyway," I added ruefully.

Bill looked embarrassed as he opened the book very clumsily and said, " Well, I realize I was more suspectable than Henry. Maybe you wondered where I came from, why I wouldn't touch you, why I was so damned determined to paint, with no obvious talent."

I put up a defensive hand and muttered, "No," unconvincingly. Then, as luck would have it, while Bill was handling the book, some of the loose sheets fell out and fluttered to the floor. I dived for them hastily, and seeing that one of them was headed, "The Case Against William Thorpe," I scrunched them up into a ball and was about to throw the mess into the fireplace when Bill stopped me.

"Give them to me," he ordered firmly.

I could hardly refuse.

He had a very difficult time straightening out the pieces of paper, but doggedly persevered.

I waited grimly for disaster to strike. It did.

"'The Case Against William Thorpe,'" read Bill in an incredulous voice. His tone changed to amusement as he read on. "'How did he know the watch was set at three seventeen?'" He grinned amiably at me. "That's easy, Mary, why didn't you ask me?"

I shrugged apologetically.

"Henry told me, of course. But I am not the detective you are and had no idea that he should not have known innocently. Now, what's my motive supposed to have been?" He read, "'Motive: revenge for being turned down by the jury of the Art Association.'"

I watched him apprehensively.

He let the book fall to the ground and buried his head in his arms, bandaged hands held carefully above. His shoulders shook.

I said timidly, "Bill, don't take it so hard. Of course it was ridiculous of me to suspect you, but . . ." I trailed off miserably.

Bill looked up, tears were streaming down his face, he was laughing so hard he could not speak.

I joined in after the first shock. But then suddenly we stopped.

I remembered Henry and soberly reproached myself, "I am just a meddling silly brat. I wish I had never even thought of any mystery, let alone provoked all this trouble."

Bill wiped his eyes and grew solemn.

"No, Henry was spoiling for trouble. If it hadn't been you, it would have been Paul, or me, or another victim. Henry had some things too easy, you know."

I looked at him in surprise.

"Oh, yes, he complained about patronage, and us poor peasants, and so on, but you know, he had the most astonishing amount of help from people here. Any sign of talent in the underprivileged, as they are called, is eagerly seized upon by the charitable Easterners with guilty consciences here. It all came easy to Henry, and somehow he never had his character properly finished by overcoming things, the way most of us have to. His wife was his only failure, and that sort of trouble is no help to the moral sense. No, don't blame yourself."

I was not noticeably cheered, because he continued, "Couldn't you think of me instead?"

I smiled encouragingly.

"Now then, that's better, and I have good news." Bill paused, watching me, so I smiled on. "I suppose I have been acting peculiar, but it isn't easy, either, to be normal when you don't know how long you are going to live, if at all. I was finally given a clean bill of health in the city yesterday, or was it the day before, so much has happened. I picked up something very obscure while in the tropics and everybody thought it would finish me off, but it turned out to be not as bad as the original estimate." He told me all this rather shyly.

I hastened to show my happiness for him. "Oh, Bill, how marvelous for you, and of you, too." Impulsively, in my relief, I went over to him, and then checked myself, seeing his hands. "But Bill," I asked nervously, "what are you going to do now?" I was thinking of his painting now with some horror.

Bill laughed, "Don't worry. I have a job all lined up. Back to being an English teacher for me. Oh, I will always paint now and again, but I'll never again get worked up about being a success as an artist. All this," he pointed to my notes on the floor, "has taught me something."

"Me too," I said, as I went happily into his outstretched arms.

CPSIA information can be obtained at www.ICGtesting.com
Printed in the USA
BVOW011724100112

280242BV00007B/7/P